tangled

Willow Springs ~ Book 2

laura pavlov

Tangled
Willow Springs Series, Book 2

❀ Created with Vellum

dedication

Dear Sissy,

When I think of strong heroines, you are always the first person that comes to mind. Thanks for inspiring me to write characters that aren't afraid to take risks, dream big, and go after what they want! Do you have to...do you have to...you know I'm such a fool for you...

Love you always,

Laura xo

one

. . .

Gigi

I MADE my way to Art History and maneuvered through the busy campus. Texas University was buzzing with students moving to and from class wearing shorts and T-shirts, enjoying these last few weeks of summer. Flags hung on every light pole with the scarlet and white TU colors and the proud bulldog mascot on full display. I still had to pinch myself at times that I was actually here. My best friend Addy and I had moved into the dorms two weeks ago, and we'd both pledged the same sorority house, Kappa Gamma.

I'd been so busy with rush week and the start of my classes that I hadn't had a moment to be homesick yet. I talked to my parents every day, and my brother Cade checked in with me a couple times a week. My three other best friends, Ivy, Maura, and Coco were all attending schools in Texas, and we had Zoom calls at least twice a week and spoke individually even more often. It was overwhelming and exciting at the same time, being here and getting situated, but having everyone's support, and having Addy by my side, had helped a lot.

"What's up, G?" Gray's voice startled me as he walked up behind me, causing me to nearly jump out of my skin.

Did I mention that my brother's best friend attended TU as well?

"Don't you have your own classes to go to? Why are you always sneaking up on me?" I hissed. Bantering with Gray Baldwin had become my favorite pastime over the years. Not that I'd ever admit that to him, because in his world, I was just someone fun to pester. Nothing more. He had a way of getting under my skin—always had. Gray was a junior and had just been elected president of his fraternity.

The boy was born to run a frat house.

He was the epitome of a cocky frat boy with a wandering eye and a red Solo cup permanently attached to his hand.

"I happen to be on my way to class right now. Don't act like you don't enjoy running into me." He nudged me with his shoulder, and I looked up to see a wide grin spread clear across his handsome face. Butterflies swarmed my belly. Again. This had been happening more and more over the past few months and it truly had to stop.

Gray was tall with broad shoulders, disheveled brown hair that was longer on the top and shorter on the sides, and green eyes that always managed to steal the air from my lungs. He was what my best friend Coco would call, *sex on a stick*. And I hated the way my body reacted to him lately. It made no sense. He wasn't my type. He was as off-limits as it gets.

A self-proclaimed player who made no apologies for it.

My brother's best friend.

And he annoyed me more often than he didn't.

But he was gorgeous and charming—and that infuriated me.

"Don't flatter yourself. Now that I'm officially done with rush, I can start going out. And I don't need you getting in my business if we run into one another," I said, trying to cover my smile because I knew that's exactly what he'd do.

Gray and Cade had been best friends for as long as I could remember.

From cradle to grave, they'd always say.

They were a bit wild when they were together, and they'd left behind a lot of broken hearts back at East Texas High where we'd all attended school. We'd grown up in a small town about two hours away from here, called Willow Springs. It was one of the oldest towns in our state and best known as *The Heart of Texas*. Gray had been around for as long as I could remember. He was a permanent fixture at our house. His parents divorced when he was young and his dad struggled with drugs and alcohol, but he rarely talked about it. His mother remarried, and she'd gone on to have two adorable twin daughters who I'd babysat more times than I could count. Because Gray couldn't be bothered and rarely spent a weekend night home.

"Your business is my business, G. I promised Cade and your parents that I'd look out for you, and that's exactly what I intend to do." Cade had always been an overprotective brother, bordering on the ridiculous, and for whatever reason, his best friend thought it was his job to do the same.

Two girls walked toward us and they both smiled as they blatantly drank him in. "Hey, Gray," they purred, and I rolled my eyes.

He nodded but kept his attention on me.

"I don't need a babysitter. When I come to your frat party, you need to stay in your own lane." I stopped when we arrived at the building where I had class.

"I've always liked your lane better," he said with a smirk, crossing his arms over his muscled chest as his gaze locked with mine, and my stomach dipped again.

Damn you and your sexy self, Gray Baldwin.

"Hey, Gray." Tiffany, the president of my sorority, walked up and stood beside him before turning to me with a flat expression. "Oh, hi, Gigi."

"Hey," I said, and Gray's eyes never left mine as he greeted Tiffany.

"So, you have this guy to thank for you and Addy getting a bid at Kappa Gamma. He can be very persuasive," she said, and she ran a hand down his bicep, and I had a sudden urge to throat punch her.

Where did that come from?

He shot her a look as if she wasn't supposed to tell me that he'd reached out and put in the good word for me and Addy. I already knew, because Tiffany had made her point perfectly clear when we received our bids that she was doing a favor for Gray and that we both owed her one.

Not exactly an empowering sisterhood moment, but I wasn't sold on the whole Greek life thing just yet, so the jury was still out.

"Oh, I'm sorry. Was that a secret?" She giggled and raised a brow at me. "Come on, Gray, we're going to be late for class."

They had class together? Were they dating? He was probably sleeping with her. Nothing would surprise me when it came to Gray. Another reason why I needed to keep my feelings for this boy in check.

Hating him was a lot easier than liking him.

"Let's go," he said to Tiffany before leaning close to my ear. "Like it or not, you best plan on seeing me in your lane, G."

I watched him walk off, and I made my way into the building and internally cursed myself for letting him get me all worked up.

I really enjoyed my classes, and Professor Benzo was one of my favorites. The hour and a half lecture went by quickly, and I made my way back to the dorms and passed Bailey in the hallway. She lived on our floor and just three doors down from us. She hadn't made the best first impression with Addy or me, but her roommate Sadie was sweet. And they'd both rushed the same sorority house as we had.

"Hey, Gigi. Awww… look at you. You're *so country* in your little dress and booties," she said, with an awful attempt at a southern accent. Why she felt the need to talk with a twang every time she spoke about my clothing was beyond me.

"I like wearing these flowy dresses in the heat," I said, looking down at my outfit, which really did keep me cool in this warm weather. Unlike Bailey's current situation.

She wore fitted black jeans and a skin-tight black T-shirt. If this was her idea of fashion in the summertime, I was just fine being *country*. Bailey was from Colorado and she clearly wasn't used to the Texas humidity just yet.

"I have to admit it kind of works for you," she said with a smile. "You have that whole girl-next-door thing going. Some guys probably find that attractive."

I laughed. Bailey was a champ when it came to giving backhanded compliments. "Thanks. I'll see you later."

When I pushed the door open to room 711, Addy was sitting at her desk studying. Our room was magazine-worthy. Addy's mother had designed the space, as southern girls took their dorm décor pretty seriously—or at least their mothers did.

Our headboards were covered in white velvet fabric, and our peach linen bedding had little white flowers all over it. We had too many throw pillows for a dorm room, but you didn't mess with Addy's mom when it came to decorating. Our walls were covered with framed photos from home and distressed wood plaques with sweet, inspirational sayings on them. We had vanity mirrors on our desks so that we could get ready in our room versus having to lug our makeup and blow dryers down to the communal bathroom.

"Hey, how was class?" Addy asked as she swiveled around in her desk chair, which matched the fabric on our headboards. Not a detail had been spared when designing our room. My mom had chuckled at Addy's mom about how serious she'd taken it on move-in day, but my mother appreciated that I lived in a space that was warm and cozy and managed to feel like home.

"It was good. Do we have our FaceTime call with the girls now?"

She glanced down at her phone and smiled. "Yep. Five minutes."

She picked up her laptop and we both plopped down on her bed, setting the computer between us. I filled her in on my annoying run-in with Gray on campus.

"I know you think he's being protective, but I swear there's something there. I see the way he looks at you." She connected our call as she spoke.

I shook my head. "Absolutely not. We can't stand each other most of the time."

I hadn't even admitted to my best friends the way I'd been feeling when I was around Gray lately, because I knew it wasn't reciprocated. I was most definitely not his type. And he'd never look at me in any sort of way as I was Cade's little sister. My only hope was that this would pass. It was a silly crush. It wouldn't go anywhere.

The girls came into focus and we all talked at the same time just like we always did. Ivy waved her hand in the air, before holding up the large leather-bound book in her hands. "Okay, we have important matters to discuss. And I decided to call our weekends home, *Willows Weekends*."

Ivy was the president of the Magic Willows, a group we'd formed in fifth grade using the first initial from each of our names. Maura, Adelaide, Gigi, Ivy, and Coco. We kept all of our memories in these notebooks, and we'd managed to fill several over the years. We were all within a few hours of one another, with me and Addy in Austin, Maura and Ivy in Dallas, and Coco going solo in Houston. Most importantly, Willow Springs was in the middle, so it would be an easy drive home for all of us. We'd committed to meeting at home at least one weekend a month.

"Why does it have to have a name?" Coco asked, with one brow raised as she stared into the screen.

"Because it does, Co. I like to name things. Why must you question everything?" Ivy said, and a tear ran down her face, startling all of us.

"You know I just like to give you shit, Ive. I love you so much." Coco's face turned serious when she realized she'd upset her.

We were all worried about Ivy. She'd dated her boyfriend Ty for years, and the two had been madly in love. Or so we'd thought. Ty had planned to attend the same school as her in Dallas, but after a crazy scandal with his family was all everyone in Willow Springs could talk about, he'd left town with his mother this summer and he'd taken Ivy's heart with him.

"I love you too. I don't know what's wrong with me lately. I just cry all the time," she said, and Maura wrapped an arm around her.

"She's been feeling homesick the past few days." Maura hugged Ivy even tighter.

"It's a lot of change." Addy's eyes welled with emotion. We'd always felt one another's hurts as we were connected in a way most people couldn't begin to understand. True soul sisters. "It's okay to be sad about Ty."

Ivy swiped at her falling tears. "I know. I just can't decide if I'm mad or sad anymore. We had a plan. And he just jumped ship and left me. Who does that?"

"I don't think it had anything to do with you," I said. "I think finding out his dad not only had an affair, but also got the woman pregnant, was more than he could handle. I mean, the Greenes were the perfect family according to Willow Springs' standards. This came out of left field. And then with his mom leaving town, I think he just needed to get away for a while."

"Let's use the word *woman* lightly. The girl he knocked up is barely out of high school, for God's sake. Mr. Greene is an old perv. It had to be so humiliating for them." Coco shook her head and rolled her eyes at the same time. Theatrics were her specialty.

"But that has nothing to do with me. Why would he cut me off? And now he's in Nashville and probably going to become some big famous country singer and never look back." Ivy broke out in a sob, and a tear rolled down my cheek. I quickly swiped it away. I hated that we couldn't hug her when she was going through so much.

"It has nothing to do with you. I think Ty is just a good guy and he was ashamed about all the talk in town, and when his mom left, I think he just wanted to go with her. And the last time you spoke to him, he said you deserved better. Knowing Ty, he carries the guilt and shame of his father and thinks he's doing you a favor by leaving," Addy kept her voice soft and I rested my head on her shoulder, wishing we were all together.

"Have you reached out to him again at all?" I asked.

"No. And I won't. He told me he was done, and he asked me to let him go. I'm not going to beg him to be with me. I have some pride left." She tipped her chin up just a bit, swiped at her tears, and forced a smile. "It's done. I'll be over Ty Greene in no time."

"Well, I can't wait to be *under* someone new. I've been in a dry spell since Shaw and I broke up, but there have already been a few prospects in my classes," Coco said, breaking up the tension like she always did.

We laughed.

"Here's to us all finding our way on this new adventure," I said. "And we'll be together in two weeks. I can't wait to hug you, Ivy."

"Me too," she said, and her smile reached her eyes letting me know that she'd be okay.

"Magic Willows for life," Maura said, and we all repeated her words.

Just like we always did.

two

. . .

Gray

I'D BEEN BACK to school for two weeks. I had a chronic headache and wondered why the fuck I'd agreed to be president of my damn fraternity. I could kiss all the good times goodbye. Jack Schwab had convinced me to go for it. He'd been president the past two years.

"It's awesome. You'll get your own room and your own bathroom. It's massive," he'd said.

And I'd probably been too many red Solo cups in to think it through. The fact that I was now responsible for anything that these dipshits did in this house was terrifying. If minors were caught drinking, I was the asshole getting cited. It would be hard to find a college party where students weren't getting their booze game on. So basically, I was fucked.

I was sure as shit not about to throw away my chances of going to law school, most especially because Simon, my dickhead stepfather would be all too happy to say, *I told you so.*

Hell, no.

The last time I saw him, he'd made a couple dozen cracks about me being a chip off the old block, and he'd reminded me that he held the purse strings for my future. He'd let me know that he was nervous about investing in someone who could later fuck up. But for now, the man had more money than God, and he seemed quite content giving me a credit card with an unlimited balance to maintain my lifestyle and to keep me far enough away.

And I was all too happy to oblige.

At least that's how it seemed. I'd been dealing with his disdain since I was seven years old, when he and Mom got married. The man had been preparing for me to fuck up my entire life. In high school I'd given him what he wanted, coming home shit-faced more times than not. Sleeping my way through most of our female senior class.

They were tough shoes to fill. But I was happy to step up to the plate.

Except when it came to school. It was the one thing I cared about. My father had been a brilliant attorney before he fell off the planet and lost himself to booze and pills and sports betting. And I'd decided somewhere along the way that I wouldn't take that path. I planned to go to law school. Probably become a divorce attorney. Hey, hopefully my mom would come to her senses one day and need good representation when she left the asshole.

One can dream.

I think it actually got under Simon's skin that I'd made the dean's list every semester since I'd started at Texas University, which also happened to be one of the most prestigious colleges in the country.

Take that, dickhead.

I might be incapable of commitment and a perpetual good time, but I was smarter than shit, and he couldn't take that from me. It was the one thing my father had clearly gifted me.

Thanks, Dad. Now sober the fuck up and step up to the plate.

Even with my dad battling his demons, he was more of a man, more of a father than Simon had ever been. Had he been a huge embarrassment over the years? Sure. He'd had one too many public intoxication charges, he'd been involved in endless fights at local pubs in town, and he'd had a pretty fierce fall from grace. And we lived in a small town, which meant everyone knew your shit. Everyone in Willow Springs was the judge and the jury.

Cue my best friend, Cade.

The Jacobs' family accepted me for who I was, in spite of my dad. Hell, Bradley Jacobs, Cade's father and my dad went way back. They were the best of friends. Bradley knew there was a good man beneath all that numbing going on.

They'd opened their doors and their hearts to me, making me feel like part of the family. When I was home, I did not stay at my mother's house. I stayed at the Jacobs' home, and they'd even given me my own room there. It had just been the way it had worked for the past few years.

I loved them. There wasn't anything I wouldn't do for any of the Jacobs. Hell, Cade was the brother I'd never had, and he knew about my struggles with Simon. He was my best friend and my wingman. He'd held my head up when I puked my brains out from drinking myself sick more times than should be required of a best friend.

I dropped to sit on my bed when I saw an incoming call from Cade. He went to school about an hour and a half away from me, but we talked often.

"Hey, asshole. How are you?" he said when I picked up the phone.

"Why did I agree to be president of this damn fraternity again?"

"Because it'll look good on your resume for law school. Just suck it up and get it done."

I ran a hand over my face and fell back to lie on my bed. "Easier said than done. I quit drinking two weeks ago because I have my hands full with these goddamn animals in the house."

He laughed. It was fair. I'd been an animal for most of my

life, so it was karma paying me back and making me deal with this shit.

"It's good to sober up every now and then. What's happening with your dad?" he asked.

"My grandparents spotted him the money. Basically, they gave him all that they had left in their retirement to give him this opportunity." I closed my eyes as the words left my mouth. My father had just entered a ninety-day rehab program. My grandparents were two of the kindest people I'd ever known, and they'd given everything up to help my dad.

"I'm sorry, brother. I know this is tough. But hopefully, getting him in a longer program will help."

This would be my dad's fourth attempt at rehab, and he'd never made it beyond two weeks. This new program would be more intensive, and he'd be living there for three months.

"Thanks. We'll see what happens." I didn't have much more to say on the matter because I'd been let down too many times in the past. Actions spoke louder than words. I hoped he could pull it off, but I certainly wasn't holding my breath.

"How's my sister doing? Are you keeping an eye on her?"

"*Is the pope Catholic*?" I said with a laugh as I sat up and pushed to my feet. Speaking about Gigi always put me on edge.

"Knew I could count on you. She seems happy about rushing Kappa Gamma. Thanks for placing that call. I guess it pays off to bang the president of a sorority house."

I rolled my eyes. Tiffany and I had hooked up one time last semester, and I'd asked her to look out for Gigi and Addy during rush a few weeks ago. I knew Gigi was nervous, even if she'd never admit it. And I'd known Addy most of my life, as well as her boyfriend Jett. The dude was a cool cat, and he'd pulled me aside and asked that I look out for his girl as well during rush week.

"Yeah, well, now Tiff keeps texting me because I asked her for a favor. We've all been on restriction for rush, but the gates have opened, and this chick is so far up my ass I won't be able to hide from her anymore."

"Gray, Gray, Gray… this is what happens when you dip your pen in company ink." He barked out a laugh.

"Whatever, dude. Don't ever refer to my dick as a pen again. It's offensive." We both laughed. "How's Camilla?" My best friend had started seeing a girl a few months ago and I'd never seen him so into any chick before.

"She's awesome. I'm happy to be back at school with her."

"Never thought I'd see the day," I said. "I'm going to head over to your sister's a little later and check on her. She wants to come to the party this weekend, and I need to prepare her for all the dickheads that she'll have to deal with."

"Dude, are you seriously giving my sister *the birds and the bees* talk?" He laughed so loud I had to hold the phone away from my ear. "This is why she's always pissed at you."

"Duty calls. Nothing's going down on my watch, trust me," I said.

"I trust you with my life, brother. Thanks for always having Gigi's back. Camilla's here. I'll call you later."

We disconnected the call, and I dropped my phone on my desk. It had been a day. Hell, it had been a rough couple of weeks. I'd been stone-cold sober, trying to keep an eye on Gigi and make sure no dickheads came near her, and also keeping my fraternity brothers in line. That meant no hazing, no out-of-control parties, and no one looking at Gigi Jacobs.

And I was fucking exhausted.

There was a knock on my door and I barked out for them to come in. It was one headache after the next lately.

"What's up, Pres," Colin said. He was a sophomore and had moved into the house a few weeks ago. The dude bugged the fuck out of me.

"Don't call me that. What do you need?" I growled. I'd become a goddamn babysitter, and I wasn't having any fun.

"The toilet on the second floor is clogged and the showers

don't have hot water." He moved around my room, pausing to look at the two framed photographs I had sitting on my dresser. There was one of my family with Mom, Simon, and the girls, and another of the Jacobs that Katie Jacobs had given to me last year. He pointed to Gigi in the photograph. "Damn, I know this girl. She's in my poli sci class. She's so fucking hot. Can you hook me up?"

"I can hook you up by your fucking balls, you douchedick. Don't even fucking look at her, or I'll throw your ass out of here so fast your goddamn head will spin. There's a plunger under the sink, go plunge some shit. And maybe a cold shower is exactly what you need." I held the handle to my door and used my hand to encourage him to leave.

"Jesus. What happened to good time, Gray?" he asked as he moved out to the hallway.

"He grew some fucking balls. Go plunge the shitter," I snarled and slammed the door in his face.

My phone vibrated and I yanked it from my back pocket and read the text.

Tiff ~ Hey Gray. Looking forward to the party this weekend. <winky face emoji>

Me ~ Yeah. Should be a good time.

Tiff ~ So, I know I helped those two friends of yours get a bid in the house. Just making sure they aren't competition for me. <shrugging emoji> <winky face emoji>

Jesus. This day just wouldn't stop. She was trying to make our one-time hook-up something that it wasn't. I'd been straight up with her that I didn't do the girlfriend thing, and she'd acted like she was on board. But last week we had a Greek meeting with both the fraternities and the sorority officers, and the girl had inserted herself the two times I'd been talking to other girls. Just talking. And she'd gone for the full cockblock both times. It hadn't bothered me too much, because I wasn't in the mood to hook up with anyone at the moment—which was a definite first. But knowing Gigi was here on campus had me on edge, and my new responsibilities at the house were way more stressful than I'd anticipated. And I'd shut Tiff down too, because I wasn't interested. But I sure as shit didn't want her taking it out on Gigi and Addy.

Me ~ Family friends. I appreciate you looking out for them.

Tiff ~ Anything for you, Gray. I'll see you at the party this weekend. We're finally allowed out. You know what happens when the cat's allowed out to play.

What the fuck did that mean? Was she the cat?

Good Christ.

There was no way for me to get out of it because the party was at our house. And I was the fucking warden of this shit show.

Me ~ Okay. I'm on babysitting duty so I won't be able to hang. I'll be keeping an eye on the pledges and making sure things don't get out of control.

Tiff ~ Ohhh, was that an invitation? Do you want to play house, Daddy?

I scrubbed a hand down my face. What the fuck was happening?

Me ~ No. It's a one-man job. See ya later.

I needed this conversation to end.

I shot Gigi a text.

Me ~ Heading over to talk to you.

Gigi ~ Stop hovering. <eye roll emoji>

I didn't respond. Because when it came to Gigi, hovering was my specialty.

I drove over to the dorms and parked my truck and jogged inside, before knocking on her door. Like a fucking hormonal teenager dying to get to his girl. What the hell was up with that?

She pulled the door open, one brow raised, trying to look annoyed, but I saw the smile fighting to come out. She had her hair pulled back in a ponytail, and she wore a white blousy tank top and a pair of jean cut-off shorts. Sexy as shit. Her tanned, toned legs were hard to look away from and I forced myself to meet her gaze.

So fucking pretty.

"What is it this time? We've already covered the basics in your last visit. I took notes, remember?" She rolled her sapphire blue eyes. "All college boys are scumbags. Nothing good ever comes from getting drunk. And my all-time favorite, sex will make my boobs smaller. What is it this time, ol' wise one?"

I barked out a laugh. No one gave me shit the way Gigi did. The girl just got me. I moved past her and dropped to sit on her bed.

"Where's Addy?" I scanned her room. It wasn't my first time here, hell, I'd helped move her in. And assisting Addy's mom was no easy task. The woman had bossed Cade and me around all day, forcing us to attach these goddamn headboards, and to hang eight million ridiculous things on the walls. I did it for Gigi. Hell, I'd do just about anything for this girl.

Because she's my best friend's little sister.

Nothing more.

"She's with Jett. What are you up to?" she asked, dropping to sit on her desk chair across from me.

"I came over to tell you not to come to the party this weekend. I don't think it's a good idea."

Her eyes doubled in size. "You came all the way over here to tell me that?"

"Did I stutter?" I lay back on her bed, and it smelled like peaches. I fucking loved it.

It reminded me of home.

And goodness.

And Gigi.

"You aren't the boss of me, Gray, so save your breath."

I knew she wouldn't listen to me. Hell, I just wanted an

excuse to come over here. For whatever reason, I liked being around Gigi.

More than I should.

"Do you disagree with me just for sport?" I asked, sliding her pillow beneath my head and making myself comfortable.

"I disagree with you because you're a pompous ass." She bit down on her juicy bottom lip, and I sat up quickly as my dick sprung to life.

What in the motherfuck is up with that?

My dick was an attentive little fucker when it came to Gigi. Especially these past few months. She didn't look like Cade's little sister anymore. Hell, she'd always been gorgeous, and I'd always had to remind myself that she was off-limits, but lately, I was feeling things I knew I shouldn't. And bickering with Gigi Jacobs had become better than sex with anyone else.

How messed up was that? I would definitely need to get my game on with some other girl this weekend to get her out of my head.

I scrubbed a hand down my face. "Have you talked to your brother? Never thought I'd see the day that Cade was pussy-whipped, but he sure seems to be spending a lot of time with Camilla."

"You're so crude," Gigi said, crossing her arms over her chest when she saw my gaze land there. I didn't miss the way her tits perked up when I looked at her.

Jesus.

I forced myself to think of my dog Duke the day we'd put him down every time my mind went in the wrong direction with Gigi Jacobs. Which was happening a lot lately.

It usually did the trick, but lately even the loss of my four-legged childhood companion wasn't working.

Fantasizing about a girl that was off-limits was not the best use of my time. I knew better. I may be a fuck up at a lot of things, but fucking up my relationship with the Jacobs was absolutely the one thing I'd never do.

"Not crude. Just being honest." I pushed to my feet.

"He likes a girl. Worse things can happen." She raised a brow in challenge.

"*Pussy*? Is that the word you have a problem with? You happen to have one and trust me when I tell you, you need to be aware of it. You're going to have a shit ton of losers trying to get in your pants at that frat party. College is not like Willow Springs." Anger rose in my chest and I moved toward the door. Suddenly needing distance from the girl I'd known most of my life.

"I can take care of myself, Gray." Now she was on her feet and getting in my face.

In my space.

Consuming my air.

"Your business is my business, like it or not. And these dudes are after one thing and one thing only." I assumed Gigi was a virgin, because I made it a point to keep tabs on her. I wasn't certain, but she hadn't had a boyfriend yet, as she was too good for all those jackasses back home.

"You're such a pig."

"Trust me, I've been called worse, G." I smiled.

"Get out." She walked to the door and placed a hand on the doorknob, raising a brow as if she dared me to fight her on this.

The door slammed in my face when I got to the other side, and I couldn't help but laugh.

I loved getting under her skin. It was far too easy.

But that was as far as I would ever allow it to go.

Ever.

three

. . .

Gigi

I PULLED out a couple of outfits to wear to the party and held them up for Addy. Living with my best friend was the best.

"I like the black top with the jean skirt and your cute booties. It's perfect," Addy said, as she sat at her desk which also worked as a vanity area. Her hair was clipped up, and she turned toward her makeup mirror and got back to work. "Has Jaden texted you again?"

Jaden was in my English class, and he'd invited us to the Sig Alpha party tonight. Not that you needed an invite. Everyone was talking about it. Even Jett had agreed to go with us, because he knew Addy wanted to go. Jett was focused on football right now, and they'd started the season strong coming out of the gate with a win against Utah. Jett had been called a freshman phenom in the local paper, and everyone was hoping he'd lead us to a winning season. Addy worried it was a lot of pressure for him, but he took it all in stride.

"Yes. He said he'd meet me there, but he's still a pledge, so he'll most likely be working the party."

She turned to face me as she pulled the clip from her hair

and let her long, dark hair tumble down her shoulders. "What do you think of him? Do you like him?"

"He's nice. But when I was leaving class, I stopped in the bathroom and when I came out, I found him getting a number from another girl. So, I think he's definitely casting his net and seeing what he catches," I said through my laughter.

She chuckled. "Typical frat boy. But it's good we're going. I saw a few guys checking you out in poli sci."

"Checking me out?" I gaped. "Who are you right now?"

"I'm channeling my inner Coco. She told me to make sure I get you to step out of your comfort zone and have some fun this year."

"I'm so happy that Coco rushed the same house as we did. I can't wait to see where Maura and Ivy end up," I said. Each of our schools held rush at a different time, and I was thankful that we were done. The whole experience had been a little stressful.

Addy's phone chimed as well, and she held it up. It was Coco FaceTiming to see what I was going to wear. "Speak of the devil."

I was so excited to go home and see my parents and the girls. We had to work around Jett's game schedule because Addy didn't want to miss any of them, which I understood. We'd gone to the first one together, and they didn't have one this weekend which was the reason he could go with us to the party.

"Hey, girls. Big party tonight," Coco purred as she came into focus. She was our resident fashion consultant, and we all benefited from her tips when it came to choosing an outfit.

We laughed. "Yep. Jett's coming over in twenty minutes and we'll walk over to the house."

"What I wouldn't give to see Gray Baldwin as fraternity president. Ah… that boy in a position of power. I can't handle it. Someone run me a cold shower. He's so freaking hot. And now he's got that face scruff making him all the sexier."

I rolled my eyes. Obviously Gray was good-looking. Quite possibly the best-looking boy I'd ever seen. But he was also arrogant, obnoxious, overbearing, self-centered, and annoying. That overshadowed his good looks.

"Whatever. Trust me, he knows he's all that. He doesn't need anyone stroking his ego. I thought you were into the nerdy chemistry guy?" I asked.

"Yes, Wallace and I are going to a party tonight. Just not sure it's going to go anywhere because he told me he has to be home by ten p.m. because he needs to be up early to study. On a Saturday. *Say what?* That's all sorts of crazy."

Addy and I fell back in a fit of giggles.

"Are you going to talk to that Jaden kid?" she asked and everyone perked up as if me talking to a guy would be the highlight of their lives.

"He's all right. I think he's a player."

"All boys are players, Gigi. At least until they meet the right girl. Don't overthink it," Coco said and Addy nodded in agreement.

There was a knock on the door and Addy hurried over.

Jett walked in and tugged her into his arms, and something in my chest squeezed. Something about the way he looked at her. It made me long for someone to look at me like that.

He moved over to sit beside me on the bed and waved at the screen. "What's up, Co?"

"Hey. Looking mighty fine, Mr. Stone," Coco said, causing us all to laugh once again.

"I try," he said with a shrug.

He patted his lap and Addy came over and sat there.

"All right, I've got to go throw my clothes on and get out of this robe so we can leave," I said, blowing her a kiss.

"Wear something hot, please, Gigi. Addy, make sure she

puts herself out there," Coco shouted, as I grabbed my outfit hanging on the closet door.

"Got it." I rolled my eyes at her. "All right. We'll call you later. Love you."

"Love you," Coco said, before ending the call.

"I'll be right back," I told Addy and Jett before heading to the bathroom down the hall to change. I hated the community bathroom. When I stepped inside, Bailey was standing at the sink applying lip gloss.

"Hey, Gigi. Are you and Addy going to the Sig Alpha party?" She flipped her long blonde hair over one shoulder and looked at me.

"Yep. Jett just got here, so the three of us are walking over in a little bit. Are you going?"

"Of course. Wouldn't miss it. Those guys are so hot. Have you seen their president this year? Someone pointed him out on campus and *Oh, my gawwwwd.* He's gorgeous. I'm going straight to the top, if you know what I mean." She winked.

I didn't have the heart to tell her it would not be a huge feat. Gray got around. Sleeping with him would be as easy as swiping her meal card. He was a sure thing. And she was pretty, so I'm sure he'd take the bait.

"Well, good luck with that. I'll see you there."

I moved to the stall to change my clothes as she continued to talk.

"Are you seriously changing in the stall? You're so adorable and private. I kind of love it."

I rolled my eyes because I knew she couldn't see me. I wasn't about to just strip down in front of her. I barely knew the girl.

I forced a fake chuckle. "Jett's in our room with Addy, so I ran down here."

I stepped out of the stall and her eyes scanned me from head to toe as I held my robe over my arm.

"Wow. You look great." She nodded as if she were

surprised. *Um, thanks?* "I mean, don't get me wrong. You're obviously stunning, but you usually just look so... I don't know. Girl next door-ish."

She burst out in hysterical laughter and I walked toward the door. I wasn't a fan. All of her compliments were backhanded. Addy and I had noticed it the first time we met her.

"Thanks." I made it to the doorway before she spoke again.

"How serious are Addy and Jett? I mean, he's really sexy too. And he's the star quarterback. I wouldn't mind a little time on the field with him, if you know what I mean." She laughed again, but it wasn't genuine, and I cringed at her words.

"They're as serious as it gets. You don't have a chance." I was surprised by how harsh my words came out, but grateful I'd put her in her place.

"Down, girl. Asking for a friend." She winked. "I've got my sights set on a certain fraternity president anyway."

I turned on my heels and left. I didn't have time for people like Bailey. And she'd just showed me who she really was. She knew Addy was my best friend. And she wanted her boyfriend. And she wanted to sink her claws into Gray.

Neither sat well with me.

"Hey. Watch yourself with Bailey. She just basically asked if Jett would stray," I said as I hung my robe on the back of the door.

"That snake. She was asking me all about how long Jett and I have been together this morning. I should have known."

"Nothing to worry about, Ace. You're tattooed here." He paused to touch his exposed inked arm, before placing his hand on his heart. "And here. I mean, you gave me half of your PB&J in third grade. Who can compete with that?"

Addy's head tipped back as he wrapped his arms around

her waist. "And of course it was organic peanut butter and jelly. Mama wouldn't have it any other way."

He leaned down and kissed her, and I swooned just a little. I loved the way they loved each other.

"Okay. Glad we're on the same page." Addy pulled away and fanned her face. "We better get going."

I glanced in the mirror one more time. My blouse left one arm exposed, and Addy had powdered on a little highlighter on my collarbone. It shimmered just a bit, and I ran my fingers through my long waves to give them some lift before heading to the door.

"Let's do this."

The dorms were in the center of campus, and Greek Row was only a few blocks' walk. All of the sorority and fraternity houses lined one street, so it made it easy to move from house to house if there were multiple parties going on. At least that's what Tiffany had told us. When we arrived at Sig Alpha, it looked like something straight out of a movie. People were scattered in the front lawn, and music boomed from the house. Gray stood off in the distance running a hand through his hair. It was longer in the front and shorter in the back, and it definitely worked for him. He didn't have his typical happy-go-lucky look on his face. He appeared—stressed. I wasn't used to seeing him that way. He picked up several red Solo cups and stacked them inside one another, before ushering people inside. He hadn't seen us yet as we were still a few feet from the front porch of the Sig Alpha house. But Gray had always been easy to spot. He was tall, and he was larger than life. Always had been.

"Wow. There are a lot of people here," Addy said, and Jett and I nodded.

Jett seemed completely unfazed. I was anything but.

"Gigi," a voice called out from the front porch. It was Jaden, and he waved us over. "Come on in."

Jett studied him and nodded. "He seems a little shady. Let's go."

I laughed because Jett was as trusting as Cade and Gray. They thought all guys were bad news. I often fought the urge to remind them that they were also boys and could be equally as shady if they wanted to be.

"Hey, Jaden. Seems like the party has started, huh?" I shouted over the booming music in the background. "This is my best friend Addy and her boyfriend Jett."

"What's up, guys? Yeah, this party is the shit. I pledged the best house on campus, what can I say? And you look fucking hot." His eyes scanned my entire body and I shivered.

Not in a good way.

He didn't even try to hide the fact that he was basically stripping me bare with his gaze. I could definitely tell he'd been drinking, because he hadn't been this bold when we'd talked in class. We stepped inside the house and made our way toward the kitchen.

"I don't like him," Jett whispered close to my ear and I nodded.

Addy squeezed my hand as we followed him.

"Drinks?" He handed a red Solo cup to Jett who turned him down.

"No, thanks."

"You're clearly not in a fraternity, because no one would tolerate that shit," he said as he handed a cup of red juice to me and Addy.

"I'm definitely not in a fraternity, you're correct." Jett's eyes were hard, and he didn't look happy as he scanned our cups. I knew that he wasn't drinking so that he could keep an eye on Addy and me as this was our first college party. Sure, we drank a little bit in high school, but we were definitely not in Willow Springs anymore. Things were louder, larger, and more in your face here.

"Drink up, ladies," Jaden purred, touching the bottom of my cup and trying to get me to down it. Before I could stop him, the cup was slapped right from my hand, spilling all over the front of my blouse and splashing onto Jaden.

"Get the fuck out of here, pledge. Don't even fucking look at her, do you hear me?" Gray hissed, as I swiped at the front of my shirt. "Give me that." He took the cup from Addy's hand quite a bit gentler than he'd torn mine from my hands.

"Sorry, Gray. I didn't know she was with you." Jaden's words slurred as he took a step back, wiping the red punch from the front of his white T-shirt to no avail. Jett used his hand to cover his smile and Addy and I stared at one another with disbelief.

"Now you fucking know. Go get a couple beers from the keg and bring them to me," Gray said, before walking over to the counter and grabbing a few paper towels and heading back toward me.

He started to wipe the liquid from my chest and my jaw dropped. He was cleaning me up like I was a freaking child. "Give that to me, you big buffoon. Could you have made a bigger scene? What are you doing?"

"*What am I doing?* Keeping you fucking safe. Don't ever drink fraternity punch. It's too strong. Drink a beer if you need to drink something. And I'll make a fucking scene whenever the hell I feel like it." The look on his face was caveman-like, then softened a tad when he finished his tirade. "You're welcome."

Jett barked out a laugh, and Addy's lips turned up in the corners before I shot her a look and she straightened. "I don't think you could do anything else to make this worse. Now I'm soaking wet, everyone's staring, and you ran off the boy I was talking to."

"Is that so?" He crossed his arms over his chest, and the muscles strained against the white T-shirt. I'd seen Gray's chest before out at the lake, and it was something one could write books about. All chiseled and tan and cut. I mean, if you were into that sort of thing, which I wasn't.

I most definitely wasn't.

"*That is so,* you big jackass." God, he could piss me off without even trying. And why did he have to look so good when he was doing it? His green eyes danced with pops of amber and gold, and I found it difficult to look away.

"First of all, that dumbass you're talking about. He's a douchebag."

"Yet, he got a bid to Sig Alpha, *your fraternity*?" I raised a brow in challenge.

"He sure as fuck did. This house is full of douchebags. And I'm currently babysitting these fuckers, so trust me when I tell you that you don't want to mess with that dude. I won't allow it," he said, leaning closer so his breath tickled my cheeks.

Is he for real?

I gasped in dramatic fashion. Coco would be proud. "You won't allow it? You did not just say that." The nerve. "Are you serious?"

"Dead fucking serious, G." He stormed across the room as I followed him with my eyes. He talked to a guy in the band, and the music stopped.

What the hell was he doing?

"Listen up. You see this girl here?" he shouted, and everyone turned as he made his way over to me and palmed the top of my head like a freaking lunatic. "If you so much as hit on this girl, I'll punch you in the fucking face. Are we clear?"

People laughed and nodded, and the music started to play again. Jaden walked over, balancing three red Solo cups as beer sloshed over the rim. All that confidence and swagger was gone. "Here you go, Pres."

"Don't call me that, you dipshit. And stay the fuck away from her." He offered Jett and Addy each a beer. Jett liked

Gray and appeared to be very pleased with the ridiculous scene he had just made. My blood boiled as I took the cup from Jaden and forced a smile. He nodded before walking away.

"How dare you speak on my behalf. Now no one is going to talk to me." I seethed before taking a big gulp of the disgusting, warm beer.

"Kind of the point."

"I'm leaving. I'm soaking wet, you just embarrassed me, and I've had enough." I tipped my head back and downed the liquid before shoving the cup at his chest. "Thanks for ruining my night."

"Happy to oblige." He smirked.

I stormed out of the party with Addy and Jett on my heels.

"Don't be too hard on him. I think he's just looking out for you," Jett said, as we made our way back to the dorms.

"He's ridiculous. And annoying," I huffed. And I hated how good he looked. Even when he was humiliating me, I couldn't pull my eyes away from him.

"I agree with Jett. He means well. He's always been protective of you. He just doesn't go about it the right way." Addy chuckled and wrapped an arm around my shoulder.

I didn't know if I was mad over the ridiculous scene he'd just made, or angry because a little part of me enjoyed it. I liked having Gray's attention, and it made no sense.

Because he drove me crazy.

In the worst way.

four

. . .

Gray

DIPSHIT NUMBER one was passed out on the couch with a half-naked chick, and I shoved at his shoulder. "Time to clean, pledge."

I'd had a shit night babysitting all of these assholes, and I'd barely slept. Thankfully, we'd survived the night without getting busted by the cops, or any unnecessary drama. Well, aside from the fact that Gigi wasn't speaking to me. I could live with it. Especially seeing the dude who was trying to talk to her last night zip his jeans up and push to his feet. Dirty bastard. The thought that he'd been pursuing Gigi did all sorts of crazy things to me.

"Come back to bed, baby," the girl whispered, reaching for his hand. A used condom sat on the coffee table next to him and I cursed under my breath.

Flush that shit in the toilet. Don't set it on the coffee table where we all live. Which I'd like to point out, Jaden did not live in the house. He was a fucking freshman. A pledge.

Not the king of the castle.

"Clean this shit up. We don't need your used condoms sitting on our table. Have some fucking decency."

He chuckled. "Sorry, Pres. Frat boy life, am I right?"

I rolled my eyes. That ridiculous name was grating my nerves and he was a lot of things, but right was not one of them. I made my way through the house making sure everyone was working and doing their part. My phone buzzed and Cade's name flashed across the screen.

"What's up, brother?" I said, my voice gravelly and tired.

"You sound like shit. Rough night?"

"Something like that." I pointed to the ground at a bra that was lying on the floor and one of the pledges hustled over and tossed it in the garbage bag.

"I just talked to Gigi. She went to her first college frat party," he said, and I could tell he was trying to keep the humor from his tone.

I ran a hand through my hair. "Fuck. She's pissed, isn't she?"

"You slapped a cup out of her hand and then told every dude at the party not to speak to her?" He barely got the words out through his laughter.

"Damn straight. These shitheads are barking up the wrong fucking tree," I hissed, pointing to the shitter as a few of the pledges huddled around the bathroom, afraid to go inside.

They had zero issue making the mess, but they were hesitant to clean it up.

No slacking on my watch, boys.

I'd been a pledge once, and I'd paid my dues.

"Thanks for looking out for her. You could probably tone it down a bit. We do want her to have a little fun," he said, as a girl's voice called out to him in the background.

"No can do. Say hi to Camilla, douchebag. Talk to you later."

He was laughing when I ended the call. I found Ricky Turlington, one of the dudes I'd personally offered a bid to because he was smart and less douchey than the others who were currently dry heaving over the toilet. I fought back my laughter.

"All right, someone else take a turn plunging. Follow me, Turlington." He was eager to get the hell out of that shit show and he trailed behind me in the trek for the kitchen. Our cook, Francie, was none too pleased to find the kitchen in a less than perfect state this morning.

"This is Francie. Make sure you're always good to her when you're over here, got it?" I asked before I paused to kiss the sweet older woman on the cheek as I'd run out of here when she'd arrived earlier this morning while I was trying to clean up the mess.

"You're lucky I love you, Gray," she grumbled as she finished wiping down the counters.

We were spoiled by this woman. She provided three warm meals a day, and she was a damn good cook. Not as good as Katie Jacobs, but much better than the private cook my mom had at her house. Francie kept two refrigerators that were locked in our oversized pantry, and that's where she stored food that we weren't allowed access to when she wasn't here. It was the only way to keep the partiers out of our food. She walked out of the pantry with a platter and set it down in front of me and Ricky before lifting the foil to show us a massive pile of donuts.

"Grab a few before I set them out for the animals," she said with a chuckle.

I pulled up a chair and motioned for Ricky to do the same as we both reached for a donut. "You left early last night," I said.

He shifted in his seat. "Is that okay? I didn't want to get too drunk because I knew I was expected to be back here first thing this morning to clean."

Ricky had been the first one to show up ready to work today. The other pledges had passed out on the couches or on the floor of one of the brothers' rooms and still couldn't get it together to be here on time when they'd spent the night under this very roof.

I noticed that kind of shit, because as much as I'd always liked to have a good time, I was all about putting in the work. I'd never been sloppy, nor had I ever slacked on my responsibilities. I'd grown up with a man who'd done that, and I didn't want to take that path. It would give Simon far too much pleasure.

What can I say… I'm petty that way.

"Totally cool, dude. Relax. I knew you were good peeps, that's why I wanted you here. We need brothers with a good head on their shoulders."

"Thanks, Gray. I appreciate it."

"Sure. Don't let those assholes push you around. Know that I have your back, so don't take too much shit. Okay?"

He took a bite of his donut and sprinkles fell all over the table and we both laughed. "Got it."

We shot the shit for a little while and I made my way to my room to grab a shower. One of the perks of being president meant a private bathroom in my bedroom. After two years of sharing that communal shitter which held memories I'd rather not recall, I was happy for some privacy.

Not that there weren't good times in there. Hell, I'd banged a few chicks in those stalls. I couldn't complain. But now that I'd stopped drinking these past few weeks, it didn't sound as appealing. It was filthy and it smelled like piss and shit, and it was certainly not the most conducive space to get your game on.

My phone buzzed and my father's name flashed across the screen. Hadn't talked to him in a few days as he was focused on surviving the first thirty days of his ninety-day program in rehab, so I tried to make myself available when he had time to talk.

"Hey, Dad. How's it going?" I asked, dropping to sit on my bed.

"Gray, glad you picked up. It's all right. Kind of feeling

like I'm ready to get the hell out of here and get back to some normalcy, you know?"

This was not my first rodeo when it came to fielding these calls. He always wavered during the first two weeks. It was like the shock of his latest rock bottom would start to become less appalling. When he'd agreed to go to rehab, he'd been disgusted with himself and ready for change.

That's the thing about addiction. It didn't matter where you came from or how smart you were—it pulled you down into the ugly abyss of darkness. My dad wasn't a bad guy. He was the smartest dude I knew, funny as hell, and loyal to the core—when he was sober. Unfortunately, he was high more often than not, and he'd gotten lost in all the numbing. I could probably hate the man if it had happened differently. My dad wasn't the guy who just liked to party and couldn't get it together. No, it had happened in the worst kind of way. He'd been in a car accident when I was five years old, and the doctor had prescribed him oxy. And that was all she wrote. He'd been fired from the firm a year later, and Mom left him shortly after.

He gave train wreck a new name.

This was a high-speed bullet train that had derailed in record time.

My grandparents lived back in Willow Springs and I saw them often when I was home. The hurt in my grandmother's eyes was enough to sober Dad up and send him off to the rehab facility in Dallas once he'd lost all the money that he'd promised to pay right back.

It wasn't the first time, and probably wouldn't be the last.

I believed in redemption, but my father had taught me to be a realist after the many times I'd put too much stock into hoping he would get it together.

"Yeah. But remember, the results work best when you follow through with the whole ninety days, right? And Grandpa took that money out of his retirement to give you the chance to get clean. That alone should be enough motivation to see this through."

"I hear you, son. But I put some money on the horses before I came in here, and it hit. Won a couple thousand bucks, and I'm ready to get out and make my money work for me. Get back in the game. Maybe talk to Larry at the firm about working my way back."

He was talking crazy. My father had been disbarred and escorted off the property after he'd been caught stealing from his partners. I didn't know all the gory details because I'd been young at the time, but I heard the talk around town, and I knew he'd fucked up bad enough that he wouldn't be going back. But it didn't mean he couldn't get his life together and do something else.

"All right. Well, that money could be used to get on your feet when you get out. Or you could start paying Grandma and Grandpa back, right?" I ran a hand through my hair. How do you tell an addict that betting money on a horse was exactly the reason he needed to stay in the program and see it through?

"You fucking punk. Are you kidding me with this shit? I shouldn't have called you, Gray. You're a judgy asshole just like your mom."

And hello, detox. Welcome back.

"I suppose so, Dad. But the difference is, I'm still here. Standing beside you and supporting you through all the bullshit."

There were days that it was too much, and I was just tired of cheering him on only to be disappointed. But that glimmer of hope, that one percent chance that this time could stick—well, it was enough to keep me here.

Keep me hoping and believing he could get better.

He was silent on the other end. "Fuck. I'm sorry, kid. It just sucks right now."

I hated when he called me kid. Like we were strangers

and not father and son. It was his go-to word when he was pulling away, so it was a trigger for me.

"Dad," I paused, giving him a minute to process the word. It was a little trick I'd picked up from a friend at one of my early Al-Anon meetings. I wasn't above guilt or emotional blackmail if it helped my father find his way. "I know how tough this is. I've stopped drinking myself these past few weeks, because I realized that I'd been doing a bit of numbing myself."

"Don't go down that path, Gray. I know that asshole stepfather of yours is hard to deal with, but don't let him push you down the rabbit hole. That's what he wants."

That was the first intelligent thing my father had said in two weeks. He was in there.

Somewhere.

Beneath all the lies and the shame.

Which was why I was holding on so hard to hope.

But he was right about Simon. And I'd given him plenty of ammunition against me. I'd partied my way through high school and the first few years of college because that's what he said I would do, and if I was being completely honest and taking some responsibility of my own, it wasn't all Simon's fault. Drinking had become an escape for me too. And being the son of an addict, I should have recognized that instead of jumping on board and playing with fire.

I had tendencies like my father, and I was smart enough to recognize that they could pull me under. So yes, stepping back because I was in charge of this house had been a good move for me. And being sober for fourteen consecutive days had allowed me to see things a bit more clearly. First off, the fact that I hadn't gone fourteen days without drinking in a few years was a big red flag. It was easy to ignore the signs when you're constantly buzzed.

I was treading in dangerous waters.

And I wasn't proud of that.

I was thankful that I wasn't having any physical withdrawals from booze. And I was grateful that I'd never been tempted by anything stronger when I was drunk. I'd always stayed away from drugs and pills because that was what had ultimately destroyed Dad's life. But booze was a conduit to that lifestyle, and it was time to check myself at the door.

"I hear you. And I'm glad for this wake-up call. I think it's easy to get lost in that escape, you know? I thought I was just having fun, but I'm not so sure anymore."

"Well, you're my son, so be careful. I'm sorry that I'm the reason you want to escape from life though. That's on me."

"That's not it, Dad. Everyone's got their shit, right? I'm just learning that it may be better to just deal with it and not run from it."

"You're a smart fucking kid, Gray. I still haven't figured that shit out. I've been running so long I don't know how to live anymore."

"Yeah, you do. Just trust the process. Take it one day at a time, okay?"

"All right. I can do this."

"Of course, you can. I believe in you, Dad."

"Needed to hear that today. Love you, Gray."

"Love you too. Call me if you need me," I said.

"I will." He ended the call, and I made a quick call to Toby, his counselor at the facility. Toby said that everything my father was saying was normal and to be expected. We had weekly calls, so he was keeping me posted on Dad's progress. After we hung up, I made my way to the bathroom to shower.

I let the hot water beat down on my back. I liked having a clear head. I'd always been able to maintain good grades while partying my ass off like I was some kind of goddamn rock star. But having a clear head was different. And I didn't mind it at all.

But I needed something good to focus on and the first

thing that popped in my head was Gigi. I could still see her storming out of the house all pissed off and full of fire. I fucking loved it. Loved getting under her skin and getting her all worked up. It wasn't right, but I never claimed to be a rule follower. I loved the way her tongue had dipped out to wet her lips after she'd hissed at me. The way her ass swayed as she exited the house.

I reached down and gripped my cock, sliding my hand up and down the shaft.

I closed my eyes and let my mind take me where it wanted to go.

Thoughts of Gigi Jacobs filled my head.

Blonde hair and sapphire eyes and a tight little body.

The thought of her soft lips made me grow even harder.

What the actual fuck?

This was worse than drinking. The absolute most forbidden thoughts I could have, and they were happening more often lately. But I couldn't stop them if I wanted to.

And I didn't want to.

I'd been torturing myself for too long.

Fantasy was okay. It would be my little secret and one I'd never act on.

I pumped harder as I thought about her perky tits. How she smelled like peaches and I imagined she'd taste just as sweet.

I groaned as the best orgasm of my life ripped through my body.

Good Christ.

Gigi was different. Special. I couldn't fuck around with her. She deserved much better.

Not to mention she was Cade's little sister.

But this wasn't my first time fantasizing about this girl.

And it sure as shit wouldn't be my last.

five

. . .

Gigi

BAILEY and her roommate Sadie had invited themselves into our room, literally just pushed the door aside and walked right in, and Addy had given me the look several times letting me know she was as annoyed as I was. I mean, who does that?

"That girl Ophelia down the hall told me she's a virgin." Bailey's head fell back in laughter. "How pathetic is that? What is she waiting for?"

"Maybe she wants to wait for the right guy. I doubt she'd be very happy that you're telling people what she shared." Sadie frowned, and I could tell she was uncomfortable with her roommate. This was the first time I'd actually heard her stand up to Bailey.

"Agreed. There's no shame in waiting," Addy said.

"Are you telling me you haven't jumped all over the hot quarterback?" Bailey flipped her hair over her shoulder and studied Addy.

"It's not something I really talk about with people I don't know well." Addy's face hardened. That was as harsh as she got, and I was grateful that she'd put the annoying girl in her place.

"Well, you're no fun. How about you, Gigi? I know you all came from that tiny little town, but you know what they say about small-town girls," Bailey said, and then forced a fake laugh.

"I don't know what they say, nor do I really care." I pushed to my feet. I was over this conversation. We weren't even friends with this girl.

There was a knock on the door, and I was thrilled for the reprieve. Gray stood on the other side, and I'd never been so happy to see him because it meant that Bailey would have to leave.

"Hey, come in," I said, and he startled. He probably expected me to ask why he was here or snarl at him like I usually did. It had been a few days since I'd gone to that party and he'd acted like a jerk. He checked in every day by calling and texting, but I'd stayed away from the fraternity house since then.

"Oh, oooohhhh," Bailey said, taking him in so blatantly that Addy and I both laughed. "How do you know Gray?"

"How do you know Gray?" he barked before crossing his arms over his chest. The boy was moody and broody these days.

"I've seen you around." Bailey fluttered her lashes at him, and I rolled my eyes. Sadie smiled nervously, as if his mere presence was too much for her.

Gray was beautiful to look at. No doubt about it. He was tall with broad shoulders and his hair was sexy in that I-don't-give-a-shit way. And those mesmerizing green eyes had most girls falling at his feet.

Lucky for me, I didn't look at him that way.

Or at least I didn't allow myself to.

"All right. Are they leaving? Because I need to talk to you." He turned his attention to me. He was on edge. I'd known this boy my entire life, and I could tell something was up.

"I guess what they say about small-town girls is true, huh, Gigi?" Bailey teased, and I wanted to dropkick her.

"Again, I have no idea what you're talking about. See you later, Sadie," I said, holding the door open for them as I hadn't moved since hurricane Gray rolled in.

"Bye, Gigi. Bye, Addy." Sadie smiled, and I decided right there to reach out to her more. Being roommates with Bailey must be the worst.

Addy and I both said goodbye and I shut the door.

"Who the fuck was that? Hell, I thought she was about to climb me like a goddamn tree," Gray hissed before dropping to sit on my bed.

"Make yourself at home, why don't you." I rolled my eyes as Addy reached for her backpack.

"You're right about her, Gray. She's the worst. Okay, I'm off to Jett's. You guys have fun. I'll text you if I spend the night there, okay?" Addy said, pulling me in for a hug.

"Okay. Have fun."

"See you, Addy. Tell Jett I'm looking forward to the game Saturday." Gray kicked off his shoes.

Addy closed the door behind her, and I moved to stand over the large boy sprawled across my comforter. "What are you doing here?"

"There she is. I thought you were a little friendlier than usual when I first arrived." He laughed.

"Well, I wanted her to leave. Your timing was impeccable for the first time… ever."

"That's how I roll, G. Just came to check on you and talk to you about that douchecanoe, Jaden. He actually just came to my room to ask me permission to ask you out like I'm your fucking keeper. Who does that? He's an asshole."

"I'm guessing someone who you threatened when he spoke to me at the party. Of course, he's asking now. You told him to stay away from me and you're the president of the fraternity he pledged. Now you've made him feel like he has to ask your permission, you power-hungry, arrogant—" I paused because I couldn't think of enough descriptive words for him at the moment. "Ball-breaking, narcissistic, pompous ass."

Not bad for a moment's notice.

He sat up and a wide grin spread across his face, and my stomach flipped. "Oh, narcissistic is a good one. That's new. Proud of you, girl."

"Shut up. What did you tell him?"

"I told him, no. I said I'd kick his ass to the curb if he so much as looked at you." He put his hands up when I gasped. "I'm kidding. I said I'd think about it. That's why I'm here."

"To ask if I like him?"

"Hell no. Of course, you don't like him. He's a putz. He woke up with another chick on the couch the morning after that party. He is not someone you want to mess with. But I wanted to tell you that so you could kick his ass to the curb."

"So, you came all the way over to the dorms instead of calling me just to tell me to turn him down? And why do you care if he was with another girl? We aren't dating. We've talked in class a few times, that's it. And you shouldn't be so judgy, seeing as you probably woke up with a random girl in your bed too. Glass houses, Gray Baldwin."

He chuckled. "I did not. My dick is on some kind of hiatus. And when it comes to you, I'll judge all day long. He's not good enough for you, and that's all you need to know."

"Please do not talk to me about your *penis*. It's more than I can handle right now," I said, nervously pacing the room.

Did it just get hot in here?

Maybe it was my virgin-self getting nervous even thinking about Gray's, er, package.

He laughed. "Good Christ, G. Don't call it a penis. That's offensive. Boys have penises. I'm a man. I have a dick. Or a cock. And it's a really good one, if I don't say so myself."

"TMI," I shouted, covering my ears with my hands. I didn't want to think about Gray and his dazzling… goods. I'm sure it was a super-powered love machine. But that didn't mean I wanted to talk about it. Or think about it.

I didn't.

I shouldn't.

I wouldn't.

"Take it down a notch. It's okay to get worked up. Most females do. No shame in that game." He dropped back down to lie on his back.

"What's wrong with you? You're off. Is your mom okay? The girls?" I asked, suddenly worried because Gray wasn't himself. I'd noticed the minute he walked through the door before getting distracted by his giant—*members-only package.*

Oh. My. God.

What was happening?

Get your head out of the gutter.

"No. They're fine. Just some shit with my dad." He pushed back up to sit when his phone vibrated in his pocket.

He reached down to grab it and read the screen, cursing under his breath.

I moved to sit beside him. "Is your dad okay?"

I knew his dad struggled with alcohol and drugs, but he never talked about it. Cade told me that Gray had a tough time dealing with it all.

"Not really. I don't fucking know, G. Being a slave to addiction is no way to live your life. And it's a battle that he's losing. You know Wren, right?"

"Wren Staub? From back home?" I asked.

"Yeah. That was him, letting me know he heard my dad left rehab early. They were friends back in the day. And when I last talked to my dad, he was getting antsy. I should have known he'd fucking bail."

My chest squeezed at his words. I'd never seen this

vulnerable side of Gray. He always seemed so on top of the world. But having a parent struggle with addiction like this couldn't be easy. Guilt engulfed me that I'd never stopped to think about how that probably felt for him. My annoyance with this boy usually kept me so distracted.

"I'm sorry. Do you know where he is? Can you call him?"

"I've tried a few times, that's why I reached out to Wren." He shrugged. "All right. I'm going to go. I didn't come over here to burden you with my shit. Just beware of Jaden, okay?"

He'd come all the way here to warn me about a boy I didn't even really like. I just wanted Gray to think I did because I knew it annoyed him. But I didn't care about any of that right now. He was hurting and I could feel it in every bone in my body.

"Wait. What are you doing now?"

He paused as he reached for his shoes and his smile was forced. "Probably just go bust some balls at the house."

"Why don't you stay and watch a movie? I'll even let you pick. Come on. I'm bored. Addy's gone. It will be a good distraction for both of us."

His tongue swiped out to wet his plump bottom lip, and I squeezed my thighs together on instinct.

Holy mother of God, this is not good.

"You want to watch a movie with me, G?" His voice was gravelly and sexy, and all the air left my lungs.

"I just thought maybe, I don't know," I fumbled over my words.

"I'm just giving you shit. Yeah. Let's watch a movie. That way I can make sure Jaden stays the fuck away from you, right?" He laughed, dropping back down to sit on the bed beside me. His weight caused me to bounce and I tipped into him. His hands came around my middle and he pushed me back up, and my skin heated instantly. Chills ran down my arms, and I struggled to gain my composure.

He kept his hands there for longer than necessary before

pulling away, and I finally cleared my throat so I could speak. "Okay, what should we watch?"

I reached for my laptop and scooted back so I was pressed against the wall. He did the same and I settled my computer on my lap.

"You pick. I don't care," he said.

"You sure about that? You know I'm a big fan of chick flicks. Last chance to choose," I said, my voice was all tease.

"Surprise me." He folded his hands together and rested them behind his head, stretching out his big body next to me as our legs hung off the bed. There wasn't really anywhere else to watch a movie in a dorm room. But it suddenly felt very intimate.

I chose *Sweet Home Alabama*. It was one of my favorites and I thought he might like it because Cade did. The movie started and I tried to relax.

But sitting this close to Gray was doing all sorts of crazy things to me.

The smell of mint and sandalwood seeped into my senses.

This wasn't the first time I was feeling things about Gray. And I hated it. We'd grown up together and he'd always acted like a big brother, but sometime over the past few years, things had shifted. I looked at him differently, and I wasn't proud of it.

This was Gray.

My brother's best friend.

He was sexy and beautiful and he stole the air from my lungs most days.

I knew he didn't look at me that way. But when I was around him, or alone with him, I felt all sorts of things. My brain was trying everything not to look over at him. His big hand rested right next to mine.

My back remained ramrod straight and I stared at the screen for two hours.

Crossing a line with Gray Baldwin was not an option.

It was a complete impossibility.

We were all going out. Jett had led the team to victory on the field, and it had been a fun day on campus. College football had a way of bringing everyone together. I'd run into Gray at the game. I hadn't seen him since the night we'd watched a movie together. He'd left shortly after. When I'd talked to my brother the next day, I didn't mention it. Nothing had happened, and it didn't mean anything—but for some reason, I felt like Gray had opened up about his father, and I didn't get the feeling he did that often. Or with many people. And it wasn't my story to tell.

I'd checked in on him every day since, and we'd texted back and forth a few times. I guess in a weird way we were becoming friends. We'd always been family, but he was showing me sides to him that I didn't know existed. He still hadn't heard from his father, and I knew it was weighing heavily on him.

We were going to a party at his house tonight, and I'd already talked to him about staying out of my business. I was in college and I wanted to have fun. Bailey's words had stayed with me—her laughing about Ophelia being a virgin. It made no sense. Bailey was not someone I respected, and her opinion didn't matter to me, but what she'd said still made me wonder when my life would start. When I'd meet someone who I'd want to take that step with. I wondered if I was the problem? Was I unapproachable? Too closed off? I'd always been a bit more on the shy side with people I didn't know, but I considered myself a friendly person.

"So, Sadie, Bailey, Ophelia, and a few other girls from our floor are walking over to the Sig Alpha house with us. Jett's on his way over now and he's bringing a few of his teammates," Addy said, wriggling her brows.

I laughed. "Okay. I'm open to that. Jaden's been texting that he's looking forward to seeing me tonight, but after what Gray told me, I don't have real high hopes about him."

"Gray sure is protective of you, right? I'm telling you, he likes you as more than a friend," Addy said, pulling out a few outfits and placing them on her bed. All the Magic Willows thought there was something between Gray and me, and they'd always teased me about it.

"Um, that's a hard no. He's a total player. I'm definitely not his type. He just feels protective because he's so close with my family." I searched through my closet, shoving hanger after hanger to the side. I loved my clothes, but they screamed country chic. I wanted to channel my inner Coco tonight.

My phone vibrated on my bed and I laughed when I looked at the screen to see the incoming FaceTime call.

Her timing was always uncanny.

"Hey, Co. What's up?" I held the phone in front of me so I could see her face.

Addy ran up behind me and waved. "Hey, girl. We miss you. We're meeting at home next weekend, right?"

All five of us had agreed to meet in Willow Springs next weekend, and I couldn't wait to see my girls.

"Yes. Can't wait. So, I figured you needed some help picking out your outfit, Gigi. I've been texting Addy and she's got a few options for you on her bed." Coco dropped to sit at her desk and applied some lip gloss.

"Those are for me? I thought those were for you. What's wrong with my clothes?" I asked, moving over to Addy's bed to look at my choices.

"It's a frat party, not a church barbecue. And it's certainly not like Addy has the sexiest clothes either, but she's got a few cute bodysuits and some sexy jeans. You can totally rock that look."

I reached for the red bodysuit that dipped low in the back. "I can't wear a bra with this one."

"Exactly. You don't need one. It's not low-cut and you don't have much there, and what you do have is very perky," Coco said through her laughter.

"Is it sad that you know my boobs better than any boy ever has?"

"It's fine. But it's time to change that. You aren't in Willow Springs anymore, where you've known everyone your entire life. That's why you're getting so much attention at school, because you're freaking gorgeous and everyone is taking notice. So, own your shit tonight. Make them beg for it."

"Jeez, Co. She's not looking for a top dollar bid, she just wants to flirt with a cute guy." Addy fell back on her bed laughing.

"Same difference. I'll wait. Try on that red bodysuit with those fitted dark skinny jeans. You've got some cute black heel boots, right?"

I handed the phone to Addy and held up a pair of booties and they both gave me a thumbs-up. I slipped on the bodysuit and tugged the jeans over my hips and butt, taking in a deep breath to get the zipper up. I leaned over and put on the booties and then turned to face Addy. She held the phone up for Coco, who whistled and cheered.

"Holy hotness, girl. Prepare to have all eyes on you tonight."

I moved toward the full-length mirror that hung on the back of our door to check myself out. Wow. It was a different look, that's for sure. I did tend to dress pretty boho in loose-fitting, flowy dresses and tops with my ankle booties. But Coco was right. This was a fraternity party. I was in college now. It was time to start acting like it.

I turned to check out my butt in the mirror and thoughts of Gray flooded my mind. He would have a fit when he saw me in this.

And for whatever reason, a big smile spread across my face.

Pissing off Gray Baldwin was quickly becoming my favorite pastime.

six

. . .

Gray

THE HOUSE WAS GOING off and I leaned against the wall and sipped my Perrier water out of a red Solo cup. I was bougie that way, and I didn't need anyone giving me a hard time about not drinking. I needed to make sure this party stayed under control, and I was on call if Wren found my father. I needed to be ready to jump in the car and head to Willow Springs to drag his ass back to rehab if needed.

So, it would be another sober party.

"You guys throw the best damn parties, Gray," Lila said as she kissed her way down my neck. Her hands moved beneath my T-shirt and ran up my chest.

I continued to look out at the party as her lips moved up to my face and covered my mouth. The girl was some kind of sex goddess and we'd banged it out a few times over the years, but it had been a while. We didn't have much in common outside of the physical, but right now this was the only kind of escape I would allow myself. I hadn't hooked up with anyone since I'd come back to school, because I'd been in a foul mood for the past three weeks.

Between the pressure of being president, keeping an eye on Gigi, my class load, and worrying about my dad, I hadn't been a whole lot of fun lately. My fingers tangled in her hair as I kissed her. She tasted like cherries just like she always did. The girl must use some kind of sexy toothpaste or something to have a mouth that tasted like the top of an ice cream sundae.

I tried to get lost in it, but I couldn't seem to get there. I tugged her mouth away and pulled her into a hug. I didn't want to be a total dick, but I wasn't in the mood for Lila at the moment. "Sorry. I need to keep an eye out on the party, so give me a bit, okay?"

She looked up at me. Big brown eyes, red lips, and a mouth begging to be fucked.

Jesus.

And yet nothing was happening down south, which was odd. Hell, I'd been hard since the football game the entire time I talked to Gigi. My best friend's little sister.

How fucked up was that?

I'd had to come home and take care of business in the shower for the hundredth time this week. I'd rubbed it out so many times I thought my dick would fall off. But it hadn't happened yet. I'd decided there was no harm in fantasizing about Gigi as long as I never acted on it.

But now I was thinking about her while a sexy as fuck girl was rubbing up against my junk, and I only wanted to get away.

This was not good.

Maybe I could get her out of my system by banging Lila tonight. That was an idea.

"Don't make me wait too long. I've missed you, Gray. We're so good together," she said, as her red lips came up to meet mine and her hand grazed my cock. He wasn't in the mood for Lila apparently.

A group of people walked through the front door and my eyes landed on Gigi Baldwin, surrounded by Addy, Jett, and a few guys I recognized from the football team. As she moved through the crowd and I got a better look at her, I was pushing Lila away and moving forward.

Hell no.

She wore a skin-tight red top and jeans that fit her tight little body like a second skin.

My dick jumped to attention as I pushed through the crowd of people standing between us.

She was laughing and talking, and I caught Jaden out of my peripheral moving toward her. Her blonde waves ran down her back which I just noticed was completely bare, and she looked sexy as fuck.

"Gray, there's a fight out front," Ricky said, reaching for my arm just before I made my way to Gigi.

Fuck me.

"Let's go," I said, beelining for the front door. The cops were looking for a reason to shut us down. I wasn't going to give them more reason than necessary.

Two drunk assholes were shouting and shoving one another. No blows had been thrown as far as I could tell.

"Hey, dickheads. Figure it out and go inside and have some fun or get the hell out of here. We don't need the cops here. Got it?"

They shrugged and then laughed. Dudes were so weird sometimes. They were ready to go to blows two minutes ago and now they looked like they might hug it out.

"Fuck it. Let's get a beer," Dipshit one said to the other.

"Well, that was easy," Ricky said, and we both laughed.

I made my way back inside and found Gigi right away. She was standing against a wall now, with Jaden all up in her business. I stayed back. I wanted to see how she'd handle him. I'd warned her about him already. What was I going to do, go yank his ass out here?

It wasn't a bad idea, but I needed to know that Gigi could handle herself.

I wouldn't always be around.

Hell, I should be in my room banging Lila, who was currently licking her lips and staring at me across the room.

Yet, my gaze kept going back to my best friend's little sister. Jaden leaned down and whispered something in her ear, and she smiled. My chest tightened. Was she falling for this bullshit? Hell, I was the king of this game. I knew how it went. But Gigi was too good for this shit.

She put her hands on his chest and pushed him back a little before shaking her head and giving what I could only assume was an apologetic look. My inner asshole cheered.

She shut that shit down with the grace of a fucking angel.

He bowed his head and stepped away, and I couldn't help but smile.

See ya, asshole.

She looked up and her sapphire blues locked with mine. She cocked her head to the side and smiled, and I swear to fucking god, my chest squeezed. My heart fucking raced. A heart I didn't even know still knew how to beat from the attention of a girl. But it was threatening to jump out of my chest.

My gaze scanned her and stopped at her goddamn nipples that were now hard enough to cut glass.

I moved toward her, reached for her hand and led her through the crowd. I didn't miss all the eyes following us. I hurried to my room and pulled her inside, before slamming the door closed.

"What the fuck are you wearing?" I hissed.

She blinked a few times as if she were stunned by my outburst.

Buckle up, girl. I'm just getting started.

"Excuse me?" She crossed her arms over her chest and glared.

"Your fucking nipples were staring at me across the room." I stormed angrily to my closet and pulled out my oversized black hoody. "Put it on."

"You're literally insane." She shoved my hand away. "I'm not wearing this ridiculous sweatshirt because you can't stop staring at my chest."

"Damn straight, G. And neither can anyone else here. I saw that fuckface Jaden talking to you and I'm sure he was looking at the same goddamn thing."

She shook her head, and her tongue peeked out to wet her pouty lips, and I nearly came undone right there. Jesus Christ. I needed to get control of this situation.

She's your best friend's sister, dickhead.

She's Gigi fucking Jacobs.

The best girl you've ever known.

Smart and beautiful.

Innocent and trusting.

Way out of my fucking league.

"I turned him down. He was nice about it. You're the only one acting crazy." She turned angrily and stormed to the door.

I wrapped my hand around her small wrist as my chest crashed into her back. She whipped around and her back pressed against the door. Her breaths coming hard and fast, chest rising and falling, and I couldn't pull my gaze away. She was fucking gorgeous.

"Your nipples weren't hard when you were talking to that asshat." My breathing was out of control, and I couldn't get close enough. I leaned forward, my lips so close to hers I could taste all that sweetness and my tongue ached to dip inside. "They didn't go hard until you were looking at me. Why do you think that is?"

She searched my gaze, and warm breath tickled my cheek. Her hands came up and fisted my T-shirt. "I don't know." Her words were breathy and laced with need, and my dick throbbed against my zipper, desperate for more than just the fantasy of this girl. To touch her. Taste her. Feel every soft curve.

My hand slid up her body and my thumb traced over one hard peak and she gasped. Her eyes closed and her head fell back. I doubted Gigi had ever been touched. I didn't know for sure, but I got the feeling she'd never allowed anyone access to her sweet body. And she certainly shouldn't now.

I nipped at her bottom lip because I just needed a taste. Something to hold me over. My hand cupped her perfect tit, and it fit there like it belonged there.

Jesus, I wasn't this guy.

I didn't take what wasn't mine.

And Gigi Jacobs was not mine. She never would be. She deserved a good guy.

And that wasn't me.

I leaned down and adjusted my angry dick, before stepping back.

"Put a shirt on or go home. This never happened." I ran a hand through my hair and watched as her desire-filled gaze changed in an instant.

"You're an asshole, Gray Baldwin."

"Can't argue with that," I said, as she turned on her heels and stormed out of my room.

I made my way back out to the party and Lila walked over. I saw Gigi talking to Addy across the room, and she glanced over, and her gaze locked with mine. Her face was still flushed from our encounter. I leaned down and covered Lila's mouth with mine. She was all too quick to tangle her fingers in my hair and tug me closer. She groaned into my mouth and I looked up to see Addy, Jett, and Gigi walk out the front door.

Good.

Mission accomplished.

I pulled away and Lila pouted. "Sorry. Not happening tonight."

I made my way through the party and looked out the

front door to see the three of them walking down the street toward the dorm.

She'd be okay.

I'd done the right thing.

And it was the hardest thing I'd ever done.

But I silently praised my angry dick for showing the restraint he did. Because the fact that I'd just held Gigi's perfect tit in my hand and grazed her soft lips against mine—I didn't know where I'd found the strength to walk away. But I had.

It wouldn't have happened if I hadn't been sober.

Another reminder that it was time to get my shit together.

I'd driven home in hopes of finding my dad. Willow Springs wasn't big enough to hide for long. My grandparents still didn't know he'd left rehab, and I wanted to keep it that way. Cade agreed to meet me there for the weekend and help me try to find him. My hope was that I could get him back in the program, and no one would ever be the wiser that he'd left. I'd spoken to his counselor there, and they were hoping I could find him and get him back there as quickly as possible, so all would not be lost.

Cade was happy to go home for a visit, and he'd told me that Gigi and her friends would all be there for the weekend.

That had nothing to do with my desire to go home. At least that's what I was telling myself. She hadn't responded to one text since the party. I'd gone by her dorm room twice and she didn't answer the door. The annoying chick I'd seen in her room before was always lurking around and told me that Gigi was at the library. I'd gone there, and there'd been no sign of her.

She was definitely avoiding me.

Hell, I understood it. But we'd need to get past it. It was a moment of weakness. Nothing happened aside from the fact that it had been apparent we both desperately wanted it to happen.

Hopefully we would just act normal when we were home. Cade expected me to stay with them, and I hadn't said anything different. I highly doubted she would want anyone to know, so it would probably be fine.

I stopped by my mom's house because Simon was at work. I wanted to see the girls as they'd just be getting home from school.

"Gray," Beatrice shouted, as she sprinted down the driveway toward me. I caught her in my arms and spun her around. "Are you going to take me out for ice cream like you promised while you're home?"

"Of course, little nugget."

Penelope raced toward me, and I set Bea down and scooped her up. "I'm so happy you're home. I miss you."

My sisters were identical twins, seven years old, and complete opposites. While Bea was outgoing and funny, Penn was sweet and quiet. They both owned my heart, and they knew it.

"Missed you too, Penny Pie. We've got an ice cream date tomorrow, right?" I asked, setting her on her feet.

"For sure. I'm wearing a dress and everything."

So much sweetness in one little package.

"Sounds good. Let's go see Mama. Your dad's still at work, right?" I asked like I always did when I came home.

"Yep. Daddy's still at work." Bea sprinted up the driveway and shouted through the house. "Gray's home."

The girl was larger than life.

"Hey there, handsome," my mother said, and I wrapped my arms around her. I loved this woman more than life itself, but her husband had put a huge strain on our relationship. I couldn't tolerate his verbal abuse, and my mother turned her cheek because she didn't want to deal with the fallout.

So, she allowed me to basically live at the Jacobs' house when I was home and we just didn't talk about it. I'm sure Simon bitched about me as much as I bitched about him, and Mom was between a rock and a hard place.

She poured me a glass of sweet tea and we both dropped to sit at the big kitchen table in their grand estate. This place had never really felt like my home. Maybe because Simon and I didn't get along. The twins ran off to get some toys that they wanted to show me.

"Any news on your dad?" Mom asked, and her eyes looked sad. I was hesitant to tell her much because I feared she would tell her husband, who would in turn throw it in my face.

"Nope. Wren hasn't seen him. I called the rehab and he's been gone for three days, but they are willing to take him back since he paid for a ninety-day program."

"Your grandparents paid, Gray." Mom's tone was harsh. She had given up on my father's recovery and I understood it. I just didn't share the same opinion. He was still in there. I believed that in the depths of my soul.

"Semantics. So, how are you?" I changed the subject.

"Good. Simon asked if we could all do dinner while you're home."

My eyes bulged out of my head. "Why?"

"I think he'd like to repair some of the damage he's done. We've had a few of my famous *come to Jesus* meetings lately." She laughed.

My mother was a kind woman, but when she lost it, she let it all out. And you listened because it didn't happen often.

"All right. Well, let me know. I'm picking up the girls tomorrow afternoon to take them for ice cream." I pushed to my feet to go check on my sisters.

"Are you staying at the Jacobs' this weekend?" she asked, and I saw the hurt there.

"That's the plan. But I'm happy to come for dinner."

I wanted to offer an olive branch. Hurting my mother was the last thing I wanted to do.

I spent the next hour playing out in the backyard before heading out. Katie Jacobs had texted me and told me there'd be a spot for me at the dinner table and she hoped I could come.

When I pulled up to the Jacobs' house, I saw Gigi's car in the driveway parked beside her brother's. I made my way inside, and Katie hurried over to hug me.

"So happy to see you. I love when y'all come home. Gigi said you've been really helpful to her at school."

Interesting.

I'd helped myself to a handful of her tit, but I'm guessing she didn't throw me under the bus.

"Yeah. She seems to be adjusting well."

"She does. I'm proud of my girl. Come on in, we're just sitting down." Katie led the way down the hall, and I followed.

"There he is." Cade pulled me in for a hug and Bradley Jacobs followed.

Gigi didn't move to her feet, and she avoided eye contact as I took the seat beside her.

My seat.

"Hey," I said, looking over at her as Cade moved to the kitchen to help his parents carry out the food.

"Hi." She didn't look at me and held her head high.

"Are you mad at me? I've tried calling a few times. Stopped by your dorm too," I whispered, leaning close and taking in all her sweetness.

She turned to look at me and shrugged. "Oh. I hadn't noticed."

I laughed and she turned away.

Okay, then.

The table was filled with platters of fried chicken and ribs.

Mashed potatoes and coleslaw. My stomach rumbled as I dropped my napkin in my lap.

It felt good to be home.

"Tell us what's happening, sweetheart," Katie said, looking up at her daughter. "What happened with that boy Jaden?"

My shoulders stiffened.

I thought we were done with that asshole?

"He asked me to dinner and a movie. We're going out when I get back next week." Gigi shifted just enough to make sure I could see the smile spread clear across her face.

My fucking blood boiled.

And I couldn't get back to school soon enough.

I had some ass to kick.

seven

. . .

Gigi

"YOU SHOULD HAVE SEEN his face. It was priceless," I said as we drove out to the lake in Coco's car. I was sandwiched in the back seat between Addy and Maura, and Ivy sat up front next to Coco.

"So, do you like him?" Maura asked.

"Of course not. I hate him."

"She likes him more than she hates him. Trust me." Addy shrugged and I rolled my eyes.

"I do not. But I know he doesn't like Jaden, so I enjoyed telling him that I was going out with him. And I am. I don't know why I was so quick to shut him down at the party."

"Um, I think you shut him down because you like someone else," Coco said over a chuckle. "And that Gray Baldwin is so freaking hot. I see why you're under his spell."

"Pfft, please. I am not under any spell. Sure, we had a weird moment in his room, but I was two beers deep and not thinking straight."

"He cupped your boob," Ivy reminded me, and I mentally kicked myself for feeling the need to tell them everything.

"Please. As a proud member of the itty-bitty-titty-committee, it barely counts." I laughed, trying to make light of it.

The truth—that moment was the most sensual experience I'd had in my life to date. How sad is that? A brief moment of weakness with a boy who didn't even kiss me. And then he followed up by kissing another girl right in front of me. After grazing his lips against mine and touching me in a way no one ever had. Sure, Tony Franco had gotten a little under-the-shirt action sophomore year, but it wasn't like that. At least not for me. I squeezed my thighs together at the thought of it. The way his thumb flicked my nipple, and his warm breath tickled my face. His words were laced with need and I'd all but combusted and made a complete fool of myself. He was messing with me, per usual. It was Gray we were talking about. But he'd never teased me this way before. Nor been so hurtful either.

Annoying was more his shtick. But he was turning up his game and I was disengaging.

"It's okay to like him, you know," Addy said, squeezing my hand. My sweet, hopeless romantic.

"I don't. You know I don't. And let's not even get started on how Cade would react if he knew this had happened. Not that anything really happened, but my brother would lose his shit if he knew Gray was teasing me this way."

"That's what doesn't make sense." Maura unbuckled when we arrived at the lake and we pulled in a parking space. "I don't think he'd do it just to mess with you."

"I agree. I think homeboy has all the feels and doesn't know what to do about it. I love it. A tortured bad boy and an angelic virgin," Coco said, as we all stepped out of the car and burst out in a fit of laughter.

"Um, tortured bad boy and angelic virgin? I think you're being a bit overdramatic," I said, as we walked down toward the water. There was a big group of people already gathered around two different bonfires.

"I think I'm spot on. Come on, just for a minute go with me on this." Coco flipped her hair over one shoulder and glanced over as she spoke. "Let's say he likes you. He has a reputation of being quite the manwhore and he's best friends with Cade, who happens to be the most overprotective brother I've ever met. Like I said—he's in a predicament."

I thought about it. Did Gray look at me like that? There'd been a few times that I'd wondered. But I'd always assumed it was just me reading into things. This was Gray, after all. Maybe it was just the chase that he liked. Maybe he truly was just messing with me. I certainly wasn't his normal type. Not that anyone was. Gray moved through girls faster than most people changed clothing. Either way, it was a huge red flag. Gray Baldwin was not the boy for me for a multitude of reasons.

He was my brother's best friend.

He was a massive playboy.

And he didn't do committed relationships.

There you have it. I'd forget what happened and write it off as a one-time lapse in judgment. I was human. We all had them. I'd go back to school and go out with Jaden and forget what it felt like to be pressed up against Gray and all his hardness.

My mouth went dry at the thought.

I shook it off and dropped to sit by the fire. It was a perfect night, and I was happy to be with my best friends.

Starting tomorrow, I was washing all thoughts of Gray away. I'd give myself one more night to enjoy him in my dreams.

"I'm glad you agreed to go out with me," Jaden said, as I reached for a piece of bread in the basket and dropped it on my plate.

"Of course. Thanks for inviting me."

He nodded. "I thought you were done with me after the

party last week. You shut me down pretty hard, but I figured I had it coming. I'm sure your bodyguard told you I hooked up with someone."

I was surprised by his honesty and laughed at his description of what I could only assume was his fraternity president and my annoying nemesis.

"Who, Gray?" I chuckled. "He's not my bodyguard. Just my brother's best friend."

"He ran me off that first time I tried to hang out with you, which is why I hooked up with someone else that night. Nothing happened. We just made out. But then I couldn't stop thinking about you and I asked him if he'd have a problem with me asking you out," he said, his ocean blue gaze locking with mine. His blonde hair was cut close to his head, and he had a perfect dimple when he smiled. Pearly white teeth and broad shoulders. Jaden was a beautiful boy and looked a lot like Chad Michael Murray from *One Tree Hill*. He appeared to be a straight shooter.

"What did he say?" I asked because I was desperate to know.

"He said you were too good for me, but that the decision was ultimately yours. I mean, he's supposed to be my fraternity brother. He hardly knows me. How the hell does he know I'm not good enough for you?"

I shrugged. "That's just Gray. Don't take it personal."

"I guess he's right. You're a big girl, you can make your own decisions, right?"

"Definitely."

I reached for my water and took a sip, trying to push away thoughts of those emerald green eyes and the way he'd been looking at me lately. I shook it off.

"So, tell me what you like to do, Gigi Jacobs." He forked a huge bite of lasagna and popped it in his mouth.

"You know, all the regular things. I love the lake, swimming, bonfires, all that good stuff. I also like to paint and create things. That's sort of my specialty."

"You're an art major, right?"

"Yep. How about you?" I asked after I'd swallowed the best spaghetti I'd ever had.

"I'm a business major. I'd like to have my own startup company someday." He oozed confidence as he spoke.

"Oh, that's cool. What kind of business do you want to own?"

His head cocked to the side and a little line formed between his brows as if he were completely perplexed by my question.

"I don't know. I haven't thought that far into the future. I just basically know I want to work for myself and make a shit ton of money."

Not the soundest business plan, but hey, I was an art major. I was all about thinking and dreaming about my future. But it seemed odd that he didn't have any idea what he'd want to own. Sort of like creating a puzzle but not taking the time to open the box.

My phone vibrated in my purse and I leaned down to check it.

Gray ~ Where the hell are you?

I rolled my eyes and put it away without responding.

"That sounds good," I said, but my words were empty. Because his plan wasn't something I related to. "So what movie are we seeing?"

"Oh, do you still want to do that? I thought maybe we could just go back to my room and watch a movie?"

My heart started to race and not in a good way.

"I'm down to go to a movie," I said, dabbing my mouth with my napkin.

"Okay. We can do that. Just thought it would be more… cozy in my room."

Of course, he did. He was showing his hand, and I was

losing interest with each passing minute. My phone vibrated again, and I leaned down to check it.

Gray ~ Pick up your damn phone. Stop ignoring me.

"You know what? That's my roommate and she isn't feeling well. I better just head home tonight."

"Okay." He didn't hide his disappointment. "Let's get the check."

When he pulled up at the dorms, he didn't get out of the car to open my door. Instead, he leaned over, catching me completely off guard and he kissed me. He all but climbed over the seat on top of me as he tugged at my cardigan and tried to pull it down. My hands pushed against his as I reared back.

A pounding on the window startled us both. "Open the door."

Gray.

Normally I'd be annoyed, but this time I was so relieved for the interruption I couldn't even be mad. I wouldn't tell him that. I shoved Jaden away from me and reached for my purse.

"This fucking guy," he said under his breath, and his tone sent chills down my spine.

This would be the first and last time I ever went out with Jaden, and I couldn't get out of the car fast enough. I yanked the door open and pushed out. There was a chill in the air, and I pulled my cardigan over my shoulders and slammed the door.

"You okay?" Gray asked, concern etched in his features.

Jaden stepped out of the car. "Do you want me to walk you to your door?"

Was he for real? He'd just pawed all over me and I didn't want him near me.

"No. I'm good." I stormed toward the entrance and pulled the door open as Jaden peeled out of the parking lot.

"Did he do something to you? I couldn't see much

through his goddamn tinted windows, but I could see him climbing over the seat. What the hell happened?"

I whipped around as he followed me down the long hallway. "Nothing. It's not a big deal. I can handle myself. What are you doing here?"

I didn't hide the anger from my tone. Was I happy he'd showed up?

Yes.

But it still didn't explain why he was there. Why he was texting me throughout my date.

Why he cared.

"I needed to talk to you, so I came over here and that fucker pulled up just after I did."

I started walking again and he trailed close behind.

"What do you need to talk about, Gray?"

"Uh, well, it's the twins' birthday next month. I don't know what to get them."

I pushed my door open and paused in the doorway and faced him. I didn't invite him in. He didn't get to just charge into my life whenever he felt like it and then send me packing when things got real.

"You texted me and drove over here to ask me what to get your sisters for their birthday?" I crossed my arms over my chest when his gaze moved down my body.

"Yes. You know them well. And you're a girl."

"Thanks for noticing," I hissed.

"I always notice, G." His tongue swiped along his bottom lip, and I squeezed my thighs together to stop the ache that always lingered when he was near.

"Why don't you ask your girlfriend? She's also a girl."

He chuckled. "Who? Lila?"

"I don't know her name. But seeing as you made out with her the other night, I assume you do. I'm obviously giving you too much credit considering your track record."

He ran a hand through his hair, and I studied the movement. I wondered how soft it was. What the scruff on his face would feel like beneath my fingertips.

"My track record? You keeping tabs on me?" His voice was gruff, and he moved closer to me as he leaned against the doorframe.

"Hardly. The whole town knows you're a manwhore."

"Does that bother you?" he asked, and his face was so close to mine I could feel his breath against my cheek.

Again.

Been there, done that.

I pulled back. "No. I don't care what you do, Gray. Just stop messing with me."

He looked wounded. Almost vulnerable, before his gaze hardened. "I'm not messing with you."

"Then what are you doing here?"

"I told you, I need to get some gifts ordered for Bea and Penn. I thought we were friends."

I sucked in a long breath. "Bea likes to paint. Go on Amazon and order her a few canvases, some paints, and some brushes. Penn likes to read. You can order her the *Junie B. Jones* series. That was my favorite at her age, and I told her about it, and she said she wanted to read them. I'll text you some links for everything, okay?" I started to close the door in his face. It had been a crappy night and I wanted to be alone. I couldn't play this hot and cold game with Gray any longer.

"Thanks. You sure you're okay?"

"You know me. I'm always okay. Have a good night." I shut the door, leaving him standing there looking completely confused.

Get in line, buddy.

He was the confusing one. Not me.

The next two weeks had flown by. My class load was keeping me busy, and I'd found a new friend, Leo, in my pottery class. He was sweet and kind, and we'd been studying together and hanging out a lot lately. I didn't feel any kind of spark with him, and I was fairly certain he was gay, but he hadn't told me yet. He was cute and funny, and I enjoyed hanging out with him.

We'd ordered a pizza and were studying in my room, while we binge-watched *Bridgerton* on Netflix.

"So, tell me your situation, girl. Do you have a boyfriend back home? I don't see you hanging out with anyone here at school aside from me and Addy," he said, over a mouthful of pizza.

"Nope. Single and ready to mingle," I said, and his head fell back in laughter.

"Oh, it's like that, huh?"

"I went out with a guy who was kind of a creep a few weeks ago, and he keeps calling and texting, but I'm ignoring him. He just isn't great at reading the signals. How about you?"

"Maybe we went out with the same guy." He raised a brow in challenge, as if he was unsure if I knew he was into guys. "The last guy I hooked up with was a capital D, douchebag."

I chuckled. "Was his name Jaden?"

"Sebastian. The dude was all about getting me in the sack. I'm apparently quite the catch," he said, wriggling his brows.

"I'm sure you are."

There was a knock on the door, and I pushed to my feet. "I hope it's not that Bailey girl I told you about. She'll never leave." I whisper-shouted.

I opened the door to find Gray standing there looking like every fantasy I'd ever had. He wore dark jeans, a black fitted sweater, and his hair was a disheveled mess.

"Hey," he said, shoving his hands in his pockets. "I

haven't talked to you in a while and wanted to see how you were. Do you want to grab some dinner?"

I sucked in a long breath because the boy literally stole the air from my lungs. I don't know when it happened, but Gray Baldwin was my kryptonite.

"I'm good. I'm actually eating now. Just studying with a friend and watching *Bridgerton*." I licked my lips because my mouth went dry when his gaze did a slow perusal down my body. From head to toe. Like he was committing every inch to memory. His eyes moved over my shoulder and he looked at Leo sitting on my bed.

"Hey, I'm Gray." He tipped his chin, looking so vulnerable, it took everything I had not to explain that Leo was just a friend. But I didn't owe Gray an explanation. We were just friends. He'd made that perfectly clear. He did his thing and I needed to do mine.

"This is Leo," I said.

"Nice to meet you," Leo called out and suddenly there was an awkward tension surrounding us.

"Yeah. Nice to meet you too. Okay, G, have a good night. Thanks for those gift ideas. I ordered everything to ship here so I could wrap it. I'll drive it down on their birthday."

There were sides to Gray that were undeniably sweet. The way he loved his sisters being at the top of the list. The loyal friend he was to my brother and the way he cared for my family were impossible to miss. There was so much more to this boy than you saw on the surface. But he was complicated and wore an invisible shield around himself that I'd recognized a long time ago. But when he let me inside, I liked what I saw.

"That's great. Let me know if you need help wrapping. It's sort of my specialty." I smiled.

What? Where did that come from?

"All right. I'll take you up on that, because I don't have a fucking clue what I'm doing when it comes to that."

"Sounds good."

"See ya, G." He backed away and held his hand up before turning and walking down the hall. My gaze lingered a little longer than it should have on his ass as he strode off out of view.

I closed the door and leaned against it as I tried to pull myself together.

"Holy hell water and fire, who the mother eff was that?" Leo bellowed.

I laughed. "He's my brother's best friend. I've known him my whole life."

"Is that so? You two have never bumped pleasantries?" He smirked.

"Um. Definitely no. I believe he bumps all sorts of pleasantries with lots of people. We're more like family."

"Girlfriend, you are not family with that boy. Unless we're talking all sorts of inbreeding and backwoods inappropriateness. He just eye-fucked you right in front of me."

I dropped to sit on the bed and laughed. "He did not."

"You are such a little innocent one, aren't you? Trust me when I tell you, I need a cold shower after watching the way he drank you in."

"Well, he's made it very clear that we're nothing more than friends."

"Actions speak louder than words, and what I just witnessed wasn't even in the realm of friendship." He laughed. "You haven't been with a guy yet, have you?"

"You mean like sex?"

He leaned forward and rumpled my hair. "Yes, I mean like sex."

"Nope. Not yet. Have you?"

"Girl, I lost my V-card when I was just fifteen. I lost it to a girl first and then realized that wasn't really my thing. And I'm guessing Mr. Sexy is treading lightly because he knows how special you are. Hell, I knew it the first time we talked.

Sweet as sugar, and pure as a nun at the Vatican City monastery."

I slapped his shoulder at his ridiculousness.

"Stop. Can we please stop talking about Gray?"

"You can stop talking about him, girl. But I don't think you can hide from it."

"And why is that?" I asked as I rolled my eyes in dramatic fashion.

"Because it's very obvious that he's got Gigi on the brain. His big brain and his little brain." We both burst out in laughter and I sat up and pulled myself together.

Maybe what he said was true.

But I knew Gray would never act on it.

eight

. . .

Gray

I'D JUST LEFT my counselor's office and we'd talked about my course load for next semester.

I drove over to Gigi's dorm. The girl had avoided me the past few weeks, and I was grateful for it. The temptation when I was around her had grown too powerful. I'd had a weak moment and driven over to her dorm desperate to see her. To feel her. Because when she was near, I felt her everywhere. I didn't have to touch her. She was a part of me, and I didn't know how that happened.

She'd been on a date, and obviously she had the attention of every fucking dude on this campus. I'd overheard that dumb fuck Jaden's drunk ass talking to another pledge at the house about how he'd tried to make a move on Gigi, and I'd fucked it up when I'd knocked on his car window. He also mentioned that he'd tried to get her to come back to his dorm, so he could bang her brains out—his words not mine. I'd seen red and stormed the fucking castle and pummeled his ass.

I guarantee that fuckhead wouldn't be going near her now. Not with a black eye and a fat fucking lip.

I'd been sober for six weeks since school started and I didn't mind it at all. What I did mind was the bad case of blue balls I was dealing with. I hadn't been laid since I'd been back to school, but I had felt Gigi Jacobs' body against mine. Nothing had happened, yet she'd ruined me for all other girls. Hell, I'd found Lila naked in my bed after the party at our house last weekend. I'd spent the whole night searching the room like a pussy for Gigi, who never showed.

The sick thing about it. I was glad she hadn't shown up because I couldn't act on it, yet I was completely broken that I didn't get to see her.

Can you say fucked up any slower than that?

And now I was driving to her dorm so she could help me wrap the gifts for my sisters before I headed to Willow Springs to celebrate my two favorite little humans. Truth was —I just needed an excuse to see her. I thought about her more than I wanted to admit.

My phone rang as I stepped out of my car with a bag of presents and a few rolls of wrapping paper.

My best friend's name flashed across the screen. We talked every day. Always had.

"Hey, what's up?" I said, pulling open the door to her dorm.

"Just going to meet Camilla for lunch, how about you?"

"You're getting serious with this girl, huh?" I asked. Cade had always been a bit of player, so seeing him settle down with one girl was surprising.

"Whatever. Sure. What are you doing?"

"I just got to your sister's dorm. She's going to help me wrap some gifts for Bea and Penn. I'm driving back home today for their birthday dinner."

"Glad to see you aren't always a douchebag," he teased. "Tell them I said hi. You know you can stay at the house when you're there. My parents are home. They don't leave for Hawaii for a few weeks. Not that you don't know where the hide-a-key is if you go when they aren't there." He knew I hated staying at Simon's house, but I could muscle through it for a night if it made my sisters happy. Katie and Bradley were celebrating their twenty-fifth wedding anniversary next month and they'd been planning this trip to Maui for weeks.

"Thanks, brother. I'll see how Simon is. We did that dinner when I was home a few weeks ago and he kept his jabs to a minimum. I mean, he still can't resist, but he definitely made a bigger effort than usual."

"Good. Maybe there's hope for that asshole," he said. "Any word from your dad?"

I ran a hand through my hair as I approached Gigi's door. "Nope. He's still MIA, which is never a good sign."

"I'm sorry to hear that. You hanging in there?"

"Yeah. Unfortunately, this is not my first time down this path with him, but it's the first time I've remained sober through it, so that's fun," I said, not hiding my sarcasm.

"You still aren't drinking? Damn dude, that's fucking amazing. Never thought I'd see the day."

I nodded. I'd had a few moments that I thought about taking a couple shots, but something stopped me every time. Thoughts of my dad. Visions of myself going down the same fucked up path as he has. Maybe his rock-bottom was my wake-up call. It sure as hell wasn't his.

"Thanks, dickhead. I appreciate the confidence." I laughed and knocked on the door. "All right, I'm here. I'll call you from the road."

"Tell Gigi I'll call her later. Give her a hug from me. On second hand, keep your fucking dirty paws away from my sister." His voice was all tease, but I knew he meant it.

A fucking endless reminder that I couldn't touch her outside of my dirty thoughts of course. Banging Gigi in my fantasies had become my favorite pastime.

"Goodbye, asshole." I ended the call and dropped my cell phone in my back pocket.

"Hey," she said, standing there with long waves cascading over her shoulders. She wore a flowy short dress with booties, showing off her tanned, sexy legs. There'd been an awkwardness between us since I'd almost claimed her in my room a few weeks ago at the party. "Come on in."

"Hey, Gray," Addy said, pulling her backpack over her shoulder. "You guys have fun. I'll be back in a few hours."

"See ya." I tipped my chin up at her. "Tell Jett I was fucking impressed with his game Saturday. The dude is a rock star."

She beamed. "I will. Thank you."

Addy shut the door behind her and the air in the room shifted. That invisible pull that always showed up any time I was alone with Gigi engulfed me. I tried to envision her with her little Princess Leia buns she used to wear, baking in her Easy-Bake Oven when she was five or six years old. If I could hold on to thoughts of her as a little girl, maybe it would push away the endless fucking vision of her sprawled naked beneath me. Writhing and begging the way I wanted her to.

Jesus.

Pull your fucking head out of the gutter, douchebag.

"Let me see what you got," she said, dropping to sit on the floor. She had a pair of scissors and a roll of tape next to her.

My dick hardened at her words.

I'd love to show you what I've got.

I set the bag beside her and dropped to sit a few feet away with my back against Addy's bed. I needed to keep some space there.

"They are going to love these, Gray. You did good." She looked through the bags.

My fucking chest squeezed. Why did getting Gigi Jacobs' approval make me feel like a fucking king?

"Thanks. You told me what to get, so I guess you did good." I chuckled.

She started cutting the paper and I watched her movements. She leaned over, setting a stack of books in the center of the paper and cutting it just so. She concentrated as if this were the most important job in the world. Hell, I could have just grabbed some gift bags and dropped the shit in them. But I'd wanted an excuse to see her.

Maybe to make amends.

Make sure we were okay.

Or maybe it was just because I couldn't stop thinking about her.

She tied some ribbon around the package and looked up to see me staring. Her cheeks flushed, and she tucked her hair behind her ear. She reached for the canvases and placed them on the paper.

"Have you heard from your dad?" she asked, and her sapphire blues looked up to meet mine.

"Nope. Wren hasn't seen him either."

Her head tilted to the side and she studied me. "That's got to be tough. I'm sure you're worried like crazy."

"It's fine. He'll turn up."

"It doesn't have to be fine, you know," she said, pulling off some Scotch tape and tucking the sides of the package down.

"What do you mean?"

"I mean, it's okay to not be fine. To be upset. To be sad."

"Oh yeah?"

"Yeah. Stop acting all tough and stoic. You can tell me you're worried. Your secret is safe with me," she said, just as she looked up and smiled, and I adjusted myself beneath my zipper as inconspicuously as possible. Hell, the girl was as innocent as they came in that department. I doubted she knew that every time I was around her my dick thought it was the fucking Fourth of July. He wanted to come out and light some shit on fire.

"I suppose you're right. It's not the first secret you've kept." Why the fuck was I going there? Bringing up that moment we'd shared was stupid. Because not only did I want it to happen again, I wanted to take it further. I wanted her in ways I couldn't begin to wrap my head around.

"You want to talk about that instead?"

"Talk about what?" I smirked.

"The fact that you almost kissed me. Well, we almost kissed each other." Her face flushed. "And you flicked my boob. Maybe it was an accident, I don't even know."

A pink hue covered her cheeks and I moved closer to her before I could stop myself. I sat beside her and reached for the package she'd just wrapped as if that was the reason I'd crawled over here. I set it aside and let my hand fall beside me. The backs of our hands grazed against one another, and my finger hooked around hers, needing to comfort her.

Needing to touch her.

I was so tangled up in this girl I couldn't see straight.

"It *was* intentional, G. And it was a hell of a lot more than a flick." I chuckled. "And it took everything I had to stop things from going further."

She sucked in a long, slow breath. Not moving her finger from mine as the heat between us burned.

"Why'd you stop?" she whispered.

"You know why. That can't happen again. Not ever." I pulled her little hand in mine and intertwined our fingers because I needed more.

"Why?" she asked, turning to face me. Her pouty lips were covered in pink gloss, and her gaze searched mine for answers.

"You know why."

"Because you don't feel that way about me?" she asked. "Is that why you kissed that other girl right in front of me two minutes later?" She yanked her hand away as if she'd just been reminded of why she hated me.

"I kissed Lila to get you out of my system. To make sure you stayed away." I admitted, before silently cursing myself for telling her this much.

"I don't understand why?"

"Listen, you're way too good to put up with my shit. And

your brother—Jesus fucking Christ. He would fucking kill me. You can do a lot better than me, G. I promise you that. That dude that was here the other night seems like a good guy, huh? Are you dating him?" I crossed my arms over my chest because I was a jealous asshole, and I was trying to tamper down my sudden anger. I couldn't be with her and I couldn't stand the idea of anyone else being with her.

"He's not into girls. We're friends. But I have a few prospects," she said, tipping her chin up at me.

I'd hurt her feelings. She was a smart girl, and she'd be wise to stay the fuck away from me.

"Good for you." I scooched away.

"Yeah, good for me." She raised a brow and clucked her tongue, and it took all that I had not to yank her closer and taste that sweet mouth.

"Jaden's leaving you alone, right?"

"About that," she said with a dramatic eye roll. "I saw him in class, and it looked like he took an ass-kicking. You don't know anything about that, do you?"

"Let me ask you something." I handed her the tape as she reached for it. My hand grazed hers once again.

Why'd I come here again?

Because I was a sick masochist who obviously enjoyed torturing himself.

The smell of peaches and goodness surrounded me, and desire stirred every time she glanced my way.

"What?" she asked, acting annoyed but unable to hide the fact that she liked bantering with me.

Hell, we'd always been good at it.

"Did that punk deserve to get his ass kicked?"

She set down the tape and looked up at me. "Probably. Yes."

"That's what I thought."

"You don't need to be poking your nose in my business," she hissed. She was as desperate as I was to push me away.

"You don't get to decide where I poke my nose," I said, and my tongue dipped out because I couldn't push away the thought of poking my nose between her legs—but I wouldn't tell her that.

She pushed to her feet and started loading the packages into the bags I'd brought them in, irritation seeping from her.

"You know, Gray. You're a lot of things, but I'd have never guessed you a coward."

Now I was standing and yanking the bag away from her. "You're correct. I am a lot of things—but a coward is not one of them."

"The definition of a coward is one who shows disgraceful fear or timidity." A fake oversized smile grew across her pretty face.

"Why the fuck do you know the definition of coward?"

"I took my SATs not too long ago, thank you very much. I assumed you'd know the definition since you wear it so well." She moved to the door and yanked it open.

"How exactly am I a coward?"

"Because you're a scared little boy who's afraid of my brother and afraid of his own feelings." She stood there all cocky and sure of herself. Hell, insulting me was her favorite pastime.

"I'm not afraid of anything, G. You're wrong about that." I moved through the open doorway, refusing to let her get to me.

"I think you're afraid of kissing me because you know it would be good and that scares the crap out of you."

I whipped around to see her smiling like she was proud that she was getting under my skin. But she wasn't. I wasn't afraid of Cade or Gigi or any of that bullshit.

I was afraid of hurting her.

But if she needed proof, I was all too happy to give it to her.

I moved into her space, dropping the bags at my feet.

Her breathing stalled and she backed up against her dresser, and the door slammed shut behind me.

"You think I'm afraid to kiss you?" I asked, my voice gruff and raw as I moved into her space. Wanting to steal the air from her lungs.

"I think you are," she whispered.

One hand hooked around the back of her neck, and the other squeezed her ass as I yanked her close. My dick was so hard I thought it might tear through the denim holding him captive. My mouth crashed into hers, and there was nothing gentle about it. My tongue slipped inside her sweet mouth as her lips parted, all but inviting me in. I groaned against her soft lips as our tongues did a wild dance charged with need and desire.

She pressed closer, and I lifted her off the ground and her legs wrapped around my waist. I rocked her slowly, moving her up and down, so she could grind up against my cock. Her breathing was erratic, and her hands tangled in my hair. She moved faster, and I knew she was close. Hell, I'd never made a chick come just from kissing her, but everything about Gigi was different.

In the best fucking way.

She cried out my name as her hips moved in frantic rhythm as she rode out every last wave of pleasure. I set her on her feet and took in her wild eyes. Her lips were swollen, and she pushed her hair away from her face. She appeared to be a bit stunned by the whole encounter.

"Not afraid of kissing you, G. Just afraid we'll both want more. And that can't happen." I kissed the top of her head before reaching for the two bags at my feet and walking right out the door.

I'd need to stop home for a quick shower so I could rub it out to my latest fantasy of Gigi Jacobs coming apart in my arms from just having my mouth on hers.

This would definitely be a new favorite.

nine

. . .

Gigi

ADDY and I walked over with a group of our sorority sisters to the field reserved for our powder puff football game. We were partnered with Sig Alpha, and my stomach fluttered at the thought of seeing Gray. I hadn't seen him in a week, when he'd made me orgasm by just kissing me. I wanted to die. I told Addy about the kiss, but not about the part of me crying out his name as I ground up against him like some sex-crazed fool. I was mortified. Something about that boy brought out sides of me that were so unfamiliar.

He'd texted me every day just as he had since I'd come to school, but he acted like nothing had happened. The whole thing was very confusing. He'd sent pictures of his sisters with the gifts he'd gotten them and given me updates on his whereabouts.

Addy found it hilarious. She thought he liked me but didn't know how to even go about it because my brother would lose his mind. But I couldn't figure Gray out. He was so hot and cold. We had nothing in common. He was a player, for starters. And he irritated me more often than he didn't. This was just a stupid crush and I needed to get over it.

"Is Jett on his way?" I asked as we dropped our bags on the sidelines.

"Yep. And his teammate Wade, the one you met at the party, is coming too. He is definitely into you because he keeps asking Jett about you."

"He's cute and he's really nice," I said, as my gaze searched the field for a certain someone who I loved to hate.

"Hey, girls." Leo walked up and gave us both a hug, raising his brows as he took in our outfits. "Football is not really my thing, but I'm so digging this look and I'm here to cheer you on."

We all wore spandex short-shorts and pink and white jerseys with our names on the back of them and our flags were a bright pink. Addy and I put our hair up in ponytails, and we wore those athletic socks that came just beneath your knee.

"If you aren't going to give it one hundred and ten percent, take your ass home," Tiffany shouted as she walked over, and it took everything I had in me not to roll my eyes at her.

Our fierce leader, A.K.A. Kappa Gamma president, was ridiculously intense over this game. She'd been sending us endless emails about the rules and the dress code. We were playing Pi Delta, and apparently Tiffany's ex-best friend, *her words, not mine,* was the president of Pi Delta.

"Wow, she's a lot," Leo whispered, and Addy and I tried to cover our laughter.

My skin prickled and I whipped around to see Gray walking my way. He wasn't wearing a shirt, he had on basketball shorts, and a baseball cap turned backward. My mouth went dry at the sight of him. A few guys walked behind him wearing the same attire. They had our sorority symbols painted on their chests.

Oh my god.

I'd seen Gray without a shirt before. God knows he liked

to flaunt himself around like he was on display in the red-light district. But I'd always looked away. But right now—I couldn't turn away if my life depended on it. Chiseled abs and defined shoulders. His shorts hung low on his hips where a deep V led down to his holy grail. He was tall, just around six foot three, and every inch of him was perfection. His tan skin glistened and my jaw hit the ground as I took him in.

He chuckled and ruffled the top of my head like I was a child, which aggravated me.

"What's up, G."

"Nothing," I hissed.

"Hey, Gray, are you ready to kick some Pi Delta ass?" Tiffany moved beside him and rested one hand on his shoulder as she pushed up to kiss his cheek.

"Down, girl," Leo whispered in my ear so only I could hear.

My hands fisted at my side as I tried to gain composure. They'd had their little fling over the summer, and she'd inquired about him multiple times. I played coy and just said he was my brother's best friend.

Because that's what he was, right?

"Yep. Let's do this. Is Addy playing QB?" Gray asked as Jett walked up and gave him one of those silly boy half hugs.

"Yeah. She's got this. I went over a few passes with her and Gigi. They ran a few plays yesterday and they're actually decent." Jett laughed and a pink hue spread across Addy's cheeks. I loved how they were together.

Why did I have to crush on an unattainable manwhore with no clue how to treat a girl?

Time to get over it.

"Hey, Gigi," Wade said, standing behind Jett as he waved.

"Hi. Thanks for coming." I beamed because I didn't miss the way Gray's head whipped around to look in Wade's direction.

"Excited to see you play," he said.

"Okay, enough small talk. Let's get out there." Gray jogged out to the center of the field, holding a ball in his hand as he spoke to the coach for Pi Delta.

Tiffany handed him a clipboard with the list of girls on the lineup, and he called out for seven of us to huddle in the center. She elbowed me as she flipped her long hair over one shoulder. I wondered how she'd possibly run with her hair down and curled, but nothing surprised me with this girl.

The first play Gray called was a pass. He wanted Addy to get warmed up. Jett stood on the sidelines giving her a few tips, and everyone laughed. She passed the ball to Heather, who moved maybe one yard down the field before tripping and falling with the grace of a toddler taking their first steps.

"No. That is unacceptable," Tiffany shouted as she glared down at the ground as Heather pushed to her feet.

So much for sisterhood.

"Are you the coach, or am I? There's no *I* in team, girl," Gray said with a smirk that caused me to squeeze my thighs together. My god, the boy was sexy. He sent Heather and Tiffany to the bench to cool off and called out two more girls from our team to join us on the field. "All right. Let's try a pass play."

Gray invited Jett out on the field with him to help coach, and Addy couldn't wipe the smile from her face.

"You ready?" she asked me.

"Yep. I'll just run down toward the end zone and hope I catch the ball, right?" I asked.

Jett and Gray both barked out a laugh.

"That's the goal," Gray said before he reminded the other girls to block as much as they could.

The whistle blew and I sprinted down the field. I'd always liked to run, and I'd beat all the boys in the high school fitness challenge in PE, so I knew I had speed on my side.

I turned around just as the ball sailed right toward me,

threatening to nail me in the face. I had a big brother, so this was not my first rodeo with a football. I held out my hands and the ball hit me hard in the chest, but I was able to hold on to it.

"Go," Jett and Gray screamed wildly, and I took off for the end zone, spiking the ball when I crossed the line.

I heard Leo screaming and making a scene as he sat on the bench with my sorority sisters.

All the girls rushed me, and Tiffany yelled out obnoxiously from the sidelines. The ref blew his whistle and told her to shut it down, and we all laughed.

"I knew you had wheels, but damn, G. That was fucking amazing," Gray said, leaning down to tuck the hair that broke free from my ponytail behind my ear.

"What can I say? I'm full of surprises." I smirked.

The heat in his eyes had butterflies swarming my belly. "You sure are."

I jogged toward Addy just as Jett set her back on her feet after spinning her around. We high-fived and made our way to the bench beside Leo.

Unfortunately, Pi Delta went on to score in the next play, tying the game up before halftime.

The second half of the game moved fast. The other team seemed to fizzle out and lose interest, but we continued to haul ass down the field. Our defense was quick, and Pi Delta never came close to scoring again. Addy and I did the same play two more times, both resulting in touchdowns, and we left the field victorious.

We jumped around and cheered and it was the first time I truly felt like I was bonding with my sorority sisters.

Even Tiffany was being nice. She pulled me aside. "Hey, so I know you're like Gray's little sister and all, so I'm hoping you can help me out with him. I mean, look at him. He's so hot. Can you put in a good word, seeing as I'm the reason you even got a bid in this house?"

It wasn't the first time she'd reminded me that she had helped Addy and me get a bid. The girl sure liked to toot her own horn. And the thought of her and Gray together—it made me sick. There was no way in hell I was going to help her make that happen.

"Um, he's my brother's best friend. I don't really have a say in who he dates."

"Come on, Gigi. Help a girl out. He trusts you. I can see that," she said as Addy, Jett, Leo, and Wade walked over.

"We're going to go grab some sandwiches, do you want to come?" Addy asked me before glancing at Tiffany who I knew she didn't care for, but she still invited her to join us because she didn't have a mean bone in her body.

"You should come," Wade said, turning his attention to me.

No flutters.

But he was really nice.

"You're coming. I'm starving and I just survived my first football game." Leo wrapped an arm around me.

Gray waltzed over and slipped a T-shirt over his head, and I studied his every move. The way his arms flexed as he tugged the cotton fabric down. The way his Adam's apple bobbed in his throat when his gaze locked with mine. My mouth went dry, and I took a drink from my water bottle to cool down.

"Good game. You two dominated," he said, and his eyes never left mine.

"It was fun. Do you want to come with us to grab a sandwich?" I asked, and my tongue dipped out to wet my lips while making every effort to act completely natural.

His eyes moved from Jett and Addy and Leo to Wade, before returning to me. "Nah. You guys have fun. Thanks for helping out, Jett. See ya."

He jogged away and my heart sank. Why was he avoiding me again?

"Gigi, go talk to him. You owe me, girl." Tiffany put her hands together as if she were praying and Addy and Leo both rolled their eyes with annoyance.

"Okay. I'll be right back, and then I'll be ready to go." I was actually happy to have a reason to go talk to Gray.

"Hey," I called out as I closed the distance between us, and he turned around.

"What's up?" he asked, crossing his arms over his chest, as if he was protecting himself.

From me?

Am I the enemy now?

"Tiffany asked me to come talk to you. She really likes you."

He studied me. "You're setting me up with Tiffany now?"

I raised a brow. "No. I mean, I don't have much of a choice seeing as she keeps reminding me that Addy and I are only in the house because she pulled a favor."

He nodded. "You going to lunch with Jett's friend?"

"Do you care if I do?" I raised a brow.

"Nope. Why would I?" he said, his eyes hard.

"No reason, I guess. I mean other than the fact that you kissed me."

"You dared me to kiss you. I told you it couldn't happen again," he said, moving closer and invading my space.

His words stung.

"Good to know." I took a step back. "I'll be off to lunch with Wade. He seems like the kind of boy who kisses you and actually wants to do it again. I guess I'll have to find out. I'll tell Tiffany to text you." I jogged off, leaving him standing there, and pushed down the lump in my throat.

Gray made it clear that it was a one-time thing.

This was a silly little crush that would go away.

I actually couldn't stand him at the moment so it shouldn't be that hard.

"He wants you to text him," I said to Tiffany before

turning to the rest of the group. "Are you guys ready? I'm starving. Turns out that scoring touchdowns works up an appetite."

They laughed and Tiffany high-fived me and hugged me before running off. We walked to the sandwich shop on campus. Addy, Jett, and Leo were a few steps in front of us and Wade walked beside me. I pushed thoughts of Gray and Tiffany out of my mind.

"So, you're from Willow Springs too?" Wade asked me. He was really cute. He had blonde hair and brown eyes and that boy next door look. He was definitely kind and sweet, which was in direct contrast to the boy who'd just hurt my feelings.

"Yeah. We all grew up there." I had a little pang of sadness as I spoke of home. I missed my parents and my brother and my best friends. Thank goodness I had Addy here with me.

And Gray.

Nope. Still hate him.

Wade and I chatted on our walk and throughout lunch and he was great. My phone vibrated on the table and I picked it up to see a text from the enemy.

Gray ~ Are you mad at me, G?

Me ~ Annoyed is a better description.

Gray ~ Fair. Are you at lunch with that dude?

Me ~ Yep. You don't care, remember?

Gray ~ I don't. Just checking on you. Have fun.

Me ~ I hate you.

Gray ~ All wouldn't be right in the world if you didn't.

I dropped my phone back on the table and silenced it. I was done playing games with Gray Baldwin.

He was correct.

All was right in the world when I hated him.

And most of the time it came easy for me.

ten

. . .

Gray

IT HAD BEEN a week since the powder puff football game and Gigi hadn't responded to one fucking text. She was pissed. Fine. But don't ghost me when I'm supposed to be keeping an eye on you. I'd gone by her dorm a few times and she didn't open the door if she was there.

It was for the better. Never should have kissed her. Now she hated me more than ever and I was fucked up over the damn kiss. Couldn't get her out of my head. My hand would probably blister with how many times I'd fucking rubbed it out in the shower to try to get over it.

Fucking Lila had shown up at my door at the frat house and dropped to her knees.

Ready and willing.

And guess the fuck what? I wasn't into it. I tried to get there. Made out with her for a minute or two and just said I wasn't feeling well.

I was suffering from Gigi withdrawal.

Fucked. Up.

"Gray, can you hang back for a minute?" Professor Lambrose called out as I made my way to the door with the rest of the students in my Business Law and Ethics class.

"Sure. What's up?" I asked, trying to think if I'd forgotten an assignment. Doubtful. I'd never had my shit more together than I did this year, and I was acing my classes so far. Turns out being sober pays off in more ways than one.

"The paper you submitted received the highest score in the class. You took the opposing side and won me over. I can promise you, that doesn't happen often." Professor Lambrose was a short, stout man and famous for being a ball-buster. This was definitely unexpected.

"Thank you, sir. That means a lot."

"Good. I don't give out compliments easily. You impress me. I assume you would like to go on to law school?" he asked.

"That's the goal, yes."

"When are you taking the LSAT?" He stacked a pile of papers beside his laptop and looked up at me.

"I was going to order the study materials over winter break and spend next semester preparing and hope to take it over the summer. I'd like to go into senior year with it behind me," I said, shifting on my feet with discomfort. I wasn't used to getting praise from professors. Sure, I'd always done well in class, scored high, but I'd never been committed enough to be top of the class.

It felt fucking good.

"I have a friend at the courthouse that takes interns based on my recommendation. I think it would be a good fit for you and allow you some real-life experience. Would you be interested?"

My jaw dropped. A recommendation coming from this man was as good as it gets. He only taught the one class for undergrads and spent the rest of his time as a professor at the TU Law School, which happened to be my top choice.

"I would absolutely be interested. Yes. Thank you so much."

He reached out a hand and shook mine hard. "Consider it done. I'll set up a meeting. Keep up the good work."

"Yes, sir." I walked out of the classroom feeling like I was ten feet tall. And the first person I wanted to tell was the one person currently not speaking to me. I dialed her number and held the phone to my ear. I glanced across campus to see Gigi on the other side of the courtyard. She had her phone in her hand and looked at the screen but didn't answer. I could see from a hundred feet away that she was smiling though, and I couldn't help but laugh. I quickly tapped out a message.

Me ~ you just rejected my call, G. Not cool. Look up.

She looked down at her screen while I leaned against a tree, taking her in.

Fucking gorgeous.

Blonde waves fell around her shoulders and she wore a little floral miniskirt, a white sweater, and some sort of short boots that all the girls wore here.

She looked up and met my gaze. Her smile was so bright my breath caught in my throat. But then her eyes hardened, and she scowled.

Still pissed.

She stormed my way, and I didn't move. I was going to enjoy this moment. The way her hips swayed and her legs shimmered in the sunlight.

"Are you stalking me now?" she hissed.

Hell, I didn't even mind an angry Gigi. I'd missed seeing her and would take her any way I could get her.

"Sure. If that's what I need to do."

"What do you want?" she asked, and I could tell she was trying to hide her smile. Gigi was good to the core even on her worst day, though she tried to prove me wrong when she was angry.

"I wanted to tell you something." I crossed one leg over the other and my tongue dipped out to wet my lips. The smell of peaches overwhelmed me, and I fought the urge to pull her close.

"Why don't you tell Tiiiiifany," she said the name slowly and rolled her eyes.

"Why the fuck would I tell her?"

"She told me you guys hung out the other day. I don't even want to know what that entails," she said, before turning on her heels and storming off.

"Hey," I shouted as I chased after her.

Never thought I'd chase after any girl before. But Gigi was different.

I reached for her and wrapped my hand around her wrist before she whipped around, her chest slammed into mine. "What!"

"Nothing happened with Tiffany. We did not hang out. She stopped by the house and brought me cookies. I don't like her that way. But something good just happened to me now." I ran my free hand through my hair but kept my fingers wrapped around her because I didn't want to risk her running away again. "And I wanted to tell you."

She looked down at my hand on her wrist and raised a brow. "What happened?"

Her tone was exasperated, and I couldn't help but laugh. I'd been told by my mother that I was exhausting my entire life. But I hadn't even gotten started on Gigi Jacobs.

I let go of her because I knew she would wait to hear what I said. She was good like that. Thoughtful. I shoved my hands in my pockets because I suddenly felt like a needy little asshole. I didn't normally do awkward, but I was feeling it at the moment.

"I, uh, well, Professor Lambrose, my Business Law and Ethics instructor, just offered to give me a recommendation for a summer internship at the courthouse."

Her head cocked to the side as she studied me, and a grin

spread across her face. "That's amazing. What made him offer it to you? Did you have an exam?"

Not many people took an interest in other people's moments, but Gigi always did. Of course, she wanted to know more.

"I guess I got the highest score on the papers we submitted. Hell, maybe it was a mistake." I laughed, trying to make light of it.

"Don't do that." She reached out and touched my forearm and I was thankful that I was wearing joggers and hoped they hid the tent currently setting up camp in my pants. "It's amazing. Congratulations."

"Thanks."

My skin heated where her hand touched me, and I was thankful she didn't pull away. "So, why'd you want to tell me? You didn't want to call Tiffany or one of your other hoochies?" she hissed at me and I couldn't help but laugh.

She was so fucking cute when she was jealous. I was treading in dangerous territory and I knew it. But I couldn't stay away.

"I haven't known them my whole life," I said. My hand came over hers because I needed to feel her even more.

She looked up at me, and her sapphire blues locked with mine. "So, call Cade."

"I will. But I wanted to call you first."

Her teeth sunk into her plump bottom lip and she smiled. It was a smile that could light up the fucking world. I wish I could bottle that shit up and keep it with me.

"What are you doing right now?" She pulled her hand away and tucked her hair behind her ear.

"Heading back to the house, why?"

"Come celebrate with me. I'm going to the pottery studio. I reserved it for an hour. I'll show you my project."

"Well, I usually celebrate with a couple shots of whiskey, but since I'm not drinking, I guess pottery works." I didn't have any desire to go to a goddamn pottery studio, but I wanted to spend more time with her.

What the fuck are you doing, dickhead?

"Let's go, my little overachiever," she said over a chuckle and my motherfucking chest tightened at her words. We were playing with fire. This couldn't go anywhere. Gigi deserved a hell of a lot better guy than me. Hell, no one was good enough for her—myself included. And I was pretty fucking impressed with myself so that was saying a lot. But Cade was like a brother to me, and his sister was very much off-limits. He knew who I was, and he would never be okay with it.

But we could be friends. We could hang out. And that's all this was, right?

We walked in the pottery studio and she signed in at the desk. I followed her into a back room. We were the only ones there and she flipped on the light. There were shelves filled with different pieces of pottery and she moved toward an oversized bowl and a vase. I took in her backside. Her skirt swayed against her thighs as she walked toward the shelves. I wanted to reach my hand beneath her skirt and touch her where I knew she was dying to be touched.

Get your fucking head out of the gutter, you scumbag.

"These are mine," she said, reaching up to grab them. I hurried over as the vase nearly tipped, my chest pressing to her back, as I reached up and took it from her hand. She sucked in a long breath before turning to face me. Chest to chest. Breaths coming fast.

"Here you go." I handed her the vase and grabbed the bowl before taking a step back.

We set them on the table, and she pulled out a basket of paints, squeezing them onto a dish with little circles to separate the colors. "Why don't you paint the vase for my mom for Christmas. She'll love it."

I chuckled as I studied the intricate piece. "I don't paint, G."

"Yeah? Well, you've also never been sober for months at a time, you've never gotten offered amazing internships by your professors, and you don't kiss your best friend's little sister. So, maybe you give this a shot?" She quirked a brow and I couldn't help but laugh.

She'd noticed I hadn't had a drink since school started. And that was a good thing because if I were a drunk asshole right now, I'd have her sprawled out on this table beneath me, doing all the things I wanted to do to her. This was another reason it was good to stay sober.

"That was a one-time thing, G."

"I know. You've made that perfectly clear and God only knows where that mouth of yours has been since it was on mine." She rolled her eyes and shivered in dramatic fashion, and I covered my mouth with my hand so she wouldn't see my smile.

"You know me too well. That's why we need to make sure that never happens again. You could do much better." I dipped my brush in the orange paint because I knew that was Katie's favorite color. I glanced over to see Gigi with her bowl flipped over as she painted the base, so I did the same.

"Agreed. But I have a question," she asked, and a pink hue covered her cheeks. She didn't look up at me, so I knew she was nervous, and I never wanted her to feel that way around me.

"Hit me with it." I covered the bottom half of the pottery in orange paint and studied my work. It was shit.

She looked over and smiled. "The first coat never looks good. You've got this."

"What's your question?"

"That kiss. Is that how it always is for you?" Her eyes were focused on her bowl and I smiled. Couldn't help it. Because that fucking kiss was haunting my dreams. Consuming my thoughts.

"You've never been kissed properly before?" My voice

was gruff, and I adjusted myself beneath the table as the mere mention of her sweet mouth had my dick on high alert.

"Not like that. I mean, what happened, you know, at the end." She chuckled and covered her eyes with her hand and shook her head. "That was embarrassing. It's never happened to me before."

Good Christ, my dick was straining so hard against my joggers I closed my eyes and tried to think of anything to calm him down.

Vomit.

Horror flicks.

Sick puppies.

Simon, my asshole stepfather.

Works every time.

"Nothing to be embarrassed about. It's called an orgasm, and it's a good thing."

"Oh my god," she whispered. "I know what it is. Did you have one? Or was it just me?"

My head fell back in laughter, and she frowned. "I'm not laughing at you, G. Just laughing at the situation. Let's just say I've had about four hundred orgasms reliving that kiss. Does that make you feel better?"

And I'm hard again.

"Oh. Good to know."

"Not really. It's a dangerous game you're playing, bringing all this up. Just because it was good doesn't mean it should have happened."

"Why? Because of Cade?" She dipped her brush in the water before covering it in pink paint.

"That's one of many reasons. He'd fucking kill me, are you kidding me? He's my best friend. My day one. And you know this can't go anywhere. You just got a little worked up because you've clearly never kissed anyone who knew how to make you feel good. Stay away from selfish assholes, G."

"Yeah, I'm working on that." She raised a brow and met my gaze, making it clear she thought she was looking at one.

"You think I'm fucking selfish? Seriously? This is the most unselfish thing I've ever done."

"Then why do you keep texting and calling? Let it go."

"So what? We kissed one fucking time and now you don't want to speak to me? We can't do that. Not happening."

"Maybe it's not up to you, Gray. You don't call all the shots."

I was fucking glad she was getting mad, because that was the only way to keep things from escalating again.

"You're right. You call the shots here. So, make good choices." I held my vase up as the outside was completely covered in orange paint and it looked like shit.

"I always do." Her face hardened and she glanced over at the vase. "You need to paint in one direction on this next coat, so the lines don't show."

"I don't have a fucking clue what that means."

She pushed to her feet with annoyance and stood so close to me I was flooded with the smell of peaches. I breathed in all her goodness. Her hand came over mine and she moved it forward to dip the brush in the paint, before guiding me to move the bristles in long strokes up the length of the pottery. Again, and again. Her little hand maneuvered mine with perfect precision.

"Take your time. Don't rush it," she whispered, and her voice was all sultry and needy.

Good Christ.

Is everything with this girl sexual now?

She moved my hand.

Long and slow and gentle.

And I wanted to flip her on the table and have my way with her.

"Okay, I got it. I got it," I hissed, yanking my hand away. She moved back to her seat with a mischievous smile spread across her face, like she was fucking proud. "You think you're funny with that shit?"

She turned to look at me. "Just making good choices, right?"

I rolled my eyes. She had me all worked up and she seemed very pleased with herself. My phone vibrated and I pulled it out of my back pocket. My dick was actually chafing against the fabric of my joggers at this point, I was irritated, and if it were possible to die of a bad case of blue balls, I may as well head to the mortuary now.

Cade.

Always there to give me a wake-up call.

My best friend.

My brother.

I showed her the screen before putting him on speakerphone. "What's up?"

"Not much. Heading to class. What are you doing?"

"I'm at this bullshit art studio with your sister. Ran into her on campus," I said, watching her because I couldn't take my fucking eyes off of her.

"Hey. He's lying. He loves it." She leaned closer to the phone and I took a step back which made her laugh.

"Why the hell are you at the art studio? This has to be a first."

"I ran into him on campus. Your bestie just got offered a summer internship at the courthouse because he got the highest score on his paper. So, I told him to come celebrate by painting a vase for Mom." She laughed, and I rolled my eyes because she was pumping me up more than necessary.

"Dude. That's fucking amazing. Congrats. And I appreciate you keeping an eye on Gigi."

She rolled her eyes. "You do realize I can hear you. He's not keeping an eye on me. I'm a big girl. He's painting a vase for Mom. And I had to show him how to do it, so there you go."

"You know what I mean, brother. Thanks for always having my back," Cade said. "I was calling to let you know that me and Camilla are going to come visit this weekend. I want to see Jett's last game and thought we could all hang out. I want you guys to meet her."

"Yay, I finally get to meet her," Gigi said, and her lips turned up in the corners. "Looks like everyone's growing up."

I didn't miss the innuendo or the way her brow went up in challenge when she looked at me.

"Sounds good. And I want to meet this dude you told me about, Gigi. The one you like. Have you met him yet, brother?"

My jaw dropped open.

She likes someone else?

What the fuck?

"I have not. But I'll make it my business to do so before you get here."

"I knew you would. See you guys in a few days."

I ended the call and stared at her.

"You have something you want to tell me?" I crossed my arms over my chest.

She laughed. "It's not really your concern, right?"

Fuck that.

Everything about this girl was my concern.

eleven

. . .

Gigi

THE EXPRESSION on his face was priceless. He'd turned and stormed out of the art studio when I refused to tell him any details and referenced the fact that he'd beat up the last boy I went out with.

I couldn't wait to fill the girls in when we had our Magic Willows Zoom call this afternoon.

Cade had caught me at a weak moment, asking me a million questions, and I'd admitted that I had a bit of a crush on a guy. I failed to mention that it was his best friend, because trust me, I was just as surprised by the revelation as he would be.

But I liked Gray.

I liked him so much.

I couldn't stop thinking about that kiss. I knew he felt it too. But he was so afraid of messing things up and I understood it. I really did. We were family. This could go very wrong. I'd never want to do anything to mess up his friendship with my brother.

But this was separate. I didn't understand why we couldn't just keep it to ourselves and see where it went before we involved anyone else.

"Hey, girl," Leo called out and moved in stride beside me.

"Hi. How are you?" I asked as we walked into our Art History class.

"Well, I've got some tea. You know that hot guy that's in our pottery class with the shaggy blonde hair who looks like a sexy-dirty-surf boy?"

I laughed. "Yes. You've pointed him out many times."

"He ran into me this morning on campus and talked to me," he said, fanning his face. "I die. But anyhoo… I was hoping he played for my team, but he asked me about you."

"Me?"

"I know. You lucky little heathen. You've got your sights set on big daddy Gray, and now you've got yourself a hot surfer boy waggling his tongue in your direction. Oh, what that tongue could do."

"You're insane. Gray just made it very clear that nothing can happen between us. And now my brother is coming to town and wants to meet the guy I like, because of course I told him I'm interested in someone when he asked but I failed to mention that it was his best friend. So now Gray is seething that he thinks I've met someone. My life is a mess."

"Girlfriend, you've got that boy all wound up over you. So, you invite our boy to go out this weekend. He sure looks the part. Maybe you'll end up liking him, or at the very least just hooking up with him. And I am happy to go out with you guys and be there waiting in the wings if he decides to jump ship on the vagina," Leo said.

"You are crazy. He is cute. What's his name?"

"Oh, honey. It's such a good name. *River.* I'd like that river to run right through me."

I fell back in my seat in laughter. "Let me think about it."

Professor Tomlin walked in and I pulled out my notebook and got to work.

When class ended, Leo pulled out his cell phone and gasped. "Oh, honey. He's already messaging me asking about you. Our little River has got it bad. He wants to know if we're planning on going to the Sig Alpha party this weekend. He wants me to give him your number so he can text you. Are you good with that?"

My stomach dropped at the thought of seeing Gray and doing so around my brother would definitely be different. I'm sure Gray would completely ignore me in front of Cade.

"Yes. I'm wasting my time with Gray. He's right—nothing is going to come of it. I need to start meeting other people."

He squealed. "I love this side of you."

I laughed and we agreed to meet up later. I hurried back to my dorm for my chat with the Magic Willows. It was always the highlight of my day when we all caught up. It made me feel close to home.

"Here she is," Addy said when I dropped to sit beside her on the bed, leaning my back against the wall.

"Hey," I called out, taking in each of their pretty faces. Coco was sitting at her desk in her dorm room that looked like something straight out of a magazine. The girl had a flair for design, no ifs, ands, or buts about it.

"Hi, G, we miss you," Maura and Ivy said at the same time. They were sitting together on a bed in their dorm room as well.

"So, give us the update. Addy was just telling us a little bit about Gray. She thinks he's totally into you and so do I. And obviously, I'm rarely wrong about these things." Coco leaned forward and flipped her blonde hair over one shoulder. Behind her sat black and white fashion drawings that she had sketched and framed.

"It doesn't matter. He won't act on it, and Cade's coming to town this weekend, so it will just be more of a reminder that it can't go anywhere." I shrugged. "But Leo just told me this cute guy in my pottery class wants to meet up at the Sig Alpha party this weekend."

"Oooohhh. Maybe it'll knock some sense into Gray." Maura took a long sip from her water bottle after she spoke.

"I agree. Maybe you need to show him what he's missing," Ivy said with a brow raised.

"I don't think he's going to do anything about it. And you know Gray. He has a ton of girls chasing him around. Ugh. Don't even get me started on our sorority president, Tiffany. She's obsessed with him and keeps coming to me for advice."

Coco laughed and shook her head before pulling herself together. "Girl's marking her territory. You better get busy, Gigi. You've got some competition."

"I am not chasing him around like a puppy. Maybe he didn't like kissing me and he doesn't want to tell me." Sure, he'd claimed he liked it when we were at the pottery studio, but Gray also wouldn't want to hurt my feelings.

"Please. Who wouldn't want to kiss you?" Ivy said, crossing her arms over her chest. "I say you just meet up with the other boy and see what Gray does about it. At the very worst, maybe you'll end up liking this other guy, which would be much less complicated."

"True," I said. "What's happening with you? Any updates on Ty?"

"His sister texted me the other day to let me know some big label is signing him in Nashville. I'm sure he'll be a big star and sleep his way all over Tennessee while he stomps on my heart and my virginity. I hate him."

"You don't hate him, Ive." Coco cocked her head to the side and her eyes filled with empathy. "It's okay to be sad about him."

"It's easier to hate him." Ivy swiped at the tear running down her cheek, before shaking her head and lifting her chin up. "Anyway, I have a date tonight. His name is Willie and he's really cute and very nice. We're going to dinner."

"Oh, I wonder if he has a big willie?" Coco said with a mischievous grin.

She couldn't help herself.

"Of course, you take it there. I'm not interested in finding out about his willie, thank you very much. Ty's penis has scarred me for life."

We all laughed.

"You're going to get through this, Ivy. I promise." Addy smiled. "Have you heard from Shaw at all, Co?"

"We text occasionally. But did you see his post on Instagram with the hot blonde? I think Shaw is doing just fine on his own." She rolled her eyes. "Do you still talk to Kyle at all, Maura?"

Kyle was Maura's high school boyfriend, and they'd split up during our senior year after he left for college.

"No, we haven't been talking, and it's okay. I'm having fun here." She smirked, and her cheeks pinked.

"Our little Maura is getting a whole lot of attention from the guys here," Ivy said, wriggling her brows. Maura and Ivy had always been relationship girls. They'd had high school boyfriends and were both putting themselves back out there now that they were single.

"That's because you're hot as hell, girl. You all are. How did we get so lucky to meet when we were so young, and we all ended up being hot pieces of ass?" Coco asked, and we all burst out laughing once again.

"Magic Willows for life," I said.

We continued chatting for the next hour, filling one another in on every little detail of our lives, just like we always did.

My brother picked me up off my feet and spun me around. "Missed you, Sis."

"Missed you too," I said, patting my short flowy dress into place and turning to face Camilla. She was gorgeous.

Long brown wavy hair, brown eyes, and a warm smile. She was a few inches taller than me, and she and Cade looked really cute together. "Hey, Camilla. Nice to meet you. I'm Gigi."

"You can call her G-money if you want." Gray waltzed up behind me and I stiffened.

"Please don't. I don't know why he insists on annoying me." I glared at the boy who was consuming my every thought, reminding myself that I hated him.

He rumpled the top of my head, and I rolled my eyes. Yeah, I get it, buddy. We're just friends.

I hear you loud and clear.

"It's so nice to meet you, Gigi. Your brother talks about you all the time." She pulled me in for a hug.

"Awww… thanks. He talks about you a lot also. I can't believe you're making her stay at that nasty fraternity house." I tried to cover my smile when I glared at Gray.

"Nasty? That room is fit for fucking royalty."

I raised a brow. "And let me guess. You're the king?"

"You know it, G. But I'm giving my room to Cade and Camilla this weekend. I'll crash on the couch."

"That's so nice of you, Gray. We just dropped our stuff off at his place and it has a private bathroom, so it seemed okay," Camilla said.

They'd gone to Gray's house first and he drove them over to campus to meet me for lunch.

"Dude, you do not need to sleep on the couch. Didn't you tell me Addy's always sleeping at Jett's? Why don't you crash in her bed?" Cade asked, and my entire body went still.

Gray glanced over at me, not making it obvious at all that that might be awkward. "Maybe. Let's play it by ear. You're coming to the party tomorrow night, right?" he asked me.

"Yes. I'm actually meeting someone there," I said, and I could barely hide my excitement to say it. I couldn't wait to see Gray's reaction.

"Ah, is this the guy you told me about?" Cade asked, and I didn't miss the way Gray's hands fisted at his side.

"Yes. It is. I don't know him well, but he seems really nice and he's really, really good-looking." I happily accentuated the last few words and Camilla clapped her hands together.

"Oh, this is so fun. I can't wait to meet him."

"Yeah. Me too." Gray's voice remained completely calm and collected.

Damn it.

"How about you, brother? Anyone on your horizon?" Cade asked as we walked into the restaurant.

"Yeah, you know me. I've got a few on the line. Gigi's sorority president will be there, and she's definitely got it bad." He wriggled his brows and I seethed as the hostess took us to the table.

"Oh yes, she's a real peach."

"You have a problem with Tiffany, G?" Gray asked with a cocky smirk.

"You don't like her?" Cade reached for a piece of bread and met my gaze.

"She's fine. She just likes to throw in my face that she's the reason I got in the house. But whatever. If Gray likes having her paw all over him, have at it. Why would I care?" I hissed, and Camilla's gaze bounced between Gray and me. My brother looked down at his phone as if he didn't notice a thing.

"You got in that house because you're amazing. Fuck her," Cade said. "No offense if you like her, brother."

Gray laughed. "I don't have to like her to bang her."

His eyes landed on mine, and he looked quite proud of himself.

"You're disgusting," I said, looking up when the waitress made her way over.

We placed our orders and Camilla filled us in on her hometown in Georgia. I really liked her. She asked me all sorts of questions about my sorority and my dorm. Conversation came easily and I ignored the elephant in the room.

The elephant being the cocky jackass sitting beside me at the table making me feel all sorts of crazy feelings.

I hated him, but I fought the urge to touch his hand beneath the table.

He aggravated me, but I couldn't shake the feeling of his lips against mine.

Most importantly, he was off-limits for a million reasons, yet I wanted desperately to be alone with him in his room again. Or my room.

Or any room, for that matter.

"You look so good," Addy said when I turned to face the full-length mirror.

"Thank you. I wish you were coming tonight." I slipped on my heel boots and glanced one more time in the mirror.

"I know. But no way Jett can go out before the big game. Coach has them on curfew, and I want to be there with him. I know he pretends he doesn't get nervous, but he has a lot of pressure on him." Addy was going to spend the night with Jett and watch movies since it was a game day tomorrow.

"I totally get it. And we'll meet tomorrow and go to the game together?"

"Yep. And you better text me tonight. My sheets are clean if Gray needs to sleep here." She winked.

"I will. Hopefully he doesn't because that could be very awkward. And the way he talked about Tiffany, I'm guessing he might go home with her. He's such a pig," I said, throwing a tennis shoe in the closet with more force than I meant to.

She laughed. "Trust me, he is not into her. Text me if you need me. And let Cade, Camilla, and Gray know Jett said he got us all clearance to come down on the field at the end of the game tomorrow."

"That was so nice of him to arrange. I'm excited to see him play. This is it if they don't win, right?"

"Yep. Fingers crossed they win, and we go on to the playoffs."

"I have one hundred percent faith in Jett," I said. "I'll shoot him a text wishing him luck tonight."

"Thanks. Love you. Good luck with River," she said, leaning over to hug me.

"Love you, too." I waved as she closed the door behind her.

River was meeting me and Leo at the party with a few of his friends. I wished I could say I was nervous or excited about it.

But all I could think about was the boy I shouldn't be thinking about at all.

Gray.

twelve

. . .

Gray

I ASSIGNED Ricky to the door to help monitor who came and left the party tonight. The dude was a freshman but had proven trustworthy, so he'd somehow become my right-hand man at the house.

"I'm on it, Gray," he said, giving me a fist bump as my best friend came walking out from my bedroom where he was staying with Camilla.

"So, this party's going to go off, huh?" he asked, following me into the kitchen.

Francie had left for the day, and I filled a red Solo cup with beer from the keg and handed it to him.

"Yeah, it'll be big. Which is why it's good I'm not drinking right now. I'm the one the cops talk to when the party gets carried away."

"Proud of you, brother." Cade held his cup up and tipped his chin before taking a long pull.

"Surprisingly, I don't miss it right now. I wasted a lot of time living in a drunken haze." I laughed, but my words came from an honest place.

He nodded. "I think it's good to step away now and again. I might need to think about that too. Camilla's been giving me shit about how much I drink with my fraternity brothers when we have parties."

"I like her. She's good for you." I pulled out a chair and he did the same. It wasn't always easy to find a place to have a conversation in this house, but there was a quiet before the storm.

Tonight would definitely be the storm.

"Yeah. She's amazing, right?" He set his cup down and shook his head. "Although she asked me if you and Gigi ever dated." He barked out a laugh and my chest squeezed with guilt.

"What? Why would she think that?" I pushed to my feet to grab a bottle of water from the fridge because I couldn't look at him right now. Cade knew me better than anyone.

"I know. Ironic, right? My mom and Gigi are always claiming girls are more tuned in to things, and Camilla pulls this out of her ass. She said she picked up on some kind of bullshit sexual tension. I nearly fell over laughing at the thought. Gigi hates you and you love bugging her. That's how it works. Talk about reading the situation wrong." He chugged the rest of his beer.

"Yeah. I guess she missed the part where everything I say annoys the shit out of your sister." It was the only thing I could think of to say that wasn't a blatant lie.

"Exactly. And I had to remind her that you're my brother. You'd never go there. Jesus, dude, your dick has seen more action than I care to speak of. Gigi is definitely off-limits. Camilla gets it now." His words stung, but he was right. I'd been a player back in high school and my first few years of college and so had Cade. But I understood why he wouldn't want me near his baby sister. Hell, even I knew I wasn't good enough for her.

"I hear ya. But look at you. You fucked around for a long time before meeting Camilla, and here you are acting all grown up and shit."

"I'm lucky. She knows who I was, and it took her a while to come around and trust me, but we got there. Do you think you'll ever want that? Gigi mentioned something about her sorority sister." I was thankful the conversation had shifted away from me and his sister, and I wanted to keep it there.

"Nah. She's a lot. Not really my type."

"Is this the one you banged over the summer?" He raised a brow with a smirk, and I rolled my eyes.

"Hey pot, this is kettle. You've never slept with anyone you regret?'

"I'm just giving you shit. I'll be your wingman tonight if you need me."

"Thanks. Glad you're here, brother."

We sat there shooting the shit for an hour before it was time to get things going. Cade and Camilla helped me make a run to the liquor store for a few more things we'd need, and before I knew it, we had a house full of people.

Drunk people.

There were a few fights that Ricky had caught before they escalated and he'd come to get me, and we were able to shut it down before anyone got hurt.

I'd selected a few brothers to be sober for the night to help me with security and monitoring the party. That piece of shit Jaden, who was on a slippery slope as it was at the house, was my first pick after Ricky. For very different reasons. I'd put him in charge of making sure my best friend and Camilla were catered to. He bitched about it, but I was ready to kick his ass to the curb and I think he sensed it, so he did what he was told. It wouldn't hurt that kid one bit to have a sober night where he actually did something to help his brothers.

I walked over to check with Ricky and my head turned to see Cade spinning his sister around as she'd just arrived. Leo stood beside her. My jaw dropped open as I took in her outfit. She wore a black top that dipped so low in the front there was no fucking way she was wearing a bra. Her black skinny jeans hugged her ass perfectly, and my mouth went dry. I stalked in her direction, closing the distance between us with just a few steps.

"Are you okay with her dressing like this?" I hissed.

Cade barked out a laugh. "She looks like everyone else here."

"I think she looks amazing," Camilla said, wrapping an arm around Gigi.

Christ, has everyone lost their minds?

"What is your problem?" Gigi snarled, tipping her chin up at me.

"Hey, Gray," a voice said beside me, and a hand rubbed down my arm. I turned to see the chick from Gigi and Addy's dorm.

"Hey, uh, Brittany?" I said, but my gaze didn't leave Gigi.

"It's Bailey. Great party, boss."

Boss? Where did people come up with this shit?

"Thanks," I said, glancing at her hand that was resting on my arm and she smiled.

Not happening, sweetheart.

I let out a long breath, and for the first time in a few months, I actually wanted a drink. I wanted to forget that Gigi Jacobs' nipples were currently sharp enough to cut glass and staring right at me.

Taunting me.

Just then, a dude with blonde hair, and an I-just-got-high swagger walked over and handed Gigi and Leo each a red Solo cup.

"What's in the cup?" I crossed my arms over my chest, forcing Bailey to release me from her grasp.

Cade was in a conversation with Leo, and I wanted to slap him upside the head at his lack of concern over the situation. I didn't miss the way Camilla studied me, her gaze ping-ponging between me and Gigi.

"Uh, just beer," the dumb shit said.

Yeah, go get your surfboard and your edibles and get the fuck out of here.

He was eye-fucking her and that shit was not going down on my watch.

"I'm sorry, Dad. I didn't know I needed your permission to have a beer?" Gigi glared at me, before whipping her hair in the douchebag's face to get her brother's attention.

"Cade, this is River."

You've got to be shitting me. Of course, that was his name. River needed to flow his ass right out of here.

"Nice to meet you," Cade said, fist-bumping the moron.

Am I living in an alternate universe?

We're okay with this now?

"You all right?" Camilla asked, moving to stand beside me, as Bailey got the hint and started talking to someone else.

"I'm fine. Are you having fun?"

"I am. Thanks for giving us your room. I feel bad about it. I don't think you should be sleeping on the couch. That's not right." She smiled, and I saw something there. It was mischievous and she glanced over at Gigi before turning back to look at me with one brow raised.

"I'm fine."

"I'm sure you are. But just so you know… Cade can be stuck in his ways. He gets worked up, but he always gets over things."

He would never get over me and Gigi. I had no doubts about that.

"I don't know what you're talking about," I said, trying to hide the smile on my face because I was somewhat fascinated by how quickly she'd recognized the battle going on between Gigi and me. That it was more than annoyance and irritation.

More than playful banter.

So much more.

"Sure, you don't. FYI, I heard River saying he'd walk her home after the party."

My hands fisted at my sides. "The fuck he will. And only because I don't trust him. I'm surprised Cade's acting all friendly with the asshole."

"Cade is four beers and three shots of whiskey deep and Gigi blasted him for being overbearing before we even arrived here, and she's right. You two need to back off, unless you, in particular, have reason to be bothered by it."

"I don't. I've just always looked out for her, that's all."

"Well, then, River appears to be a nice guy and she seems to like him."

"She does not," I hissed. She only acted that way to aggravate me, but how in the hell was I supposed to explain that to Camilla.

Gigi's head fell back in laughter as she and Cade listened to River as if he were the wisest person they'd ever heard speak before. What could he be sharing? How to roll a joint in record time, or what his favorite jellyfish looked like? Give me a break with the overzealous laughter. I glared at her and she refused to look in my direction.

"There you are," Lila said, slipping her hand around my waist as she sidled up against me. Her tits were pouring out of her low-cut top. Lila was voluptuous, to say the least.

Gigi's head whipped around in my direction and her gaze locked with mine.

Yeah, I can dish it out just like you, G.

I introduced her to Camilla, and her hand slipped inside mine. Fingers intertwined.

We all made our way over to Cade, and I introduced Lila to the group.

"Big daddy, Gray, this party is lit," Leo said, and everyone laughed at his slurred words.

Gigi sipped her beer and refused to look at me. The surfer boy stoner fist-bumped me like we were buddies.

We were not.

"Sweet party, dude," River said.

I nodded and my eyes zeroed in on his hand resting on Gigi's lower back.

"Thanks. Would you like a tour of the house? We have a cool rooftop terrace," I said, desperate to do anything to get him away from Gigi. She narrowed her gaze at me, silently asking what I was up to.

"Really? Fuck, yeah. I didn't pledge because I'm not big on commitment," he said, and I had a hard time hiding my smile.

Commitment-phobe. Strike one, asshole.

"I hear ya. Yeah, come on." I turned to lead him away and he didn't let go of Gigi's hand. She looked up at me as if she dared me to do something about it.

"Stay with your brother. It's cold outside and I'm taking him to the rooftop." My gaze purposely zoomed in on her nipples that were once again aware of my attention.

She huffed and crossed her arms over her chest after she slyly flashed me the bird.

I couldn't help but laugh as I walked away with the douchebag on my heels. I didn't mind at all. Leo joined us on the bullshit tour.

"You don't like him, do you?" Leo leaned in so only I could hear him, while River walked across the terrace and looked over the edge once we were outside on the rooftop terrace.

"He annoys me, but that isn't saying much because most people annoy me," I said with a shrug.

"I hope I don't." He laughed, and his drink sloshed over the sides of his cup.

"Oddly, you don't." Leo was becoming one of my favorite people. He had Gigi's back and I saw that the first time I met him.

And that fact that he wasn't trying to get in her pants didn't hurt either.

"Do you mind if I vape out here?" Surfer-douche asked.

"Not at all. Take your time." I crossed my arms over my chest. The longer I could keep him out here, the better.

Leo laughed. "You're a man with a plan, aren't you?"

"No idea what you're talking about," I said with a chuckle.

I shot the shit with Leo for the next hour while surfer-douche got baked off his ass.

"Dude. Thanks for bonding with me up here. Spiritual, man. This whole experience has been—real. I haven't had a lot of *real* since I came to school. But I feel you both now."

Feel your ass home, River.

He'd clearly been drinking the hard stuff because he pulled me in for a hug and he reeked of bourbon.

"Good to know. I need to get back downstairs." I was getting text updates from Ricky every ten minutes and things were going strong at the party.

Leo and River followed me through the house and River turned into a room where two dudes were playing Fortnite.

The universe was aligning all the stars for me at the moment.

"I'm going to hang here. I'll see you downstairs." His words slurred.

Fabulous. He struck me as the kind of guy who could spend hours gaming.

Leo and I made our way back to the group and I was happy to see Cade and Camilla dancing and having a good time.

"Where's River?" Gigi asked, looking bored as her gaze met mine.

"Your boyfriend could give Snoop Dogg and Marth Stewart a run for their money when it comes to dipping in the herbs. He's currently blitzed off his ass and playing video games. Sorry about that." I tried not to smile but it was impossible not to.

Gigi grabbed Leo's hand, glaring at me as she led him out

to dance with her brother and his girlfriend. I checked on a few things and gave into Lila who dragged me into the sea of sweaty college drunkards currently jumping up and down to techno music.

We laughed and danced, and my eyes were never far from Gigi. The party started to weed out as people made their way home. Jaden did a decent job of cleaning up and making sure no one was driving. Ricky was helping people who were making themselves comfortable on the couch find their way out of there, and even called a few Ubers from their phones for them.

"Love you, brother. And Camilla thinks you're great," my best friend said, pulling me in for a bro hug.

"Love you, too, man."

"All right, we've had way too much to drink. Your house officially throws better parties than mine." He slapped my shoulder and saluted me, as Camilla waved before leading him down the hall to my room. "Hey, make sure Gigi gets home okay, will you?"

"Of course," I said, and Camilla wriggled her brows at me behind Cade's back.

I rolled my eyes and turned to see River making his way down the stairs. "Hey, sorry. I passed out in one of the rooms."

"We were just coming to look for you," Leo said.

Gigi crossed her arms over her chest. "It's fine. I'm going to head home."

"Can I walk you?" River asked. The kid was sloppy, and he was in no shape to walk anyone home, including himself.

"I'll give you guys a ride," I said, shaking my keys in front of me. "I promised your brother."

Gigi stormed out of the house in front of me and River stumbled behind her, completely clueless. Leo moved in stride beside me. "I don't think she's happy with you. She thinks you sabotaged her night with River."

"Thanks for the heads-up, bro. And I totally sabotaged it." I shrugged. I had no shame. I didn't want her wasting her time on a dude like that. I did what needed to be done.

He barked out a laugh. "Well, at least you're honest."

"I am that, my friend."

They piled in my truck and Gigi was tucked up front between me and Leo. Surfer-douche was in the back seat completely sprawled out and snoring before I even started the engine.

"Where does everyone live?" I asked.

Leo informed me that he and River lived in the same dorm right up the street from Gigi's. Perfect. I would make sure ol' River made it to his dorm safely.

I pulled up and Leo helped me get River out of the back of my truck and he came to and thanked me for the ride. I nodded as they both walked inside the building.

When I got back in the truck, I received the silent treatment, which didn't surprise me. She'd moved across the seat as close to the passenger door as one could get. We pulled in front of her dorm and she turned to face me.

"Are you happy with yourself?"

"I actually am, thank you."

"What is your problem?" she asked, and my gaze moved down once again and stared at her tits. They were small, but perky as hell, especially in my presence.

"My problem is the fact that your nipples are hard every time I look at them."

"Then stop looking at them." She swung the door open and stormed to the front of her building. I thought about parking and chasing after her. Crashing in Addy's bed so I didn't have to sleep on the couch. But I knew myself too well. If I went to her room right now, there would be no way my mouth wouldn't be on hers.

The pull was too strong.

My phone vibrated and I looked down to see a text from her.

Gigi ~ I hate you.

Me ~ Keep it that way. Sweet dreams, G.

Gigi ~ <middle finger emoji> <middle finger emoji>

I laughed.

I pulled out of the parking lot and drove home.

It was the only way I'd be able to stay away from her tonight.

thirteen

• • •

Gigi

THE NEXT WEEK flew by in a blur. My brother and Camilla had gone back to school, and I'd found a new friend in Cade's girlfriend. I loved her. Jett had arranged for us to come down on the field after TU had won the game and made it to the playoffs and I was so happy to experience that with my brother.

His best friend was another story.

I'd ignored Gray after he'd managed to run off River during the party—yet he wanted nothing to do with me romantically.

Hypocrite much?

River had reached out the next day to apologize for getting so trashed that he could barely say my name. The truth was—I wasn't interested in River, or anyone for that matter.

Gray had ruined me with his kiss.

And I hated him for it.

I thought about that kiss. I dreamed about that kiss.

And I longed for another one.

I'd been ignoring his texts all week, because that had just

become our routine. He'd piss me off and I'd ignore him for as long as I could until he wore me down again.

He'd made it clear that nothing could happen between us, yet every time I tried to date someone else, Gray had a meltdown.

Frustration didn't begin to describe the brewing feelings that resonated deep within me. The more he pushed me away, the more I wanted to be close to him.

Yet I hated him at the same time?

What was wrong with me?

I'd never been one to lose control of my emotions or feelings, especially when it came to boys. I'd never actually liked anyone enough to get a reaction out of me. And now I was bursting with feelings and emotions that were so foreign I didn't know what to do with them.

So, in typical crazy hormonal, irrational fashion—I was going to a Sig Alpha party tonight. Yep. That's where we were with this. I'd been ignoring his texts where he pretended to be a family member just reaching out to check on me and I was going to show him what he was missing.

Addy, Leo, and I walked to town where there was a cute boutique to find something to wear tonight.

"I can't believe you get to date that delicious football star. Man, he looks like he's chiseled to perfection, and I've only seen him fully clothed," Leo teased, and a pink hue spread across Addy's cheeks.

"He's as close to perfect as you can get." She beamed.

"Yes, girl. He sure is. And big daddy Gray is, mmmm-mmmmm, you two have fabulous taste in men."

"Gray is not my boyfriend. Hell, he's nothing. Maybe my nemesis," I hissed as I pushed a few tops down the rack as I wanted something that would jump out at me, and I'd yet to see it.

"Sure, he is. That's why he ran that poor sexy River around his house until the boy dropped."

Addy laughed. "I agree. He's definitely into you, but he's scared of what will happen with Cade."

"Why, your brother's fine ass seemed perfectly reasonable to me." Leo held up a black see-through blouse and I scrunched my nose and shook my head. I didn't want to show everything, just enough to leave him waggling.

"He's not reasonable about things like that," I said.

"She's not kidding. He would lose it if Gray tried to date Gigi. Gray has a bit of a reputation back home," Addy said, pausing to look at a white turtleneck bodysuit. Conservative, yet sexy, just like my bestie. "But so does Cade, and he's turned things around for Camilla."

I held up a blue blouse with a little denim miniskirt and studied it. "Exactly. He's ridiculous. He'd get over it. But maybe Gray's afraid he couldn't stay faithful to me. That's the truth of it. He probably just wants a one-nighter, and he knows that will cause a lot of trouble with Cade. And I'd hate him if he did that too. So maybe he's right and we shouldn't go there at all."

Leo laughed. "One-nighter. Oh girl, you make it sound so dirty. One-nighters can be amazing."

"I'm sure they can, but seeing as I'm sort of a no-nighter at this point, I should probably not attempt a casual fling. I've never had anything. And I want the real deal. Like what Addy and Jett have." I admitted before turning to let them see the outfit I was admiring.

"And you deserve that. And hells to the yes on this outfit. Classy, sexy, and very Gigi. Go try it on," Addy said.

"I agree. You deserve the best, girl. And that outfit will have all the boys dropping at your feet. Why don't they make anything sexy like that for guys?" Leo said, and we all laughed.

Leo waited on the pink velvet love seat while Addy and I went into the dressing rooms to change. We modeled a few different things, but they both voted for the blue top and skirt for me and the white turtleneck bodysuit and new jeans for Addy.

The weather was changing as Thanksgiving was right around the corner. I couldn't wait to go home for a few days. The girls would all be home, but Addy would be going with Jett to the bowl game that weekend. But we'd have a few days where we'd all be together, and I was looking forward to it.

"Well, I might not have an outfit with any sass, but I'll be walking in with the two hottest girls on campus on my arm, so that has to bring me some attention, right?" Leo was a character, and I'd grown close to him.

"You always look amazing," I said as we gathered our bags and made our way out of the shop, laughing all the way back to the dorms.

I'd been asked to dance so many times I could barely feel my feet anymore in these booties. The outfit was clearly a hit. I'd also been drinking more than usual, and you know what, I didn't care.

I wanted to be a normal college kid. I was tired of always being so responsible. And I made a special point to drink the red juice that Gray had insisted I avoid at my first party.

Because Gray Baldwin was not the boss of me.

He'd come over to say hi, and I'd turned my back on him. I didn't want to look at him because I knew the minute I did, I'd be desperate for more. I was breaking myself of him, not that I minded the way he drank me in when he first saw me. I'd watched as his eyes had slowly perused me before I turned away quickly when he tried to meet my gaze.

I made my way over to Addy, Jett, and Leo. Joshua, the boy I'd just been dancing with, ran off to get me a drink. My head was a little fuzzy, and I touched my lips to make sure they were still there because I couldn't feel them, which made me laugh. Joshua walked over and handed me another delicious red punch.

"You sure you want to drink that?" Addy asked me, concern laced her pretty face.

"I'm totally fine. Soooooo good, actu… actually? Is that a word? Actually?" I said it slower and tried to remember the meaning.

Joshua wrapped an arm around my shoulder, and Jett moved in his space. "I think she's had enough, buddy."

"Are you her father?" Joshua asked.

"No. I'm her friend, and you most definitely are not." Jett's face hardened, and I stepped back, unsure why he was angry.

"Come on, Gina, let's get out of here," he said, and I cracked up that he called me the wrong name. Hell, I only met him on the dance floor, we'd never had a conversation outside of him handing me a couple drinks.

"Beat it, asshole," a voice said from behind me, and I stiffened.

Gray.

"And who the hell are you? Her stepfather?" Joshua pressed, and I closed my eyes because I knew this wouldn't end well. Poor bastard didn't even know me, yet he was willing to piss off Jett and Gray.

"I'm your worst fucking nightmare, motherfucker, that's who I am." Gray raised his hand and before I could process what was happening, Joshua was ushered out of the party.

"Are you going to kick out every guy I talk to?" I hissed as he took the cup from my hand and set it on the table beside us.

"Probably."

"You're an asshole." I turned on my heels and headed for the dance floor.

"Where do you think you're going? You can barely walk,"

he shouted from behind me and wrapped his hand around my wrist.

I shoved him away. "I'm going to dance, and you can't stop me."

Before I took one step, I was thrown over his shoulder as he moved through the crowd with ease. I slapped at his back and looked up to see Addy, Jett, and Leo smiling. Of course, they would side with him. Everyone was against me having a good time tonight.

He pulled me into his room and dropped me on the bed, before slamming his door shut.

"What the fuck are you doing?" he shouted, pacing in little circles in front of me, as he ran a hand through his hair.

"What the fuck am I doing?" My words were slurred, it made me laugh. I fell back on his bed as the room started to spin.

"Jesus, G. I told you not to drink that shit." He came to sit on the side of the bed and pushed the hair out of my face.

"You aren't the boss of me, Gray." I hustled off the bed and moved to my feet. "I'm the boss of me."

He stood, hovering over me.

"All right. What's the plan, boss?" he asked, his voice gravelly and strained, for reasons I couldn't understand in my hazy state. But I liked it.

And I am the boss.

"You want to know the plan?" I asked, poking him in the chest.

"I do." His hand was cupping the side of my face, and I closed my eyes at his touch.

No. Nope. Not getting distracted from what I wanted to do.

"The plan is this. I'm tired of being a virgin. And you ruin it for me every time I try to talk to anyone else. So, you'll have to do the deed. I don't care about Cade or anyone else. *Make me a woman, Gray Baldwin.* Have your way with me and teach me all the things. I am an empty canvas dying to be painted." The last line made me smile because I didn't expect to go so deep. But here I was. Begging the boy of my dreams to make love to me. And I'd thrown in an art spin, which should be the cherry on the cake. I mean, I doubted Gray's usual bimbos put this much thought into it.

"Good Christ, you can't say things like that," he hissed and moved closer.

"Well, too bad for you because I'm saying it, you stubborn ass."

His thumb grazed along my bottom lip, and I squeezed my thighs together because maybe this was actually going to happen, and I was ready for it.

Something twisted in my stomach, and with no warning, my head fell back, and a gush of liquid exited my body.

I'd projectile vomited all over the boy I wanted to make love to me. He stood there staring at me in disbelief.

Because, hello, nothing about tonight was going my way.

And I'd worn the cute outfit.

"Oh my gosh, did I ruin my outfit?" I whispered and looked down.

He laughed as if I'd said the funniest thing in the world. "Nope. You somehow managed to contain all your vomit for me. Come here."

I followed him to the bathroom, and he yanked his vomit-covered T-shirt over his head and dropped it on the floor before turning on the shower. My palms started to sweat as I watched him in the mirror as he stood behind me. His muscles flexed as he pushed his jeans down.

"We're showering?" I asked before swooshing water in my mouth and spitting in the sink.

He raised a brow. "You have no reason to shower. I'm the one covered in puke."

He pushed his black briefs down and my mouth dropped open. I hadn't seen many penises in my life, but I was fairly certain this one could win some sort of award for its... *grand-ness.* A true overachiever, just like everything about this boy. "Oh, my gosh."

He raised a brow. "You like what you see?"

I nodded slowly before my hand went to my stomach as a sick feeling flooded me again. He lifted the toilet seat before stepping in the shower.

I dropped to my knees and unloaded what was left in my stomach.

While Gray was naked behind the curtain looking like every fantasy I'd ever had. Was I dreaming this? Had he just stripped naked in front of me?

Well, after I'd just begged him to have sex with me and then puked on him.

He wasn't the one that should be scrutinized right now.

I wiped my mouth and pushed back to lean against the wall and groaned. The room was spinning, and I was sick to my stomach.

The water turned off and he opened the shower curtain. I forced my head up to look at him one more time. If this was the last time I was going to see him naked, I didn't want to forget what he looked like. And damn it, my head was so hazy I'd never remember this moment.

"Would it be completely inappropriate to ask you to grab my phone and take a picture of yourself for me to look at later? When I'm hiding in my room and mortified by everything that just happened."

I was feeling a little better after that last dumping of vomit and bile, and I opened my eyes and looked up at him.

He cinched a towel around his waist, his hair dripping wet, green eyes looking at me with anything but judgment, and a sexy smirk that melted my heart. He bent down to meet my gaze. "There's nothing to be embarrassed about, G."

"I just begged you to make me a woman and then puked

on you. And then I vomited while you were naked behind the curtain," I said as the tears started to fall.

He used his thumbs to swipe away the tears. "Trust me, you're already a woman, G. Having sex does not make you more complete. You're already perfect to me."

I buried my face in my hands and sobbed. "Then why don't you want me?"

I couldn't believe the words coming out of my mouth. Talk about liquid courage. I'm sure I'd regret every word tomorrow, but I couldn't keep this in any longer if I tried.

And I didn't want to.

"You think I don't want you? I'm going out of my fucking mind every time you show up here with a dumb fucking dude hanging all over you. I want you so much I can't see straight."

I leaned my head against the wall and calmed my breathing. "What are you afraid of?"

"Hurting you. Hurting Cade. Messing things up."

I nodded. "We don't have to tell anyone. We can see where it goes first."

He smiled and pulled me to my feet. "Let's talk about this tomorrow. You're drunk and nothing's going to happen tonight."

He led me into his bedroom and pulled out a T-shirt and placed it on the bed before walking to the door.

"Where are you going?" I asked, dropping to sit on the soft mattress.

"I'm going to grab you some toast and a bottle of water. Put on the T-shirt and get in bed. I'll be back in a bit."

"I'm sleeping here?" I asked, wrapping my arms around my shoulders as chill bumps covered my skin.

"I'm not letting you out of my sight tonight."

I smiled, because I couldn't help myself. He walked out the door and I pulled off my booties and then dropped the skirt to the ground and unbuttoned my blouse. I slipped his large T-shirt over my head and breathed it in. It smelled like Gray.

Mint and sandalwood.

I wanted to pick my clothes up off the ground, but I was spinning again, so I rested my head on the pillow and closed my eyes. Things may not have gone as I'd hoped tonight, but I couldn't complain.

I was exactly where I wanted to be.

fourteen

. . .

Gray

WARM BREATH TICKLED MY NECK, and I stirred. The feel of soft hair feathered through my fingers like silk, and my eyes slowly opened. Gigi was staring up at me. Her concerned sapphire gaze was filled with confusion.

"Hey," I said, liking the feel of her warm legs tangled with mine.

"Oh my god," she whispered, before pulling the navy comforter on my bed over her face.

I waited a minute to see if she'd come out. She did not.

"Hello," I said, pulling the blanket off her pretty face.

"Did we?" A pink hue covered her cheeks, and I tried to hide my smile.

"Did we, what?"

"You know," she said, refusing to meet my gaze.

I tipped her chin up and forced her to look at me. "Did I *make you a woman*?" I couldn't help but chuckle as the words left my mouth. "No. And trust me when I tell you, you wouldn't need to ask. You would know if I had. You'd feel me long after I was gone."

Her gaze searched mine and she nodded. Something crossed her face and she paled. "Oh. My. God. I asked you to make me a woman, didn't I? That's why you said that. This isn't happening."

She tried to tug the comforter over her face again, and I yanked it back down. "Stop. It was cute. And very tempting."

"Yet nothing happened?"

"Well, I wasn't going to do anything when you were shit-faced."

She continued to study me and then gasped. "I puked on you. And I saw your... manhood. Oh my god, what is happening? I'm never drinking again."

"You weren't complaining about seeing my *manhood* last night."

She fanned her face. "Did I do anything inappropriate?"

"Other than projectile vomit red juice all over me? No. You were an absolute lady." I barked out a laugh because I couldn't help myself. Shit, I'd been drunk more times than I could count and had my fair share of embarrassing nights. This was nothing.

"Why am I here?" she whispered. "Why didn't you send me home with Addy?"

"Because I wanted you to stay. If you hadn't been drunk, we would have done something that we would both probably regret today." I ran the pad of my thumb over her bottom lip, and she trembled in my arms.

"What would we have done?" she asked.

I chuckled. "What do you think, G?"

"So, you admit that you want it to happen?"

"I've never denied that I'm attracted to you." She moved closer, her body rubbing against mine and my dick was enjoying every minute of it.

"But you don't want to give it a chance because of Cade?"

"It's more than that, but yes, he's a huge factor. The dude is like a brother. And your family—they've been so good to me. But aside from that, I'm not good for you, and we both know it. I'll fuck it up and everything will be weird after that.

And for what? So we can scratch an itch? You really want to play with fire like that?"

Her head cocked to the side, and my breath lodged in my throat. I'd woken up with my fair share of girls over the years, and none had ever looked like this in the morning. Gigi Jacobs was gorgeous with no makeup, hungover after puking her brains out, looking at me like she had all the faith in the world in me.

Her hair was a wild mess splayed out on my pillow.

"What if I'm not good enough for you? Did you ever think of that?"

I ran my fingers through her hair because I couldn't help myself and I laughed. "No. Because we both know that's not true. Everything about you is good."

"Why are you so hard on yourself?" she whispered, and her fingers grazed my jaw, and I closed my eyes as I reveled in her touch.

"Because it's easy."

"I think that needs to change starting now." Her nose rubbed against mine and it took every ounce of restraint not to kiss her. "Does my breath smell like puke?"

"You used my toothbrush and mouthwash last night, so your breath smells minty. And how do you always manage to smell like peaches?"

She smiled and bit down on her plump bottom lip. "It's my lotion. You noticed that, huh?"

"I did. Peaches are my favorite fruit." I tugged her closer, wrapping both of my arms around her because I needed to feel her, but was wrestling with how badly I wanted her.

"Why does my head feel like it might explode?" Her breath tickled my chest as she spoke.

"You've got yourself an award-winning hangover." I chuckled and my phone vibrated on my nightstand. I pulled back, assuming it was a sign from God to put some space between us. "It's Wren. I need to take this."

She nodded and sat up in bed. My T-shirt was pooled around her, and she looked cute as hell as she tried to comb through her hair with her fingers.

"Hey, what's up?"

"I'm sorry to do this to you, Gray, but your dad was here last night, and he placed some hefty bets on a few fights that I'm guessing he can't cover." Wren owned a warehouse where underground local fights took place. "These are not guys that he wants to mess around with. He took off and I can't find him. But if they find him first, it won't be pretty."

Good Christ.

Could the man not get his shit together for one minute? Just see through the program at rehab.

Do better.

It was exhausting.

I scrubbed a hand down my face. "All right. I'll get in the car now. I know where to look for him. Do you know how much he owes?"

"No. But if you could get him back in the program, they won't be able to touch him there, and we could figure out how to get him out of this mess in the meantime." Wren had been a good friend to my father, and I was thankful he still had someone looking out for him. He'd burned every other bridge in Willow Springs.

"I'm on my way," I said, pushing to my feet and ending the call.

"What happened?" Gigi asked, and her gaze zeroed in on my morning wood, which was more prominent than ever. My dick would have to sit his ass down. I had to deal with my dad's shit per usual. Exactly why this girl did not want to get mixed up with me.

"My dad's in some trouble. I need to go home for the night. Fuck. I don't want Simon to find out he fucked up yet again. Jesus, this is a never-ending nightmare." I dropped to sit on my bed and ran my hands through my hair.

She moved beside me and wrapped her little arms around me and somehow managed to offer more comfort than anyone else ever had in just the small gesture. "I'm going with you. You don't need to do this alone."

"The hell you are." I pushed to my feet. "This is why we can't fuck around with this, G. You don't need to be brought down with my shit."

She pushed to her feet and pulled the T-shirt over her head, showing me her perfect tits and causing me to groan. She slipped on her bra and tugged the blue blouse over her head, before shimmying into the little jean skirt she'd worn last night. "You're not the boss of me, Gray. And whether you never want to act on this..." She motioned her hand between us. "Whatever this is. I'm still your friend, and I'm going with you."

She dropped to sit and slipped her ankle booties on and hurried to the bathroom to splash some water on her face. I pulled on my jeans and tugged a T-shirt and hoody over my head. I didn't have time to argue with her, or maybe I just liked the idea of her coming with me.

I shouldn't.

It wasn't a good idea to get tangled up with Gigi Jacobs, but I didn't know how to stop it.

It was an unfamiliar force that I'd never experienced in my life, and I didn't have time to dissect it.

"You ready?" she asked.

I rumpled the top of her head and pulled the door open. "When did you get so stubborn?"

"It only comes out when I'm dealing with you." She laughed as she followed me into the kitchen. Francie wasn't there yet, and the place was a fucking disaster. Ricky came around the corner holding a broom. Damn, the kid was as dependable as it gets. I grabbed us two bananas and a muffin and wrapped it in a paper towel and handed it to Gigi.

"Dude, I have a family situation I need to deal with.

You're in charge. Anyone gives you shit, you call me and I'll talk to them."

"You got it. Hey." He smiled at Gigi and his cheeks flamed red. I tried not to laugh. I got it. She was fucking beautiful. It was a fair reaction.

"Hi," she said with a wave, as I grabbed two water bottles, and placed my hand on her lower back to lead her out of the house.

"The dude has a major crush on you," I whispered in her ear as I pulled open the passenger door for her. She climbed in and I reached over to buckle her seat belt.

She slapped my hand away. "I know how to buckle myself, Gray."

I shrugged. I liked doing things for her. I jumped in the driver's seat and started the truck. "Sure you want to come with me? Last chance to get dropped off at your dorm."

"Nice try. I'm coming with you. We can stay at my house tonight. My parents are in Maui." She crossed her arms over her chest, proud that she was solving all my problems for me. I didn't want to have to stay at my mom's house and tell Simon why I'd come home for the night. Staying at the Jacobs' was a good idea.

"You've just got it all figured out, don't you?" I asked as I merged onto the freeway.

"Most of the time." She shrugged. "Tell me about your dad. I know your parents split up when you were young, but I don't know much about him."

I let out a long breath. Maybe it was good for her to hear about all the shit that was part of my life. Like it or not, my dad was a part of me.

"He's a great guy when he isn't fucked up, which unfortunately isn't often lately. He was such a good dad when I was young. He got in an accident and got hooked on pain killers, and it's been a vicious cycle ever since."

She nodded. "Is he still hooked on pills?"

"Well, now he's hooked on everything. Booze. Pills. Gambling. Who knows what else the dude has going on."

"How does that make you feel?" Her voice was soft, and I glanced over at her. The look in her eyes made my chest squeeze. No one ever asked how I felt about the shit with my father, or the divorce, or the fact that my stepfather was a complete prick.

"It's fine."

"You don't need to say you're fine for me. He's your dad. It wouldn't be normal if this didn't hurt you or fill you with worry."

I let out a long breath. "It sucks. He's my dad. Everyone talks shit about him in town, including that asshole, Simon. My mom doesn't want to talk about it because it's too painful, so I only have my grandparents and Wren that still hold out hope that he can come out of this."

She moved to the center seat in my truck and buckled herself in before reaching for my hand in my lap. My shoulders stiffened but I didn't pull away.

"Addiction is brutal. He's very lucky he has you in his corner. If I had to have anyone in my corner, I'd want it to be you," she said.

"Is that because you saw my *manhood*?" I teased, still finding it humorous that she wouldn't say dick or cock or even penis.

"I mean, it doesn't hurt the argument." Her cheeks pinked and she laughed. "But, no. It's because you're strong and resilient. I've known you my entire life, and you don't let things stop you. You just push through and keep on trying, and I think it's admirable. Most people would fall apart if they were dealing with all this."

I squeezed her hand. "Don't give me too much credit. I don't really have a choice, right?"

"You always have a choice, Gray. Your mom walked away.

Most of his friends walked away. You made a choice to stand by him, and he's lucky to have you."

"When did you get so wise?"

"I was born this way," she said, and a wide grin spread across her face.

We spent the rest of the drive talking and laughing and sharing things we'd never shared before. Like the fact that we'd both never had a serious relationship—but for different reasons. Gigi hadn't found anyone she cared about that way, *her words not mine,* and I'd never met anyone who made me want to stop banging other girls, *my words not hers.*

She wanted to be an artist because she liked creating things, she loved her best friends and had her entire life, and her family meant everything to her. She wanted to be a mom someday but wanted to have a career of her own because her mother never did, and she didn't want to regret not filling those needs first. She loved Cade but didn't appreciate that he treated her like a little kid because she was a grown woman. I laughed when she said it because she was so worked up—but she was right. She wasn't a little girl anymore, and her brother needed to respect that.

Hell, I needed to respect it too.

Although I'd been fantasizing about her for a while now, but that was different.

I pulled up at Dad's apartment, because Wren thought he might be hiding out there, but he hadn't picked up the phone nor answered the door when he'd tried to reach him. I had a key, so if he was there, I was going to haul his ass back to rehab. I let Wren know I was close, and he was meeting us over here.

Again.

"You wait in the car," I said when I stepped out, but I heard her door shut behind me. "What are you doing?"

"You might need backup. You don't know what you're walking into."

I rolled my eyes as she followed me up the cement stairs. "Anyone ever told you that you're exhausting?"

"Only you," she said, pausing to stand beside me at the door.

Dad lived on the second story of a sketchy duplex. I was fairly certain the people downstairs were porn stars because I always heard moaning when I came here, and there were dudes with cameras coming in and out of the place.

Shady as fuck. I hated that this was where he lived. He'd lived with my grandparents for a while, but he didn't like them knowing when he came and went—which is code for *fell off the wagon*.

My father had had it all at one time. We'd lived in a gorgeous house on the lake when I was young, he was practicing law, and my mom and dad had always seemed happy together. At least that's the memory that's stayed with me.

I knocked on the door and listened for any movement.

Nothing.

I pulled out my keys and we both jumped when a car door slammed from the parking lot and I looked over to see Wren making his way up the stairs.

"Did you knock?" he asked.

"Yeah. I don't hear anything, but that doesn't mean he isn't in there." I put the key in the door and pushed it open. "Dad," I called out.

Wren moved me to the side and stepped in first. "Let me check the place out first."

I knew why he'd met me over here. I wasn't stupid. If my father continued down this path, there'd come a day where we'd find him lying facedown on the floor. Wren didn't want me to see that.

"You shouldn't have come," I said, looking down at Gigi. This ugliness was not a part of her world, nor should it be.

"Stop being dramatic," she said. "You're not getting rid of me, you stubborn ass."

I closed my eyes and looked up at the ceiling when Wren called for us to come in from the back room. "He's all right."

Relief engulfed me, and I let out a breath I hadn't even realized I'd been holding.

"Come on." I reached for her hand and led her into his room.

It smelled like trash and stale booze and misery.

My dad was slumped in the corner of his room with his face buried in his hands.

"I'm sorry, son. I fucked up."

It wasn't the first time, nor would it be the last time. But I dropped Gigi's hand and moved in front of him, bending down to meet his gaze.

His eyes were dilated and lost and lonely.

A reminder that I never wanted to be here myself. I'd always avoided drugs at all costs, and this would be a forever reason to continue down that path. And booze had become an escape for me, and I needed to remember that.

I never wanted to be here.

"Can we get you back to get the help you need, Dad?" I'd seen a therapist over the years to deal with being the child of an addict as well as attended more Al-Anon meetings than I could count, and I knew better than to get angry at him right now. My father was drowning in addiction. Putting him on the defense would only make him run. I'd been in touch with his counselor at the facility and they were willing to take him back.

"Yeah. I'm sorry, Gray." He glanced up and focused on Gigi. "Who's this?"

"This is my friend Gigi," I said, offering him a hand but he didn't take it.

"Pretty girl."

The door flew open behind us and we all startled, with the exception of my father. Two shady-looking motherfuckers strolled in the apartment, and I moved to stand in front of Gigi on instinct. My hand found hers behind me and I knew she was frightened. I cursed myself for bringing her here.

"Who the fuck are you?" my father snarled, and Wren moved toward the two men.

"I told you I'd get back to you when I found him," Wren hissed and glanced over at me, and the look he gave me made the hair on the back of my neck stand on edge.

This was not good.

"Well, it looks like you found him." The dude with two sleeves of tats on his arms said, staring at me and craning his neck to see Gigi.

Jesus Christ. I'd fucked up big-time bringing her here.

"He doesn't have the cash. He'll get it. Give him a few days." Wren crossed his arms, standing tall and bowing up just enough for me to notice.

We might throw down right here, and what the fuck would Gigi do?

"Time is money. He's going to pay more with each passing day, and if he doesn't pay up, we'll find other ways to make him pay," the other guy said. He had a scruffy beard and stood maybe an inch shorter than me, and his eyes were filled with hate.

"Get the fuck out of here. You'll get your money soon." My father was on his feet and waggling a gun in front of his face and all the air left my lungs.

"Fuck, Dylan. Put that down." Wren moved beside my father.

"Get the fuck out of here or I'll blow your fucking heads off! You'll have your money by the end of the week." Dad had lost all reason, and he looked like a madman, swinging his pistol and raging.

Gigi had buried her face in my back and her hands fisted my hoody. I had one hand behind me, holding her there.

"All right, man. You've got a week, with interest. You've

got our number, Wren." They turned on their heels and left, and I stood there staring at my father in shock.

"What the actual fuck, Dad? Have you lost it?" I shouted, pulling Gigi in front of me and wrapping my arms around her.

Wren took the gun from my father and hurried to the door and locked it.

"These guys are not fucking around, Dylan. And now they've seen your fucking kid. This is not good." Wren paced in front of me and my stomach wrenched.

"I'll get the money. Don't worry about it. I'll go back to rehab and I'll clean my shit up. I'm sorry, Gray." It was the most coherent he'd been since I'd gotten there.

Yeah, putting others in danger had a way of sobering his ass up apparently.

"Listen to me, Gray. I'll take him back and get him squared away in his program. You just go back to school and I'll keep you posted."

"What about the money?"

My father walked to his dresser and pulled open the drawer. He reached his hand inside and moved it around before taking out a box. He handed it to Wren. "This will cover it."

When Wren opened the box, my father's Rolex was inside.

"I thought you hawked it with everything else a long time ago?" I asked, unable to contain my anger now. Gigi's cheek rested on my chest and I kept her close. She hadn't said a word, but I was fairly certain she was either in shock or too terrified to speak.

"It's the one thing I kept because I wanted to pass it down to you. The last fucking thing I have to my name." He lost it. Tears streaked down his face and he dropped to the floor, slumping against the wall. I felt nothing. He wanted sympathy about a piece of fucking jewelry when he'd failed his family in every way? I couldn't muster any today. Not after what he'd just pulled.

"I don't give a fuck about a watch. But it sure would be nice to have a father." I looked at Wren and he nodded to let me know he'd handle it from here.

I guided Gigi out of the apartment and down to the truck. Somewhere between looking for my father, being approached by two sketchy dudes, and Dad pulling a gun, the weather had changed. Should have known the storm was coming when I got here, both literally and figuratively. It was pouring rain and we hurried to the truck. She didn't stop me when I buckled her in, and she hadn't said a word yet.

Because what was there to even say at this point?

fifteen

• • •

Gigi

MY HEART WAS STILL RACING when Gray pulled down the dirt road at the end of the lake. Rain was pelting the windshield, and I pushed my wet hair away from my face. We hadn't spoken a word. I sat as close to him as I possibly could, needing his warmth.

Water dripped down the side of his face as he opened the door and got out. He paced in front of the truck and I jumped out and made my way over to him.

"It's pouring rain," I shouted, reaching for his hands.

"I'm so fucking sorry, G. I never should have brought you here." He tugged me close and wrapped his arms around me. Rain pounded against the back of my head and I didn't care.

"I'm glad I came with you. I wouldn't want you to have been there alone," I was yelling over the falling rain.

"This is the only place that calms me. This lake. The water." He led me down to the shore and he stood staring out like he was fighting the urge to dive in. The way the rain pelted against the water looked like diamonds dancing on the surface.

"Let's go in." We were already soaked, and I knew he was

struggling. I'd do just about anything to help him right now, and the warm air made the rain tolerable.

"You want to go in?" he asked, studying me like I held all of life's answers. The look in his eyes nearly brought me to my knees.

Sadness.

Hurt.

Pain.

Disappointment.

He bent down and pulled off his shoes and reached for my foot. I held on to his head and let him slip off my booties.

"Clothes or no clothes?" he asked when he stood back up and his nose grazed mine.

"It's daytime. Someone could see us. My clothes are staying on." I shivered at the thought of being naked in the water with Gray.

He grabbed my hand, and we ran into the water. I fell forward when the bottom dropped out from beneath my feet. Gray caught me and tugged me against his body. He stood easily as the water came up to his chest, and I ran my hands over his muscled shoulders. I looked up at him, just as the rain seemed to lighten up all at once and I didn't miss the heat in his eyes.

"My dad is so fucked up. I can't believe he'd pull this shit."

I reached up and grazed his jaw with my fingertips. "I'm sorry. I know he loves you, he's just an addict. And addiction always wins. He isn't thinking rationally."

He nodded, and his head tipped back to look up at the sky. The rain halted. The sun appeared out of nowhere and he looked back down at me. "I've never jumped in the water fully clothed."

"Sometimes you've got to do what you've got to do," I said.

"You're right about that, G." He leaned down and

captured my mouth. My limbs went weak, but he wrapped an arm around my waist, holding me firm against his body.

His tongue dipped in and I groaned into his mouth. My hands tangled in his hair because I needed him closer. He lifted me and my legs wrapped around his waist and I ground up against him. So lost in the moment.

Lost in this boy.

He took control of the kiss. Tilting my head back to gain more access. His hand stroked the back of my neck as I continued to grind against all his hardness.

Thunder boomed behind me and he pulled away.

"Please don't stop," I whispered when he set me on my feet. My hands reached up to grip his white shirt, forcing him to look at me. To stay in the moment.

"I don't think I could stop if I wanted to. And I don't want to. I can't stay away from you anymore." He shrugged, leaning down and kissing the tip of my nose. "You're my addiction, Gigi Jacobs."

A wide grin spread across my face and I reached for his hand. He led me out of the water, and we both laughed when we bent down to get our shoes. "We're soaked."

"My truck has seen worse. You think it's all right to go to your house? I really don't want to deal with Simon and all his judgment right now."

"Of course. I'm sure you remember that my parents are in Maui for the big anniversary, seeing as it's all they've talked about for months. I sent my mom a text when we were driving here and just let her know I'd come home to grab a dress for an upcoming dance," I said when he picked me up, soaking wet, and set me in his truck like I was a delicate piece of china. I slid over to the center seat and reached for my seat belt and he smiled.

Gray's smile did things to me that I'd never experienced. I swear my heart doubled in size every time he looked at me.

We drove to my house and talked about his father. He

asked me to send a quick text to Wren from his phone to see what was going on.

"Wren said they are on their way back to rehab now. He has the watch and he'll take care of it," I said, reading the text when it came in.

"I'd be in deep shit without that man. Can you respond and thank him for me?"

"Of course," I said when we pulled into my driveway. The sun was just dipping behind the horizon and I jumped out of the truck. The leaves had all changed colors. Fall was my favorite season as it meant Thanksgiving and Christmas weren't far behind. It was still surprisingly warm for this time of year, but I wasn't complaining because otherwise jumping in the lake with Gray would not have been tolerable.

I put the key in the door, and we made our way upstairs. I flipped on a few lights and paused when I got to my room.

"I have to get out of these wet clothes," I whispered.

"Yeah. Me too. Thankfully I have some stuff here." Gray leaned against the doorframe, watching my every move.

"I need a hot shower. I probably smell like puke." My heart raced and I walked into the bathroom and reached for a towel. I patted my face and rubbed it against my hair, waiting to see what he would do.

"You smell like peaches." He smirked and my legs went weak. "It's my favorite scent now."

"Is that so?"

"It is. Do you want to shower together?" His voice was gruff and full of need.

"I've never showered with anyone before," I admitted. Gray knew I wasn't experienced, but I didn't know if he knew just how deep that ran. I hadn't done much with anyone outside of kissing.

"I've never showered with anyone either." He closed the distance between us and stood in front of me.

"You haven't? That surprises me."

"One-night hookups do not typically lead to bathing together. Wham-bam, thank you, ma'am has always been more my speed."

I rolled my eyes, annoyed by his words, but equally excited by his nearness. "Well, I'm not a one-night hook-up."

His hand cradled my cheek and his thumb stroked me there. "I'm very aware of who you are, G. That's why I've been fighting this—because I don't want to fuck it up. And there's a very good chance that I will. But I'm willing to try."

My hand came over his large hand. "Okay."

He leaned forward and kissed down my neck and my head fell back. His hands settled at the hem of my blouse and he pulled back to look at me. Asking me with his emerald gaze if it was okay to keep going. I nodded. He lifted the silk fabric over my head, and I stood there in my pink lacy bra and my denim skirt. Goose bumps covered my skin as he took his time perusing me.

"You're so fucking beautiful." His words were laced with need, and my breath caught. I reached for the buttons on his shirt and my hands trembled as I unbuttoned each one. He helped me push it off his broad shoulders. My fingers traced every line and muscle on his chest and he sucked in a long, slow breath. He unbuttoned my jean skirt and I helped him shimmy it down my thighs and we both laughed. Wet denim was nobody's friend.

He tugged down his pants and briefs with no hesitation and stood there like it was perfectly normal to undress in front of me. I understood his confidence because he was chiseled to perfection. Strong arms, a muscled chest, and six very distinct cuts down his abdomen. I had visions of him standing in front of me last night naked, but my memory was blurry. So, I was going to enjoy this moment.

I reached behind me and unsnapped my bra, and he dropped to his knees and kissed my stomach as he rolled my panties down my legs.

I couldn't breathe with the feel of his mouth there. His warm breath teasing my skin. He looked up at me and smiled, and I bit down hard on my bottom lip.

"Don't be nervous. We aren't going to do anything you aren't comfortable with and we aren't having sex, so don't start stressing about something that isn't going to happen." He pushed to his feet and turned on the water in my shower.

I wrapped my arms over my chest, hugging myself as I let the sting of his words settle in. "Why not?"

He came closer and chuckled just a little as his forehead rested against mine. "It's certainly not because I don't want to. But there are a lot of things we can do without having sex. And until we figure out what's going on with us, we'll stick to those things. I promise to make you feel good."

"I don't doubt that at all."

He took my hand and led me into the shower. I didn't know what it would be like to shower with someone, but this exceeded all expectations. Gray squeezed some shampoo into his hands and washed my hair so gently that my back fell against his chest, enjoying every minute.

"I love your hair. Everything about you is pretty, you know that?" he whispered against my ear.

I turned in his arms and reached for the soap, taking my time as I washed his hard chest, and my hands made their way down lower. Enjoying the feel of his abs beneath my fingers, the way the muscles were so defined. My hands moved lower and I gripped his erection, and he hissed. I slowly allowed my soapy fingers to stroke him until he fell back against the wall and covered my hand with his.

"We're taking this slow, G. Tonight I want to give you pleasure." He lifted my hand and kissed it.

"I want to give you pleasure too."

"Trust me. Seeing you get off is all the pleasure I need." He turned off the water and yanked two towels off the rack and wrapped me in one. He used the other to dry my hair as he stood there buck naked and dripping wet.

"Oh my god," I whispered.

"Do you trust me?"

"Yes."

"That's all I need to know." He wrapped the towel around his waist, and I walked into the bedroom and grabbed some sweats. Gray went into the room that he stayed in when he was here and came out wearing a white T-shirt and navy joggers. His hair was wet and fell around his face. I sat on my bed brushing my hair and he leaned against my doorframe.

"Hungry?"

"Starving," I said, pushing to my feet.

"Pizza sound okay?" He stared down at his phone.

"Yeah. That sounds good."

"It's on the way." He moved toward me and dropped to sit on the bed beside me. "I'm really sorry for dragging you into my shit."

"Stop saying that. Would you let me walk into that situation alone?" I asked.

"Fuck no. But that's different."

"It's not. I'm only upset because I know it hurts you."

"Fuck," he said, falling back on the bed. "I don't want to fuck this up, but I don't know how to do this."

I dropped back and rolled onto my side to face him. "Don't overthink it. I like you and you like me. There's no pressure. Let's just see where it goes."

"And what about Cade? He's going to lose his shit. First, I take you to see my father who pulls a gun on a couple thugs who are chasing him. And now we're talking about dating. You're a fucking virgin, Gigi. I don't want to take anything from you that I don't deserve."

"First of all, can we please stop talking about my virginity? Yes, I happen to be one. But my god, why is it such a big deal? Everyone's a virgin at some point in their life." I rolled my eyes. "Secondly, I chose to go with you to your dad's. We're all fine. No one got hurt. Don't make this bigger than it is. And I think we should keep whatever this is between us right now. Why risk all the drama with Cade if we don't even know if it's going to work?"

"You've always been wiser than me." He chuckled as he pushed the hair back from my face.

"You finally admit it." I smirked, and he flipped me on my back and tickled me, and I burst out in a fit of laughter.

"So, this is our secret for now."

"My lips are sealed," I said, and he leaned down and kissed me hard.

"Not if I have my way about it."

The doorbell rang and we were both panting when we sat up.

We made our way downstairs and ate a few slices of pizza on the couch. Somehow, I'd ended up on his lap and we talked more about what had happened today.

"Did you know your dad had a gun?" I asked.

"No. I'm still pissed about that. What the fuck is he possibly thinking? Drunk and high and swinging around a pistol? I swear to you the man is brilliant, but he's just all fucked up now."

I rubbed his shoulder and studied him. He was so stoic. This had to be eating him up inside. A lot of things were making sense to me now. Why he liked to be at our house all the time. He probably craved the simplicity and normalcy of our family life. There was rarely any drama here, aside from Cade getting in my business.

"I know he is. He's still in there, Gray. And he needs you to have faith in him."

"Yeah. It's getting harder and harder," he said, and his tongue swiped out to wet his lips.

"Do you think those guys will go after him?"

"Not if they get paid. I'll call Wren tomorrow to make sure the watch will cover everything."

"You're a really good son," I said, and he tipped me back on the couch.

"I need to kiss you right now. Make you feel good. Think about something other than my fucked up father. And you happen to be my new favorite pastime."

My breaths came hard and fast, and my chest moved up and down rapidly.

"I'm fine with that."

"Yeah?" he asked, searching my gaze.

I tugged him down, and his mouth came over mine. He propped himself on one arm, so he supported his own weight as he kissed his way down my neck. His hands slipped beneath my T-shirt and they slowly moved up my sides. His thumbs grazed the sides of my chest. I arched into him, desperate for him to touch me where no one ever had. His hands moved across my breasts and he flicked my nipples and I groaned against his mouth. I'd never wanted anyone or anything more.

He pulled back and looked at me. "Is this okay?"

I couldn't speak. My breaths were too rapid, and my body trembled. I nodded and he chuckled. He looked so sexy. His hair a disheveled mess and his hooded gaze drinking me in. Plump lips, swollen from kissing me already. He tugged my shirt over my head and his mouth came down over one breast. My eyes closed and I tried desperately to keep it together. He continued to worship me, giving each breast equal attention.

"I want to carve these tits in clay so I can have them with me all the time," he said against my skin and I gasped. "So fucking perfect, G."

He pulled back to watch me as his hand slipped beneath the waistband of my leggings. I nodded.

Don't stop.

He paused for a moment when he realized I didn't have any panties on. He found my most sensitive area and I gasped at his touch.

Holy mother of all things…

Even my subconscious wasn't making any sense.

I bit down hard on my bottom lip to try to calm myself down.

But it wasn't working.

This building need took over and no matter how hard I tried, I couldn't stop it.

"Stop thinking, and just let yourself feel good. You're so fucking wet it's making me crazy," he said as his lips grazed my ear.

I stopped thinking.

My hips moved against him and I pulled his mouth back down to mine. He slipped a finger inside, and I got lost in the moment.

Lost in this boy.

Lost in all things Gray Baldwin.

My body took over. Seeking what it needed.

More.

I cried out my release, and he didn't ease up until the last ripple of sensation worked through my body.

He pulled back to look at me, and a wide grin spread across his face.

"You're so fucking beautiful."

"You are," I whispered. Somehow this boy had hidden all of these different sides of himself from me all these years, but now I was seeing everything.

All of him.

And I only wanted more.

sixteen

. . .

Gray

GOOD CHRIST. If anyone had ever told me what it would be like to see Gigi Jacobs come apart in my arms, I would have straightened my shit up a long time ago. Blonde waves falling all around her. Blue sapphire eyes glazed over and sated. Lips swollen from where I'd kissed her.

It was better than any fucking thing I'd ever witnessed.

I pulled my hand out from beneath her leggings and slipped my finger in my mouth. Desperate for a taste. I wanted to bury my face between her legs. Bury myself deep inside her.

"Oh my god," she whispered as she watched me pull my finger from my mouth.

I was using all the restraint I had to move slowly with her.

There was a very good chance that I'd fuck this up before things even got going.

I'd agreed to keep this from Cade for now because she was right, it would cause a shit ton of drama before we even knew where this would go. The truth was… I didn't want to share this with him because he'd tell me I wasn't good enough for his baby sister—and he'd be correct. And right now, I just wanted something good in my life. Something that felt right.

And everything about this girl felt right.

But look what I'd already exposed her to over the past few hours. I should leave her alone. Walk away now before we both got in too deep.

But I couldn't do that right now.

I needed Gigi Jacobs like I needed to take my next breath.

"Let's get some sleep. It was a tough day. You must be exhausted."

"Are you going to sleep with me?" she asked, and something in my chest squeezed. The way she looked at me like she had all the faith in the world in me. Like I'd keep her safe no matter what. It made me want to be that guy for her.

"I was planning on it." I lifted her off the couch and carried her upstairs and she laughed.

"You know I can walk, right?"

"I just like keeping you close."

I carried her into my room and set her on the bed.

"You want to sleep in here?"

"It feels wrong to sleep in your princess room."

She shook her head and she smiled. "I don't care where we sleep, Gray. As long as it's together."

She climbed up the bed and pulled back the covers, and I flipped off the light and slipped in beside her. I breathed in all her goodness.

"Thanks for coming here with me," I whispered.

"I'd go just about anywhere with you." Her voice sounded sleepy and her head settled on my chest.

Sleep took us both quickly.

It felt completely natural waking up with Gigi in my arms. Like she'd always been there. Maybe in a way she had.

Maybe I'd always wanted her there but been too afraid to admit it. But for the first time in my life, I wasn't trying to get away from a girl that had woken up in my bed. Hell, I wanted to keep her there for as long as she would stay.

"Hey," she said when her eyes opened.

"How'd you sleep? Did you have any nightmares about thugs and guns and drug dealers?" I teased, but there was some truth in my words. I had no idea who my dad was messed up with.

"No. I had the sweetest dreams that I would be waking up with you again," she whispered.

So fucking sweet.

Gigi had always been that way. I remember when we were young, she was always baking cakes in her little oven for all the neighbors. Everyone was outside playing, and she was determined to make sure everyone got something. Cade and I used to tease her about it, but the truth was, I always admired her kindness.

She was instinctively good to her core.

"I like waking up with you too. But we should probably get up and head back to school here pretty soon."

She pushed up on her elbow, one hand tracing along my collarbone. "I was thinking maybe we go and see your sisters and your mom while we're here. They'd be so happy. Wouldn't it be fun to surprise them?"

I stiffened at the mention of going home. It wasn't that I didn't want to see my mom and sisters, but that meant seeing Simon. If he knew I was here to help my dad, I'd never hear the end of it.

Her head cocked to the side, and all that blond hair tumbled over one shoulder. "If you're worried about them wondering why you're with me, I can stay here. Or we can just say I grabbed a ride with you because I needed something from home. No one has to know anything."

She tried to hide the hurt from her tone, and I placed my

thumb and pointer finger on each side of her jaw, forcing her to meet my gaze. "Hey, this has nothing to do with you. I have no problem with you coming with me. They all love you. It's Simon I'm worried about."

Her eyes softened and she nodded. "Tell him I begged you for a ride to grab this dress. I really did need to get it, so it's not a complete lie. And we'll say my car is having trouble and you offered to bring me home. They don't have to know we came yesterday. We'll say it's a one-day trip, and you wanted to surprise them."

"You sure have the answer for everything, don't you?"

"It's all in a day's work." She chuckled, and I flipped her on her back and tickled her again.

My dick was unhappy. He'd been taunted and teased more than he was used to. Hell, I had no problem getting chicks, and this was definitely the longest I'd gone without sex since high school.

I'd just need to service myself a little more often to survive until we figured this shit out. Rushing Gigi was not an option. She paused when I pressed against her.

"Oh my," she said, covering her mouth with her hand. "Do you have a situation down there?"

"You think that's funny, do you?" I buried my face in her neck and rubbed my scruff against her as she yelled out in laughter.

"I could help you with that," she said, her eyes searching mine when she stopped laughing.

"Yeah? Have you ever done that before?"

She bit down on her bottom lip and shook her head. "No, because I haven't wanted to. But I want to now. I want you to be all of my firsts."

Good Christ, this girl was going to destroy me. My chest squeezed and a lump formed in my throat.

"I like the sound of that." I rolled off of her and settled on my back.

"Me too," she said, and her sapphire blues darkened as she slipped her fingers beneath my waistband and pulled down my joggers. I sucked in a strained breath as the anticipation was killing me. This certainly wouldn't take long.

I chuckled, feeling like a damn hormonal thirteen-year-old. I wrapped my hand around hers as she gripped me, and I guided her up and down my shaft. I closed my eyes and hissed as my hand fell to my side.

Gigi Jacobs was a rock star at all things, and this was no exception.

"Damn, baby." I pulled her head down and kissed her as her hand continued to move. The combination of her hand on my dick and her lips on mine—was too much.

I moaned into her mouth as I went over the edge.

"Jesus, that was fucking amazing," I hissed as I grabbed my T-shirt and cleaned up the mess.

Her cheeks were flushed, and she smiled. I pushed up and kissed her hard. "Shower?"

"Yes, please."

I pulled her to her feet. My new favorite activity was all things with Gigi. Hell, showering was awesome because I got to be wet and naked with my girl. A hand job with Gigi was better than sex with anyone else.

And we were just getting started.

"Oooh, I love Violet's Floral shop. Are we getting flowers?" Gigi asked when I came around to her side of the truck and helped her out.

"Yeah. I try to bring my mom and the girls a little something every now and again, especially since they don't know I'm home." I rubbed the back of my neck because it was Sunday, which meant Simon would most likely be home.

I could handle the criticism, but I didn't want Gigi to witness it.

The man thought my father was a piece of shit and he was convinced that I would follow suit.

Maybe she'd believe it if she heard the things he said.

"Oh, my. To what do I owe the honors? Gray and Gigi, you are a sight for sore eyes," the older woman said as she came around the corner and hugged us both. Violet had owned the flower shop for as long as I could remember, and she was a permanent fixture in Willow Springs. Everyone knew her and everyone loved her. "When did you get home from school?"

"I just gave Gigi a ride to pick up a dress she needs for a dance," I said, patting the fragile woman on the shoulder.

"My sweet girl, you and Addy decided to rush a sorority?" she asked, because nothing got past this woman. Her gaze ping-ponged between us as if she were trying to solve a puzzle.

"Yes. We are both Kappa Gammas."

"Oh, my word. Isn't that something. And you two are at the same school. You sure seem to be getting along better than you used to?" She raised a brow and smiled.

Gigi stiffened beside me. Violet was the town gossip.

"Trust me. I still bug the hell out of her most of the time. She just needed a ride."

"Ah, I see. So what would you like today, Gray?"

"Make it three bouquets of azaleas and two daisy bouquets, please."

Violet disappeared behind the counter and Gigi turned to face me. "Sorry. I know we're keeping this between us, and we probably should have thought of that," she whispered.

"We used to go places together back when you despised me," I said against her ear so only she could hear. Her fingers tangled in my hair and she smiled up at me.

"I did despise you, didn't I?" She tugged me close and her lips grazed mine.

"Did you despise me when my hand slipped beneath your panties last night?" I nipped at her ear this time.

She laughed and pulled back as Violet's footsteps made their way back out.

I righted myself, but my dick was still raging with anger. He'd had a reprieve this morning, but he was sick of me toying with him like this.

I adjusted myself, making sure Violet couldn't see me from the other side of the counter, but Gigi noticed. She raised a brow, and her eyes went wide before she turned to face the sweet older woman holding up five bouquets.

"Are these okay?"

"They're perfect." I handed her my card.

"Do you get them flowers often?" Gigi asked.

"He pops in here every couple months." Violet gave me my card back and handed me the bouquets. "He started getting his girls flowers since he got his first job when he was sixteen years old."

Maybe I should have Violet talk me up to Simon as well. This was good PR.

We both hugged her goodbye and made our way out to the truck. I handed her one of the bouquets and she beamed.

"Gray Baldwin, you're much sweeter than you let on."

"Only with you, G."

Gigi was quiet on the drive over to my house and when we pulled in the driveway, she turned to face me.

"I don't know why I always thought you were just an arrogant asshole."

"Gee. Tell me how you really feel," I teased, tucking her hair behind her ear.

"You were always such a jerk to me when we were younger."

"I think I may have had a massive crush on you for a long

time, but I didn't want to admit it. Hell, I wouldn't even admit it to myself. But I always wanted to be around you."

"I'm sorry that I didn't take the time to see the other side of you before now."

"Trust me, it was me, not you. You're the nicest person I know. I gave you good reason to despise me. I messed with you constantly. I was probably drunk around you more than I was sober these past few years," I said.

"But then you do things like get flowers for your mom and sisters too." Her hand found mine on the seat.

"Trust me. I'm an asshole most of the time. Yes, I get my family flowers because I love them. And maybe it's because I feel fucking guilty that I never want to be here because of Simon. Don't give me too much credit, G." I jumped out of the truck and came around to open her door.

"I don't think you give yourself any credit," she said, setting her bouquet on the passenger seat.

"What? I think I'm fucking amazing." I laughed. "I mean, I may suck at being a boyfriend, but I know I look good. There are no self-esteem issues here."

She laughed. "There he is."

I held the bouquets in my hands, and we walked up to the front door. She didn't question me when I knocked, because she knew I was surprising them. But even if I wasn't surprising them, I'd be knocking on the door. This place had never felt like home. This was Simon's house. Not mine.

Mariana, our housekeeper, opened the door and gasped. "My sweet boy."

I handed her a bouquet of azaleas, and she hugged me. She turned to Gigi and wrapped her in a hug as well. Gigi babysat for my sisters many times, so they knew one another well.

"Where is everyone?" I asked.

"They're all in the kitchen having lunch. Simon's here." Her words had an edge. She was more than aware of the tumultuous relationship that I shared with the man, but he also signed her paychecks so she couldn't say much about it.

Simon wasn't a bad dude to anyone else. He resented me for reasons that I had no control of—being born the son of a man that he despised. Living with him had been hell. The Jacobs had saved me by opening their doors to me.

Did Simon financially support me in every way? Absolutely. The man was filthy fucking rich, and he loved flaunting his money over everyone's heads.

Was he a good father to the twins? Yes. I hated to admit that, but he genuinely loved them. And he loved my mother. So, I just stayed away so I didn't rock the boat.

"Hey," I said, walking into the kitchen with Gigi beside me.

Pen and Bea jumped from their seats and squealed. They both charged me, and I caught them with ease.

"Sweetheart, what are you doing here?" My mother moved to her feet and came around the table to hug me. I set the girls down and they took turns fawning all over Gigi.

"Gigi's car wasn't working, and she needed to pick up a dress for a dance. I offered to give her a ride. We're heading back now, but I wanted to say hi before I left."

I handed the girls their flowers and then gave my mother her bouquet. Her eyes were wet with emotion because she always got weepy when I was home.

"Nice to see you, Gray," Simon said, pushing to his feet and offering me his hand. "How are you doing, young lady?"

"Simon, you don't need to be so formal. Gigi has babysat the girls dozens of times." My mom moved to grab some vases, just as Mariana came into the kitchen and took the flowers from her.

"It's great to see you too." Gigi smiled and glanced over at me.

Mariana poured us some sweet tea, and Mom asked that we sit with them while they finished up lunch. They offered

Gigi and me some food, but we declined. I was anxious to get out of there.

"Gray, are you going to play Barbies with us before you go?" Bea asked as she scooted her chair closer to me.

"Not today, Munchkin. I need to get back to school."

She pouted and I kissed the top of her head.

"So, did you hear that your dad left rehab again?" Simon asked, pushing his plate away.

"Yeah. I believe he's on his way back now. How do you know about that?"

Gigi's hand found my knee beneath the table and it rested there.

"Everyone knows what a screw-up he is. It's all over town. I figured that's why you were here? Getting dragged into his world like you always do."

"Simon." My mother's voice was harsh.

That was new.

He nodded. "Just saying. You want to go to law school and make something of yourself, you're not going to achieve much by following in your dad's footsteps. You know that, right?"

My shoulders stiffened at his words. "I'm aware."

"Like father like son, but it won't carry you far, Gray." His gaze locked with mine and I was ready to get the hell out of there.

"Gray got the highest grade in his Law and Ethics class and has been offered a summer internship at the courthouse." Gigi's lips were pursed as she stared at my stepfather.

Mariana set some cookies on the table and I didn't miss the smile on her face. No one had ever come to my defense like that. People rarely stood up to Simon.

"Is that so?" Simon looked back at me with surprise.

"That is so. All right, we need to get going." I pushed to my feet and Gigi followed me to the door.

I hugged my sisters goodbye and did the same to my mom.

"I'm sorry, baby. He means well," she whispered in my ear. "He just doesn't want to see you go down the same path."

I nodded. "Yep. I'll see you at Thanksgiving."

"Will you join us for dinner this year?" she asked, and her gaze was full of hope. The thought of sitting through a lengthy dinner with Simon did not appeal to me.

"The Jacobs invited me, but I'll stop by for sure."

When we stepped outside, Gigi walked beside me. "He's such an asshole."

"Yep." I paused when I opened her door. "Thanks for having my back."

"Always," she said. And a small part of me wanted to hold her to it. But I knew better.

This couldn't last forever.

Because nothing good ever lasted forever.

I'd just pulled her into my father's shit storm, and I knew better.

I knew I needed to end this now because I'd already allowed it to go too far.

seventeen

. . .

Gigi

I'D ARRIVED home Wednesday afternoon for Thanksgiving break, thankful that the drive to Willow Springs was less than two hours. It made the commute fairly easy. I made my way over to Addy's house after having lunch with my parents and Cade. We were all looking forward to having our Magic Willows meeting in person versus Skype. I had a pit in my stomach all day at the thought of seeing Gray as it had been almost two weeks since we'd spoken. And my heart was still hurting because he'd literally flipped the switch on me.

"Hey," I said, hugging each one of the girls before dropping to sit on the fuzzy rug under the Edingtons' coffee table in their basement. We all sat in our same places. Maura beside me, Ivy, Addy, and Coco on the couch across from us just like we'd been doing since fifth grade.

Ivy opened the book and let out a long sigh as she held the pen over the page. "I ran into Ty's dad last night in town. My parents and I went to dinner at The Rusty Pelican and he was there with his mistress, I mean, new wife."

"*Awkward AF,*" Coco said, shaking her head. "Did you talk to him and thank him for running the love of your life out of town?"

Ivy rolled her eyes. "I did not. Ty was just my first love. He most definitely will not be my last love, not after the way he just disappeared from my life. Who does that?"

"I'm sorry, Ive." I leaned forward and squeezed her hand. I knew she was still hurting about the way things ended with Ty. "What did his father say?"

"Well, he went on and on about Ty becoming a big star with this label that signed him. Apparently he is going to start touring and we should expect to hear him on the radio soon. Can you believe that?" she hissed, and we all laughed because her flair for the dramatics was always entertaining.

"Good riddance. You're onto bigger and better." Coco leaned forward and high-fived her.

"Technically, he's onto bigger and better. But my dating card is full, so there is that. And Monday night at our sorority house meeting, I had a slew of gifts from a few fraternity guys." Ivy forced a smile.

We all knew she was hurting, but it wasn't in her nature to wallow. She was all about rising above and moving forward.

"She's not kidding. Our whiteboard outside our door at the dorms is bursting with notes from different guys. The girl is on fire," Maura said over her laughter.

"Please. Half of those messages are for you. Maura is right up there with me in the dating game."

We all chuckled before Coco turned her attention to me. "And how about you and sexy Gray? Is he still ghosting you?"

Gray and I had an amazing time after I puked on him at the party and woken up in his bed. We'd taken a trip to Willow Springs together and it had been an emotional roller-coaster. We'd spent two nights together, and he'd all but rocked my world. And then he'd dropped me at my dorm and gone radio silent on me. We'd taken two steps forward and four steps back. He'd kissed me goodbye and I hadn't heard from him since.

"I texted him twice, and he never responded." I shrugged, a lump forming in my throat. I had no idea what happened. He'd completely cut me off. Even before we'd had anything romantic between us, he'd always texted me daily. Now he'd just shut me out. "I didn't go to the fraternity party last weekend because I'm not chasing after him. He obviously doesn't want a relationship with me. It is what it is."

I swiped at the tear falling down my cheek because it still stung. We'd gotten so close, and he'd completely flipped a switch on me.

"I think he's just freaking out about Cade and bringing you into all the drama with his dad," Addy said. The girls knew what happened between us and I shared most of what happened back home, aside from the part about the gun. I didn't feel like I needed to tell them that because I knew they would have all freaked out.

Just like Gray did.

He'd completely vanished from my life.

"He's a coward. We weren't even going to tell my brother unless it turned into something serious, which obviously Gray isn't capable of," I hissed as anger moved through every inch of my body. I'd spent the first few days crying myself to sleep because it hurt so badly, but now I was just mad. I'd been there for him and he'd turned his back on me.

"Yeah, he showed you all his sexy moves and then he taps out? Ridiculous," Coco said, holding up her two fists and banging them together, imitating Ross in his classic move from *Friends*. "You just need to show him what he's missing."

"And he'll be at your house tomorrow for Thanksgiving, right?" Maura asked.

"I think he's sleeping over tonight." I crossed my arms over my chest and tried to tamper down my anger. "Cade was on his way to meet him at the lake when I left, and then I'm sure they're coming back to our house. I'll just ignore him the way he's been ignoring me. It's for the better. Things could never work between us. He's not the committed type. He's probably out there tramping it up now."

"You make it clear that you are not sitting home pining over him." Coco gives me a knowing look. The girl has every guy wrapped around her little finger.

"Even if I am?" I said because it was the truth.

"Remember when Jett pushed me away? It took us some time to find our footing. I see the way he looks at you. He's crazy about you. I think he's staying away because he thinks he's doing the right thing." Addy was always the voice of reason. And I loved her for it. She'd been sleeping at the dorms all week with me because she knew I was down in the dumps.

"Well, he's about to see that she's got plenty of options. Bonfire tonight, girls? Everyone's home from school. Let's get dressed up cute and go to the lake and strut our shit." Coco was on her feet now and clapping her hands together.

"Strut our shit? Who are you?" Maura said over her laughter.

"It's going in the book. All the shit strutting will make for good memories. Let's meet up later tonight." Ivy finished writing and then shut the book.

We all hugged goodbye and planned to meet up in a few hours. I made my way home and heard laughter in the kitchen. Cade and Gray were perched on the counter talking to my mom.

"Sweetheart, you're back. How are the girls?" my mom asked. I glanced over at the couch where Gray had kissed me and made me cry out his name just two weeks ago and my body heated at the thought.

"They're great." I grabbed a bottle of water from the fridge and my brother pulled me in for a hug.

"Hey, G," Gray said, and I refused to look at him.

"Oh. Hello," I snipped, leaving all emotion out of my tone.

"I thought you two were done hating each other," Cade said when he barked out a laugh.

"You thought wrong." I forced a smile and kissed my mom on the cheek.

"Stop that nonsense." My mother shook her head. "You and Gray are family."

"Okay." I shrugged because I was uncomfortable with the conversation and I wanted to get out of this kitchen now. "I'm going to go take a nap before dinner, and then we're going to bake pies tonight, right?" It was tradition that my mom and I baked all the pies the night before Thanksgiving. It was one of my favorite holiday memories. We'd bake and listen to music and laugh. I looked forward to it every year. And then afterward, I'd go to the bonfire.

"Are you all right, honey?" Mom asked, placing the back of her hand on my forehead.

"Yeah, of course. Just tired. But I'll get up and help you with dinner and then we'll bake all the desserts tonight." I didn't have the heart to tell her that Gray had ripped my heart out and now I had to deal with him living at my house.

"I'm looking forward to it. I'm going to run to the market to grab a few last-minute things."

I nodded before leaving the kitchen. I went upstairs and stretched out on my bed. I heard the garage door open and close as it was beneath my room.

"Hey." Gray's voice startled me when he stood in my doorway, and I squeezed my eyes closed to pretend I was sleeping. "Cade went with your mom to the store. I know you aren't asleep yet."

"What do you want?" I refused to open my eyes and look at him.

"You seem mad."

I sprung up to sit on the bed and glared at him as he stood in my doorway. "I seem mad? Are you serious?"

He scrubbed a hand down his face. "I'm trying to do the right thing. You don't have to make this harder for me."

"Harder for *you*? I'm sorry if I'm not making this easy for you. You spend the weekend with me, we shower together and—I thought we had a great time. And then you completely ghost me, and now you're a permanent fixture at my house. Sooooo sorry that makes *you* uncomfortable." I was on my feet and in his face.

He was so gorgeous I tried not to look at him. His chiseled jaw flexed and he ran his hand through his hair. It was overgrown on top and looked sexy as hell. My fingers ached to touch him, and I shoved them in the pocket of my hoody.

"I'm doing this for you, not for me," he snipped as if he was irritated with me.

"Don't you dare pretend you're doing this for me. You're a coward, Gray. You don't know what you want, and you think you can jerk me around every time you change your mind." I whipped around to walk back to my bed because I needed to put space between us.

He stalked behind me and grabbed my arm, turning me to face him. My chest slammed into his. The look in his eyes was one I'd never seen before. He was completely wounded.

Is he for real?

"You think I changed my mind?"

"I don't know, because you don't talk to me. But you sure go hot and cold awfully quick," I hissed.

"You couldn't be more wrong, G."

"Oh, please. I'm sure you've been bouncing from bed to bed these past two weeks, you... you… *dirty pig*." It was the best I could come up with at the moment, with his warm breath tickling my cheeks, and his chest pounding against mine.

His head fell back in laughter and it infuriated me. "Dirty pig? Wow."

I stomped on his foot. "Let me go and leave me alone."

He held on to my arms and calmly looked down at me. "You were the last girl in my bed. And I haven't been in anyone else's bed either."

A maniacal, crazy laugh escaped my lips, and I was shocked by how angry I sounded. "Well, throw me a ticker-tape parade! Do I get some kind of prize for being the last one in your bed? You're such a jerk!"

I shoved against his chest, but he didn't move. His gaze searched mine. "So that's what you think of me, huh?"

"That's exactly what I think of you, Gray. I think you used me and tossed me aside because you were bored. At least we don't have to worry about telling Cade anything. We had a shorter life span than a piece of raw fish." I spewed all the ugliness I could muster, and he stood there watching me with surprise.

He dropped my arms and walked out of the room.

Fine by me.

I slammed my bedroom door, my hands were shaking, and I lay back on my bed. I needed to pull myself together. I was so angry and hurt, and once I opened that can of worms there was no stopping it. I squeezed my eyes shut, praying for sleep to take me. Everything hurt right now, and I just wanted to escape for a few hours.

Knowing that the boy who hurt me was just down the hall did not make it easier.

I woke up to someone's hand on my shoulder. "You must have been really tired. You've been asleep for almost two hours. Are you sure you're feeling all right?"

My mom sat on the edge of my bed and I blinked a few times before I could completely make out her features. "Yeah. I just needed to catch up a little."

"Okay, sweetheart. Dinner's just about ready."

"Oh, no. I wanted to help you," I said, and my mom stroked my hair away from my face. She had a gift for soothing me, and I loved her so much. I wanted to tell her that my heart was hurting, because I'd always told her everything. But being with Gray or not being with Gray, either way, it made things complicated.

"Don't be silly, darlin'. We're going to make all the pies tonight. I'm glad you got some much-needed rest. Come on down when you're ready." She kissed my forehead before moving to her feet.

I nodded. "I'll be down in five minutes."

It was much darker in my room than it had been when I fell asleep. I sat up and immediately thought of my conversation with Gray, and my chest tightened. I knew it was silly to be hurt over something that never even went anywhere. Gray and I weren't anything. But it felt like everything. Maybe because I'd never dated anyone seriously, so I was clueless about this stuff. But the way I felt when I was with him was something I'd never experienced in my life.

He got me.

When I was with Gray I was so happy.

He also completely infuriated me, and I knew logically that this couldn't go anywhere. I needed to get over it. Meet someone else and put this behind me. Why did the first time that I actually liked someone have to be a guy who was completely unattainable?

I walked to the bathroom, brushed my hair, and splashed a little cold water on my face. Tonight, I'd go out and have some fun. I was determined to forget about my short time with Gray.

I just needed to get through dinner.

I made my way downstairs and laughter bubbled through the house. Butterflies swarmed my belly when I heard Gray telling them about some of the drama he'd dealt with at the fraternity house.

"Hey," I said, as I took the seat beside Gray because sitting anywhere else would make it clear that something was going on.

"Hi there. How's my girl?" Dad asked and his whole face lit up when he looked at me.

"Good. My classes are going well. But I'm happy to be home."

"Mom said you came home when we were in Hawaii. I was disappointed that we missed you," he said.

My entire body stiffened at the mention of my trip home two weeks ago.

"You did? For what? You didn't tell me that," Cade asked as he scooped some salad on his plate.

I rolled my eyes to cover for the fact that my heart was beating double-time. "I just came home for a day to get a dress for an upcoming sorority dance."

"Why didn't you just get it this weekend?" he pressed, and my palms were sweating beneath the table.

"Because it's next weekend and I would have needed time to order one if it didn't work. But Addy thinks it's perfect, so I'm all set."

Please let someone change the subject.

Gray cleared his throat beside me. "Who are you going to the dance with?"

Asshole.

"I don't know yet. I'm not even sure I want to go anymore. This guy that I was talking to turned out to be a *huge disappointment*." I internally gave myself a pat on the back for that zinger. "So, I might just skip it."

"Don't waste your time on losers. You're too good for that," my brother snipped.

"Very true." I handed the basket of rolls to Gray and I couldn't wipe the smile off my face.

"Why don't you go with Gray? I always found it more fun to go to those things with a friend versus a real date," my mother said.

"That's a great idea. Unless Gray already has a date?" Dad asked.

Gray's shoulders stiffened the slightest bit. No one else would notice, but I'd studied every movement of this boy for a while, and I noticed. "I don't have any plans to go, those aren't really my thing. But I could take you if you want."

This boy was going to give me whiplash.

"I don't need a pity date," I hissed.

"Don't be stubborn. It would be a good way to go and have some fun without having to worry about some dude getting handsy," Cade said, forking some mashed potatoes and popping them in his mouth.

"Handsy? You do know that I can take care of myself, right?"

"Stop being difficult. Let's just go and have a good time." Gray turned to me and flashed his brightest smile and I wanted to punch him in the throat.

I didn't know what kind of game he was playing.

But game on, Gray Baldwin.

eighteen

. . .

Gray

THANKSGIVING DINNER AT THE JACOBS' had been nice, aside from Gigi completely ignoring me. I was still reeling from the whole dance fiasco. I was trying to stay away from her, and there I was pressuring her to go with me. Because I couldn't stand the thought of her going with someone else.

I was an asshole, there was no arguing that.

We'd all gone to a bonfire the night before down at the lake. I didn't miss the way Gigi kept looking over at me when Samantha Brown, a chick I'd hooked up with many times in high school, was hanging all over me. Nothing happened, but I liked seeing Gigi all worked up.

The bottom line was—I was fucked up over this girl. No one had ever gotten under my skin this way. I drove over to see Wren. I wanted to make sure everything had been taken care of with the guys my dad owed money to. He was back in rehab and Wren had handled everything shortly after. I was still processing the fact that I'd brought Gigi into that situation. I was drowning in guilt over it and I'd cut her off when we returned home.

Gigi Jacobs was my weak spot.

My blind spot.

My heart.

This was a lot to process, seeing as though I didn't even know I still had a working heart.

I'd been fucking miserable these past two weeks trying to stay away from her. And seeing the hurt in her eyes made it all the worse. She thought I'd changed my mind, and that stung. Because everything between us was real. I couldn't explain it to her right now because she would double down and ignore the fact that I might be putting her in danger. I'd stayed away for her own good. I'd kept my eye on her in my own way from a distance through social media and I'd assigned Ricky with the undercover task of checking on Gigi on occasion too.

I knocked on Wren's door and he shouted for me to come in. "Happy Thanksgiving. Are you coming from your mom's house?"

"No. I was at the Jacobs'. I'm heading over to see my mom next. Just wanted to stop by and make sure those guys are taken care of."

He gripped the back of his neck. "I sold the watch and paid them off. As long as your dad stays away from this shit, I think they'll leave him be. I told you there was a few thousand dollars left over which I have in a safety deposit box at the bank. I don't want to give it to him right now."

"I agree. Thanks for taking care of that shit for him. It gets exhausting, right?"

"Listen, I know it's tough for you to watch him go down this path. But we're all he has left, Gray. If we throw in the towel, I'm afraid that'll be the end of him."

I nodded. Wren was the brother my father never had. "Thank you for always sticking by him."

"Always will. He's my best friend. Even if he's an idiot sometimes. He's got his demons, but there's a good man underneath all that," he said.

"Do you think this time it'll work? If he sticks with the program?"

"I think it's his only shot. He may slip again, but as long as he keeps fighting, there's always hope."

I closed my eyes and shook my head. It was never easy with my dad. I'd wondered a million times what it would have been like if he was the father he should have been. Could have been. If pills hadn't taken over his life. If he was there to support me and hadn't left me to be reliant on a man who hated me.

"Yeah. I hope you're right."

"So, you still hanging out with Gigi Jacobs? How's that going to sit with her brother?" He had a smirk on his face as he studied me.

"We're friends."

He barked out a laugh. "Friends, my ass. I saw the way she looks at you. Don't run from everything good just because your dad has got some issues. That doesn't define you, Gray."

"Some issues? That's a bit of an understatement. Fuck. I can't believe I brought her into that shit. I've been trying to put some distance there for her own good," I said, shaking my head.

"Everyone's got their shit, Gray. It doesn't make you a bad kid because your dad's an addict. It makes you honorable that you keep showing up for him. And Gigi sure didn't seem to mind being there at all. It's good to have people like that in your corner. Although I'm sure you're going to take some shit from Cade if you go there." He chuckled and crossed his arms over his chest.

I nodded. "That's for sure. And I think Simon would argue with you about me paying for my father's sins."

"Simon is an asshole. Always has been. I'm glad he's good to your mom and your sisters, but he's always been a judgmental prick."

"I can't argue that. All right. I'm going to head over to my mom's. What about you? Did you have turkey yet?" I asked, pushing to my feet.

He nodded. "Yeah. Mae Stone invited me over to have Thanksgiving with her, Jett, and her mom."

"Glad you went there and had dinner. Jett kicked ass this season. The dude is such a badass."

"Yeah. He's a good kid." Wren's chest puffed up and I chuckled. He was a man of few words, but I could see that he had a weak spot. I just hadn't known it was Mae and Jett Stone.

I clapped him on the back. "Thanks for everything. Happy Thanksgiving."

"You too, son. Hang in there. Don't let that prick Simon give you shit."

He patted me on the shoulder before I made my way down to my truck.

When I arrived at my mom's house, the Sheldons, who lived across the street, were over as well. My mom hugged me tight. "So glad you came. Thank you."

"Of course. Where are the chicken nuggets?" I asked, because they were truly the only reason I'd made the effort to be here.

"Gray," a little voice shrieked, and they both ran toward me.

I caught them in my arms, and they tugged me into the living room to greet everyone.

Louise and Paul Sheldon and their two little girls Rosie and Mabel were close family friends and they'd always been nice enough.

The girls ran off to play, and my mom encouraged me to sit on the couch and join them.

"There he is. Our future lawyer," Simon said, and his cheeks were bright red, which meant he'd been drinking.

Fuck.

Simon was not a friendly drunk. He'd pick a fight with me for sure.

I prepared myself for what I was certain was coming.

He handed me a glass of scotch. His drink of choice. I hadn't told him that I hadn't had a drink in a few months. I didn't like to allow him to know much about what was going on with me. He'd use it against me if he could. I set the glass down on the coffee table in front of me.

"You still want to be a lawyer?" Louise asked, and her warm eyes made it clear that she was genuinely interested.

"Yep. That's the plan."

"Well, pending he doesn't fuck it all up like his old man." Simon dropped to sit in the chair across from me and his icy stare let me know he was just getting started.

Why the fuck did I come here again?

Oh, yeah. I was trying to be the bigger person.

"Simon," my mother said in her calmest voice. Why didn't she ever get mad? Why not call him out for being an asshole when she knew he was?

"What? I'm not saying anything he doesn't know. Hell, I'm funding this project. *The Gray Project.* Giving him the opportunity to make something of his life."

I saluted him. "Thanks for that."

He didn't miss the sarcasm, but the Sheldons appeared to, or they were just too many cocktails deep to pick up on the tension.

My sisters yelled for my mom, and she and Louise both left the room to go find the kids. Great. Alone with Simon the asshole, and a drunk Paul who was studying Simon's books that lined the shelves in this grand room and paying us no attention.

"The day you stop believing in your old man is the day I'll believe you might actually pull this off. I mean, how many times does he need to fail for you to realize he isn't coming back?" Simon sipped his drink and leaned back in the leather chair.

"I'll let you know when I get there."

"You do know that he left you and your mother with nothing when he derailed his life. Did you know that your mom couldn't pay the bills when I met her? You didn't have electricity or power. That piece of shit walked out on his wife and kid." He was spewing ugliness like he'd been holding onto this for so long and he needed to let it out. I'd heard a lot of things about my dad from Simon, but this was new.

"I don't know all the details. I just know that we were on our own for a while before she met you. And you saved the day." I raised a brow. *There's your bone, asshole. Now step the fuck off.*

"You're fucking right I saved the day. Your mother found that son of a bitch getting his dick sucked by some whore. That's right. That's the man you're protecting."

I leaned forward and reached for the glass, tipping my head back and letting the cool liquid travel down the back of my throat. I couldn't listen to much more of this, but I knew he wasn't going to let up any time soon. I'd been sober for a fair amount of time, and I was ready to jump back in the numbing game. Hell, I was tired of feeling so many things.

"Thanks for the visual. You love telling me what a failure he is, don't you?" I hissed, moving to my feet and pouring a double for myself.

"Is that what you think? That I enjoy hurting you?" he asked.

I barked out a laugh before taking a long pull and letting the alcohol numb all the raw edges that were currently exposed.

"Yeah. I think you enjoy it."

He nodded and I filled my glass again and returned to my seat. The alcohol was already taking over as my threshold for booze was definitely not what it once was. I was warm and relaxed when I settled back down and faced him. Paul had disappeared from the room. I didn't know where he'd gone or when he left but I knew that Simon was just getting started.

"You're wrong, Gray. I want better for you. I see your potential. But you continue to worship that sick fuck. Do you know that he never paid a dime of child support? He wanted nothing to do with you or your mother once he started using. Yet you continue to stand beside him."

"He's a goddamn addict. It's a disease."

"He's a selfish piece of shit. And you are at a fork in the road. Cut his ass off and take the smart path. That's when you'll earn my respect," he said, lips pursed and face hard.

"I won't hold my breath." I slammed the drink and moved to the bar for a healthy refill.

Simon was behind me now. "Do you know why I pay for your college and hand you a credit card with no limit, allowing you to get whatever you could want for?"

I slammed my drink and turned around to face him. "I actually don't know. To keep my mother happy is my best guess. Or to wave some bullshit power over my head."

"Wrong. When I met your mother, you were just a little kid. And I saw how smart you were. My father was a drunk, Gray. And everything I have is because I went out and earned it. I didn't look back or live in the past. I want that for you. And I have the resources to do it."

"You have a funny way of showing it," I said, stepping around him and leaving the room.

I stumbled to the bathroom and locked myself inside. Fuck. I was wasted. But his words were spinning in my head. I dialed Cade's number.

"Come meet us at the bonfire," he said, and his words slurred.

"You're out? Fuck. I need a ride. I have to get out of here and I'm too fucking drunk so I can't drive."

Ubers weren't big in Willow Springs, and the last thing I wanted was some nosy ass local in my business anyway.

"I'm texting Gigi as we speak. She's at home. Okay. She's on her way to get you," he said. "I'm sorry, brother. Don't let that dickhead get you down."

"All right. I'll see you later," I said, ending the call.

I made my way out of the bathroom and toward the front door.

"Gray." My mother's voice was calm, as always.

Did the woman ever get pissed?

"I'm leaving. Thanks for," I paused and threw my hands in the air, "the enlightening conversation about what a dead-beat my father is."

My mom rushed toward me and reached for my hands. "I'm sorry, son. He shouldn't talk about your dad that way."

"Why don't you ever stick up for me? You're my fucking mother. How have you allowed this to go on for so long? Dad may be a pill-popping junkie, but at least he has a valid excuse for why he's a shit parent. What's yours?"

I'd never spoken to my mother like this before. I didn't know why I was now. Maybe being sober these past few months had made me question things for the first time in my life.

"I-I-I'm sorry." Her words broke on a sob and I walked out the door, leaving her standing there. Headlights came down the driveway.

Gigi.

I opened the passenger door and climbed inside.

She studied me for a minute and then leaned over me and pulled my seat belt across my body and clamped it at my side. The car smelled like peaches and I closed my eyes and breathed her in.

"Are you okay?" she whispered as she backed out of the driveway.

"I'm fine." I scrubbed a hand down my face before leaning

forward and punching her dashboard. I thought of the words Simon had said. The words I'd said to my mother. The way she looked at me when I'd said them.

Gigi pulled the car into the parking lot of a park up the street. She unbuckled and climbed over the seat and settled on my lap. She wrapped her arms around me and hugged me.

And I fucking lost it.

I cried for the first time ever. I wasn't one who believed in breaking down. It was for the weak. But at the moment—that's exactly how I felt.

Weak.

Broken.

Sobs left my body and I hugged her even tighter.

"Fuck," I said when I finally pulled my shit together. "I'm sorry about that."

She put a hand on my cheek and studied me. "You don't have to be sorry. What happened?"

"Just another life lesson from Simon about what a shitty father my dad was and is. How he never wanted me or my mom, and we weren't worth fighting for."

"That's not true, Gray. You know that's not true. He's an addict. He's not using rational judgment," she said, and her sapphire blues locked with mine.

So fucking pretty.

So fucking perfect.

So fucking good.

"I know. I actually think this is his way of showing he cares, but he has a shitty way of doing it. He's worried about me. Of me turning out like my father," I said, tucking the hair behind her ear. Her nearness settled me.

"You have all the good qualities of your father, but you aren't your father, Gray. You've never done drugs and you've made it clear you never will. And you weren't drinking for the past few months, well, until tonight?" She smiled and raised a brow.

"I couldn't take listening to him anymore. I fucked up. I drank. I told my mother off." I shook my head and groaned.

"What did you say to your mom?"

"I asked her why she's never stood up for me. I think I told her she was a shitty parent like my dad but at least he had a good excuse." I flinched because I couldn't believe I'd said those words to my mother. She was doing the best she could.

"I think it's good you said it. I think it's a fair question. She's your mom. She should stand up for you."

"Why are you being nice to me? You hate me, remember?" I couldn't stop my hand from stroking her face.

"I don't hate you, Gray. You just hurt me, and I was angry."

Her mouth was so close to mine, and my dick was hard as a rock. "I'm sorry for hurting you."

She nodded. "So, why'd you do it?"

I was three sheets to crazy town, and I'd already said more than I should to my mother, so what the hell. "I freaked out when we got home. Thinking about the fact that I brought you around two deadbeats that are involved in God knows what. My father dangled a gun around and you were there. Fuck, Gigi. Your family would be so fucking mad at me."

Her gaze narrowed. "Why didn't you just tell me that?"

"Because you're a stubborn ass and you wouldn't have listened."

She raised a brow. "Fair enough. What else? I can see those wheels spinning," she said.

I shook my head. "I'm fucked up, G. I have a fucked up family. Who knows who my father is messed up with? And I'm in a whole lot of trouble with you and I don't know what to do about it. It scares the shit out of me."

"What kind of trouble?" Her lips grazed mine as she spoke, and her fingers were tangled in my hair.

When did that happen?

"I'm in fucking love with my best friend's little sister, and she's too good for me." There. I said it. It was the truth. I was tired of keeping it in.

"I love you, too," she whispered, eyes full of emotion. Her lips were on mine and my hands wrapped around her tighter, because I couldn't get close enough.

"I missed you so fucking much," I said against her mouth before my tongue dipped in for a taste.

She was grinding up against me and it was the first time I'd felt good in two weeks.

Because Gigi Jacobs had a way of making everything better.

nineteen

• • •

Gigi

THE WEEKEND HOME had been an emotional roller coaster. Gray and I had found our way back to one another, but we'd had to keep our distance while we were home. But since we'd returned to school, we'd been inseparable. Addy, Jett, and Leo were the only people at school who knew that we were together, and of course, Coco, Maura, and Ivy all knew what was going on as well.

We weren't ready to tell my brother, because we didn't want to add that pressure. This was new. Gray was dealing with a lot of stuff with his father, and he still struggled with feelings that he wasn't good enough for me. That killed me in a million ways, and I was determined to prove him wrong.

I loved him. And that's really all that mattered to me.

We were going to this dance tonight together per my brother's insistence, which was comical considering there was so much more going on than Cade knew. My parents had also given the thumbs-up to the idea, which made it all too easy. I was a little nervous about how Tiffany would respond. She thought Gray and I were just friends. I'd avoided her question when she'd asked me at our Monday night dinner dozens of times who I was going with tonight. Gray said she'd called and asked him to go with her, but he'd told her he already had plans for the night and hadn't said anything because it wasn't her business. He said he didn't care what she thought.

I'd spent every night this past week at the fraternity house with Gray, as he had the bigger bed and his own bathroom, but so far, we'd been able to keep a fairly low profile. Tonight, we would be out in public, and I was anxious about it. I didn't like keeping secrets. But I also wasn't ready to start a full-on shit show with my overbearing brother.

We weren't there yet.

I slipped into my navy blue dress that hugged my body like a second skin. I'd curled my hair and then pulled it back in a long ponytail. Addy and I both looked in the full-length mirror at the same time and smiled.

"You look gorgeous," she said.

"Thank you! So, do you. Jett's going to lose his mind."

There was a knock on the door, and I didn't miss the disappointment in Addy's eyes when Bailey walked in. Being in the same sorority meant she would be going to the dance as well, so there was no escaping her. "Hey, hey. Haven't seen you two around since Thanksgiving break. Just making sure you're both going tonight. It's going to be so lit. I plan on getting totally wasted."

She turned around and shook her ass and laughed. She wore a red sequined dress that was barely there. It dipped low in the front and stopped short in the back. Way short. Leaving very little to the imagination.

"Yep. We're going." Addy dropped to sit on the bed.

"Well, I know who you're going with, but who's taking *you*?" She narrowed her gaze and looked at me.

"I'm going with Gray."

"Awww… that's sweet. Your brother's best friend is taking you. Hashtag thank god for big brothers and small favors, right?" She smirked. I saw Jett and Gray appear in the doorway when I looked over her shoulder.

Gray moved right past her, walked up, wrapped a hand around my neck, and kissed me hard. I was breathless when we pulled apart and I'm sure my eyes had doubled in size.

"Hey, beautiful." He stared down at me, and Jett and Addy laughed behind him.

"Oh, ooohhhhh," Bailey said, and it felt damn good to put her in her place.

"Damn straight. Nobody's thanking god for her big brother here. Just a guy who's crazy about his girl. You good with that?" He turned to look at Bailey as she gawked in shock.

"Yes. Of course."

My fingers intertwined with his and I let out a breath that I hadn't even realized I'd been holding. "You look really pretty, G," he whispered in my ear.

"Thank you. You look great." I leaned into him because I could feel my cheeks heat. Addy and Jett led Bailey out of the room, and I looked up at Gray. "Should you have done that? Isn't this still kind of a secret?"

"She was being a bitch to you. And she doesn't know Cade. You worry too much." He kissed my forehead and I melted.

We loaded a party bus, and the booze was flowing. Gray wasn't drinking again and hadn't since we'd returned from Thanksgiving. We hadn't run into Tiffany yet, but she'd just stepped on the bus, and I sipped my drink because I was a little anxious about how she'd treat me once she saw he was here with me. She had been hot and cold with me every time we were at the house. She really only acknowledged me if she needed me to do something for her; otherwise, she didn't give me the time of day. He wasn't fazed by her, but I most definitely was. She could make my life very difficult at the house.

"Well, well, well, I guess I know who you're busy with tonight, don't I?" She raised a brow at Gray.

"I guess you do," he said confidently, as if they were discussing the weather.

"So, what? You're her sympathy date? Is it your best friend duty to take his little sister to a dance? You did get her in the house after all." She smirked and took a long pull from her red Solo cup. Her words slurred a bit and my stomach twisted because she looked at me like she was ready to scratch my eyes out.

Gray lifted my hand with his and showed our fingers intertwined. "No sympathy date here. G wouldn't need me to do her any favors, so go ahead and take your shots because we don't give a shit what you think. Why don't you focus on who you came here with."

Two guys from Gray's fraternity stumbled past us and gave him a high-five in greeting as they moved to the back of the party bus.

"Really?" she hissed before reaching over and snatching the cup out of my hand. "Did I not tell you that you are going to be a *sober sister* tonight? It's about time you start paying your dues for getting in this house." Her smile was forced, and it sent chills down my spine.

"No, you didn't mention it, but that's fine. I don't mind not drinking." I cleared my throat.

Addy leaned forward and handed her cup to Tiffany. "I'll join her. I've clearly not earned my way in either, since you did us *such a big favor* and all."

Jett laughed, and Gray's face remained hard. "Are we good now?"

"We're far from good, Gray." She crossed her arms over her chest and studied him.

"What is this? We've barely spoken in months. We got together once over the summer. Nothing has happened since.

What is happening here?" he said, not hiding his irritation even a little bit that she was pulling this.

"Listen. That's not how this works. Sure, if you're a player, I can get on board with that whole *fear of commitment* bullshit. But if you think I'm going to stand by while you fuck around with some… freshman when I've made it clear that I'm interested—you're dearly mistaken. You and I are not finished."

"There is no you and me." He raised a brow in challenge. "Who I date is not up to you."

"I guess we'll see about that." She glared at each of us before storming off.

"Jesus," Gray said, wrapping an arm around me. "I think she's just drunk. That was batshit crazy."

"Some of the girls in the house were telling us that she's unstable," Addy said, looking over her shoulder to make sure no one was listening. "Apparently she's been bullying a few of the girls that live in the house. They all can't wait for her to graduate this year and be out of there."

"You let me know if she gives you two a hard time at all after this. I'll take it to the board. She can't throw a fucking hissy fit every time she doesn't get her way."

"Yeah. What the fuck was that?" Jett said, shaking his head. "Don't take any shit from her crazy ass."

Addy and I both laughed, but a pit settled in my stomach because I highly doubted this was just going to go away. A few of Gray's fraternity brothers and two players on the football team with Jett were there, and they came to sit with us, and we laughed and talked all the way to the event location.

"You okay?" Gray whispered in my ear.

"Yeah." I nodded.

"I promise it will be okay. Don't let her ruin your night."

"We could just Uber home when we get there. I don't even care to be here."

"Nope. These are experiences you only get once. Fuck

Tiffany. We're staying." He pulled me close and we stepped off the bus when we arrived.

The night ended up being a lot of fun. Tiffany apparently vomited in the bathroom and had to be taken home early, and I definitely relaxed after she was gone. Gray was the life of the party on and off the dance floor. He even got pulled up to the DJ booth because the DJ was a Sig Alpha Alumni. He was hilarious the way he got everyone to come out and dance, and my heart melted because Gray announced that he was there with the prettiest girl he'd ever laid eyes on.

"Wow. Do you think you guys will tell Cade soon? Gray seems okay with letting everyone know tonight," Addy said while Jett chatted with a few friends.

"I don't know. I'm sort of dreading that whole conversation. You know how crazy Cade gets and he won't take this well."

"Yeah, it's definitely going to be added pressure. But how long can you keep it a secret? You guys are so cute together. I'm really happy for you," she said, leaning forward to hug me.

"Thanks. I don't know. And I'm a little freaked out by the whole scene with Tiffany. She's going to be a total bitch to us when we see her next."

"She's a bitch to us now. I don't care. We were doing this for fun, and if she wants to make it awful, we can quit. I'm not letting her bully you or me. Got it?"

I laughed. I loved when Addy acted like a badass. Jett had been so good for her as far as finding her voice and standing up for herself. We all noticed how she'd come into her own and we loved him even more for it.

"Coco is going to freak out when we tell her about Tiffany."

"She will want to come here and put her in her place for sure," Addy said over her laughter. "She doesn't think you and Gray should tell Cade yet either. She makes some valid points."

"She does. It will add a lot of pressure. And what if he ends up wanting out of this but feels obligated because my brother will freak out if things don't work out. That would be horrifying. I wish Cade wasn't a factor, because things are going so well. And Gray has so much drama to deal with about his father as it is. He doesn't need the added pressure of my brother's anger."

"Maybe that's your answer. Give yourself some more time. After winter break, you won't be home with Cade for a while. By then you'll know where you stand. But I'm telling you, you guys are so stinking cute together. I think you better prepare to tell your brother at some point that you're in love with his best friend."

I nod. Because I am. But telling Cade is a different story. Thankfully he's been so busy with Camilla and his classes we just haven't talked as much lately. He was happy that Gray was taking me to the dance because he had no idea that we were actually together.

"Yeah. It would be nice to give it some time before we involve him."

"You've slept over there every night since we've been back. Everything still going well?" She smirked and her cheeks pinked.

"Nothing to report. I mean, I'm starting to wonder why we aren't doing anything more. I'm not complaining, because..." I bit down on my bottom lip and shook my head. This boy made me feel things I never knew were possible. The way he touched me was like nothing I'd ever experienced. But I wasn't about to get into the details here. "Well, it's all good. But he isn't trying to have sex with me, and he always stops things before they go too far. He keeps telling me we should wait. That's what makes me wonder if he is really all in with me. I mean, why wouldn't he want to do... everything?"

"Have you asked him?"

"No. It's kind of embarrassing. Obviously, he's been with lots of girls, so it makes me feel like maybe he doesn't want me that way."

"I promise you that is not the case. I think you're the first girl he's actually ever cared about and loved." She bumped me with her shoulder, just as Gray slid in beside me.

"You guys having fun?" He nuzzled my neck and I leaned into him.

"Yes. Thanks for doing this. It's been a lot more fun than I expected."

"Are you guys ready to get out of here?" Jett asked, taking Addy's hand in his.

"Yeah. I'll call an Uber now." Gray led us out the door and we made our way to the car.

We dropped Addy and Jett off at his apartment and drove to the fraternity house. It was quiet since everyone was out tonight. I slipped into one of Gray's T-shirts and climbed into bed and he went to the kitchen to grab us a few waters. When he slid in beside me, I was sleepy, but I had a lot on my mind. He pushed the hair out of my freshly washed face and his legs tangled with mine.

"Did you have fun tonight?"

"Yeah. Did you?" I asked.

"I did. I always have fun with you. Are you okay that people know about us now?" he asked as he pulled me closer.

"Yeah. I don't feel the need to keep it a secret aside from Cade, and that's only because I think once he knows there will be a lot more pressure, mainly on you. And that's not fair to you."

He pulled back to look at me. "I don't give a shit about pressure. But I do give a shit about losing my best friend, and

I don't think he is ever going to be okay with it." He leaned forward to rest his forehead against mine.

"He'll just have to get over it." I tugged his mouth down to mine and he kissed me hard.

His tongue slipped in and explored my mouth and I arched into him. His hands moved beneath my T-shirt, making their way up my back. He tugged it over my head as his mouth moved down my neck and wrapped around my breast. The sensation was so strong I couldn't stop the moan that escaped my mouth. He gave equal attention to each side, and his mouth made its way down my abdomen as his fingers settled on my lace panties. I paused and tangled my hands in his hair to stop him. This had become our routine.

Gray giving me pleasure, and me doing the same back to him after.

But I wanted more.

I wanted everything.

"Are you okay?" He looked up at me before pushing up and propping himself above me. "Do you not want me to do that tonight?"

I laughed because the fact that I'd just stopped him was ridiculous because I knew how good he would make me feel. But I wanted to know why we weren't taking things further. I was breathing heavy and he dropped to lie beside me and we both rolled on our sides to face one another.

"Why aren't we doing more?" I whispered.

His eyes went wide, and he looked very caught off guard. "What do you mean? Isn't this all new for you?"

"Yeah. But we love each other, right?"

"Of course I love you. You've lost me," he said, tucking my hair behind my ear as he studied me.

"Obviously you've had sex before. Do you just not want to have it with me?" My voice wobbled as the words left my mouth, and as mortified as I was for asking, I knew we needed to have this conversation.

"Is that what you think? That I don't want you?"

"It's crossed my mind." A nervous laugh escaped, and I let out a long breath. "If you aren't attracted to me *that way,* you need to let me know."

His mouth dropped open and he stared at me as if he couldn't believe the words coming out of my mouth. "G, that is not the case at all. I want you so bad I'm going out of my fucking mind."

"Then what's the problem? I love you. I'm ready for this. For everything."

He chuckled and nipped at my bottom lip. "I have never wanted anyone or anything more than I want you. If that means taking it slow, that's what I'm willing to do. This is all new for you, and I want to make sure you're ready. When we finally talk to Cade about this, I don't want him thinking I pressured you into anything."

"You have to take Cade out of this conversation, Gray. I'm a grown woman." I tried to remain calm, but I was frustrated that this was becoming such a factor.

"He's my best friend. And you're…" He paused.

"I'm what?"

"Listen, Gigi. I haven't had a lot of good in my life. I have a drug addict father, a mother who is too submissive to stand up for me, and a stepfather who hates me. Your family has been there for me when no one else was. And you… you are the best person I know. In all the years I've known you, I've always been blown away by how pretty you are. How smart you are. *How good you are.* I still struggle with the idea that I'm deserving of any of that light. But I'll be dammed if I tarnish it, I can promise you that. So, me waiting, is because I love you so damn much, I want to do right by you."

Tears streamed down my face at his words. "You are doing right by me. You deserve to be happy too."

He used his thumbs to wipe away the liquid rolling down my cheeks. "How do you know you're ready?"

"Because it's all I think about. I want you, Gray. I want us to do everything together. No more holding back. This has nothing to do with Cade. Not this part of it. This is just ours. We can tell him that we love each other when we're ready, but this—this is something I want to share with you. Please."

He rolled me on my back and leaned forward and kissed me.

He kissed me like he was never going to stop.

I only hoped he wouldn't.

twenty

. . .

Gray

I WASN'T PREPARED for her to tell me she was ready. Maybe a part of me was holding back because the thought of making a mistake with this girl would be the worst decision of my life. She deserved the best of everything, and I was damn well going to try to be that person. And one thing I was the fucking best at—was sex. I'd obviously tread with caution because it was her first time. And I wanted to both rock her world and take it slow—and I was up for the task.

I kissed her until I knew her lips were aching because mine were. And I didn't fucking care. I could kiss Gigi for the rest of my life and never tire of it. She was grinding her hips up against me, and it was driving me wild. She tugged at the hem of my shirt and yanked it over my head, and I chuckled against her mouth. I kissed my way down her body and the frantic breaths coming from her mouth were all the motivation I needed to keep going. I loved the way her body reacted to my touch.

"Gray," she whispered. "Please."

I moved back up to her mouth. "You sure, baby?"

"I'm positive."

There's no one I wanted to please more than this girl. I

reached over to my nightstand and pulled out a condom from the drawer. She pushed up on her elbows and watched me with wide sapphire eyes. I tore the foil packet open with my teeth and rolled it over my erection. My dick was on high alert as he'd been anticipating this moment for a long time.

I leaned down, propping myself above her on one arm. "We're going to take it slow, okay? If it hurts, just tell me and we can stop. There's no pressure."

She nodded, her eyes were hooded, and she bit down on her full bottom lip. I nearly came undone right there. I positioned myself at her entrance and kissed her as I moved forward so slowly it took every ounce of restraint that I had.

"Jesus Christ, you're so wet. You feel so fucking good."

She tangled her fingers in my hair and kissed me. She stiffened at the intrusion and I paused.

"Don't stop."

"Am I hurting you?" I asked as I moved slowly.

"It hurts and it feels good. Is that normal?" She looked up at me like I hung the fucking moon, and I swore in that moment that I would spend every day trying to.

"Yes. Totally normal. But if it's too much, just tell me, okay?"

I moved a little further and waited for her to adjust to me for a moment.

If I died right here, right now—it would be totally worth it.

Nothing had ever felt better.

"You were fucking made for me, Gigi Jacobs." I groaned into her neck.

She started to move, which let me know she was okay. We found our perfect rhythm and when I say it was perfect—it was fucking mind-blowing.

Her body arched off the bed, and I covered her breasts with my mouth, one at a time. My lips came back up to meet hers as we moved together, like we'd done this a million times before. She was moaning, so I knew she was enjoying it as much as I was. My hand moved between us, finding her most sensitive spot, and her head fell back at my touch.

"Gray," she groaned, and I moved faster, knowing exactly what she needed. Somehow I always knew what she needed. She went over the edge on a gasp, and her body shook and trembled beneath my touch. It was the hottest fucking thing I'd ever seen. I pumped a few more times and went right over the edge with her. We were both gasping and shaking and I fell forward, making sure to keep my weight off of her. Every ounce of pleasure racked my body before I fell to the side and pulled her on top of me as we both fought to catch our breath.

"Oh my god," she whispered before pushing up to look at me.

I laughed because I couldn't help myself. "That good, huh?"

"Um, yeah. Is that how it always is? I thought the first time was supposed to be terrible?" she asked, her fingers grazing the scruff on my jaw.

"Yeah. This is not the norm for a first time. Or any time. That was fucking unbelievable. We're clearly made for each other, baby."

She smiled. "We are."

I pulled out of her and pushed up to walk to the bathroom and dispose of the condom.

"How do you feel?" I stood in the bathroom doorway taking in her mess of blonde hair falling all around her as she lay naked on my bed. It was a vision I'd remember forever. I took my time, memorizing every line and curve of her beautiful body. Perfect tits, flat abs, and toned sexy legs. Her eyes were hooded, lips plump, and she fucking smiled. Two little dimples that I'd always teased her about decorated her cheeks.

"I feel good. Maybe a little sore." She sat up and wrapped a sheet around her shoulders.

"Let me run you a hot bath. You can soak for a little bit."

"You're running me a bath? You're just full of surprises, aren't you?" Her voice was a little hoarse and sexy as hell.

I turned to start the water and moved toward her. "Only with you."

She took my hand and we walked into the bathroom. I stepped in the tub and dropped down to sit and she burst out in laughter. "You're taking a bath with me?"

"Yeah." I wriggled my brows. "Get in here."

"You're a little big for that tub." She was shaking her head and laughing as she climbed in.

"Lucky for me, you're small. So, it works."

She pulled her hair up on top of her head and used an elastic that was around her wrist to tie her wild mane of hair in a messy knot.

She settled between my legs and her head fell back against my chest. I reached for the soap and rubbed it between my hands and ran them down her chest and stomach.

Her eyes closed. "You don't have to wash me."

"I like doing things for you." I moved my hands between her legs, gently stroking her.

She gasped. I moved my fingers back up her body and wrapped my arms around her as we sat in the quiet. Our breaths the only audible sound.

"Listen, G. We need to tell him. We'll do it over Christmas break. I can't keep this from him anymore. Not now."

"Why? It's none of his business. He's going to freak out. It's going to complicate things," she said. "He's going to tell you we shouldn't be together."

"Baby, I'm not going anywhere. He's going to be pissed. But I'll show him how real this is for me. I'll make him understand."

She rolled over in the tub and faced me. Her eyes were watery with emotion. "Okay. Promise me you won't let him come between us."

"I promise."

And I meant it.

Because for the first time in my entire life—I was completely content.

At peace.

And happy.

I was in my truck and driving an hour and a half to see Cade because I'd gotten a frantic call from him this morning, and he said he needed me. Cade was my brother in every way outside of actual blood. We'd been best friends since we could talk. College was the first time that we weren't together every day, but we still talked almost daily aside from when we had finals. He'd been a little distant lately and I hadn't pressed matters because I was in deep with his fucking sister. I dreaded the day we'd have the conversation because I already knew the outcome. I knew him as well as I knew myself.

It.

Would.

Not.

Be.

Okay.

But I was going to make him understand. There was no other option anymore. I'd found something that I never knew I could find, and I wanted it. I wasn't walking away, not even for my best friend.

He'd been a protective brother since day one. It's who he was. And I always understood it, because she was special, and I wanted to protect her too. Hell, she was the most important person in my life.

I left Gigi in my bed and told her that her brother needed me, and she'd nodded in understanding. She knew how close we were. We were all heading home in three days for Christmas, and we'd talked about discussing our relationship with Cade over break. Gigi and I could probably win some sort of record for the amount of sex we'd had over the past two weeks. I couldn't get enough, and neither could she. I'd never been big on repeat visitors, but this girl was different in every way. And it was time to tell her brother, because this thing between us was the real deal. I never thought I'd say the words, but here I was willing to die on the sword for this girl.

I sent her a text when I arrived at his fraternity house.

Me ~ Hey, just got here. I hope you went back to sleep. I'll keep you posted. Love you.

Gigi ~ I can't sleep. I'm worried about him. Will you call or text as soon as you know what's going on.

Me ~ Yes. Xo

I jogged up the steps and dialed Cade's phone. The door flung open while my phone was still ringing, and my best friend stood there looking like he hadn't slept in two days.

"Come in." He led me up the back stairs and my stomach dipped. Could he know about Gigi? We had been seen together in Willow Springs when we'd snuck home to check on my dad. Could someone have seen us out at the lake that day?

"Brother, you're freaking me out. What the fuck is going on?" I dropped to sit on the couch in his room. Being a junior, he'd managed to get his own room, so he had a loft bed built above a little couch area.

Cade paced in front of me. "Camilla's late."

"Late?" I searched his face, unsure what we were talking about.

Oh. Late.

"Her fucking period, dude. One time. One fucking time I was a lazy asshole and convinced her that we would be fine." He ran his hand through his hair.

I pushed to my feet and put my hands on each of his

shoulders. "Stop. You're human. You made a mistake. You'll deal with it."

"Gray, I'm not fucking ready to be a father. I graduate next year. I'm still in fucking college."

I nodded. I understood his fear. But I also knew my best friend. He was a stand-up guy. He'd never walk away from his responsibility. And he'd respect whatever Camilla wanted to do.

"I get that, but you're jumping the gun. Did she take a test yet?"

"No. We had a fight before I called you. She's been really distant lately and I didn't know why. I thought she was breaking up with me. But she finally broke down and told me that she's been freaking out for two days."

"How late is she?"

"A week." He shrugged. "What the fuck am I going to do? She's going to blame me for the rest of our lives."

"Cade, brother, you are not the first couple that this has happened to. Stop beating yourself up."

"No, Gray, this is serious shit. I'd beat the fuck out of anyone that did this to Gigi. So, I'm a total fucking hypocrite. This is why Gigi can't ever be with a dude like us. We're selfish assholes. Camilla has a brother. What the fuck is he going to think of me?" He dropped to sit and buried his face in his hands.

I stiffened at the mention of his sister. We'd always been careful. But that didn't matter. I was having sex with his baby sister. He would lose his motherfucking mind.

"Let's take this one step at a time. She needs to take a fucking test."

"I know. I wanted to go with her to get one from the drugstore, but she was crying and angry, and she stormed out of here," he said. I could still smell the booze on his breath, so he'd obviously been out last night, and the fight was probably fueled by alcohol. It was times like these that I was happy I was cutting out the booze. Sure, I'd had that one slip, and I'd probably have more in my lifetime, but I'd come to the conclusion that nothing great came out of alcohol binges. I hadn't minded being numb for most of my high school and college years, but I was thankful that I was present lately. I was able to jump in the car and be here for him. I'd help him get through this, no matter what the outcome.

"All right, listen to me. Let's get in my truck and go to her apartment. I'll talk to her and you sit in the car until she calms down, okay?"

He pushed to his feet. "Okay. Thank you, brother. I'm so glad you're here."

"Always. Let's go."

We drove a mile away to where Camilla lived. She wasn't taking his calls, as he'd obviously pissed her off. I knew Cade, and my guess was that he'd freaked out, which hadn't helped the situation.

"She's not answering," he groaned.

"What's her apartment number?"

"She's on the first floor. Apartment 102. It's right there." He pointed to the outside door and he scrubbed a hand down his face.

"Wait here." I jogged to the door and knocked three times.

The door opened and Camilla stood on the other side. Her eyes were swollen. Nose red. Lips trembling. I opened my arms and she walked into them. "It's going to be fine, Camilla. I promise. We'll figure it out."

She broke out in sobs, and I stood in the doorway with my arms wrapped around her.

"What if it's not, Gray? My parents are going to freaking kill me." She shook and quaked and let it all out.

"I promise you, it will be okay. But you need to find out if you're even pregnant. My mom had a ton of false alarms when she was trying to get pregnant with the twins. Stress is a huge factor and you're in the middle of finals." I patted the back of her head and she looked up at me and nodded.

"You're right. That's very possible." Her gaze was hopeful for the first time since I'd walked in. "Where is he?"

"He's out in my truck. He doesn't think you want to see him."

"I'm just scared." She threw her hands in the air. "And him freaking out does not help me."

"All right. Listen. Do you need me to go get a test?"

"I got it on my way home. I was just trying to find the courage to take it," she said, tears streaming down her face.

"Camilla, you need to take the test before you freak out. Let's first make sure you're pregnant." My voice was calm, and she studied me.

"Okay. I'll do it now."

"Do you want me to go get Cade while you do it?" I asked.

"Yeah. Thank you."

I walked back out to my truck to find my best friend with his face buried between his hands.

"You need to pull your shit together before you come inside. She's taking the test now. You need to be the rock, brother. Just show her you're there for her." I clapped a hand on his shoulder as we walked back in her apartment.

We dropped to sit on the couch and sat in silence.

Camilla walked out of the bathroom holding up the white stick with tears streaming down her face. "It's negative."

Cade rushed over to her and wrapped his arms around her as they both cried. I pushed to my feet and walked outside to text Gigi.

Me ~ Everything is okay. I'll fill you in later. I'm going to hang with your brother for a few hours before I head back.

Gigi ~ Are you sure he's okay?

Me ~ Positive. All good. Love you.

Gigi ~ Love you more! Xo

I deleted the conversation just in case Cade were to look at my phone. He and Camilla walked outside to find me.

"Well, that was scary," Cade said, and we all laughed.

"It was really nice of you to come here." Camilla intertwined her fingers with my best friend.

"Of course. Nowhere else I'd want to be right now."

"You always have my back, brother. You're my day one." Cade clapped a hand on my shoulder.

"Hey," Camilla said over a chuckle.

"You're my forever, baby. He's my day one."

We walked toward the truck because apparently pregnancy scares made you hungry and they were both starving. The air around us was lighter now. I was happy I'd been here and relieved that things had worked out.

"No more being stupid, I promise," Cade said once we took our seats at the diner up the street. "Safe sex from here on out."

"Um, not sure this is the appropriate time for this conversation," Camilla said, dropping the menu to the side after she looked it over.

"Hey, he knows everything. We've both been stupid assholes most of our lives, so I don't hide anything from this guy." Cade tossed his menu on top of his girlfriend's. My chest squeezed at his words. I was keeping a secret from him.

A big fucking secret.

"Day one," I said, guilt engulfing me as I spoke.

His phone vibrated and he looked down at his screen. "I need to take this. It's Gigi. Will you order me a burger and fries?"

"You got it," Camilla said, as Cade strolled out of the restaurant.

The waiter came by and took our orders, and I chugged the water that he'd set down. It had been a long day already and it was barely noon.

"Thanks so much for being here, Gray. And for bringing him to me. I really appreciate it."

"Not a problem. Glad I could help," I said, as I sipped my water.

"So, how is Gigi?" She had a big, goofy grin on her face.

"She's good as far as I know." I quirked a brow in challenge.

She laughed. "I thought Cade told me you took her to a dance just recently?"

"Yep. He asked me to take her."

"I'm sure you didn't mind," she said, reaching for a fry when the server set our plates down.

"Something on your mind, Camilla?"

"I just want you to know that I like you and Gigi a lot. And I know Cade loves you both, and that's all that matters, right?"

What the actual fuck are we talking about?

She was being cryptic as hell. She obviously suspected something.

I nodded just as my best friend came back to the table.

"How's Gigi?" Camilla asked, but her gaze locked with mine as Cade reached for his plate.

"She's good. She's seeing some guy and she seems really into him. She sounds… happy." He shrugged.

"Is she? Have you met him yet, Gray?"

"I have not. I've been busy with finals." I wanted to talk to him about it, but this was not the time. This shit was going to end soon though. I couldn't do it anymore.

She nodded, and her lips turned up in the corners. "Well, you'll have to let us know what he's like when you meet him."

"Yeah, dude. We need to make sure my sister stays clear of assholes like us," Cade said, before taking an enormous bite of his burger and continuing to talk over a mouthful of food. "That's the last thing she needs. You'll check him out for me?"

"Sure," I said, looking at Camilla who couldn't wipe the smile off her face. Fuck me. It was time to come clean but not here. Not now.

"You're the best, Gray. My brother for life." He slapped me on the back.

A sick feeling settled in my stomach.

And all I wanted to do was get back to school.

Back to Gigi.

Back to my best friend's little sister.

twenty-one

. . .

Gigi

I'D JUST FINISHED my last final and I was going to meet Gray at the frat house. I couldn't believe I was halfway through my first year of college. Time was flying, and I was enjoying every minute of it. Our group chat with the Magic Willows was blowing up because we were all going to be home within the next twenty-four hours and we were looking forward to having two weeks together.

Gray and I had decided to talk to Cade about our relationship over break. Things were going so well, and he felt strongly that we needed to get this out in the open. This was the first serious relationship either one of us had had, and bringing my brother in to stir the pot or involving my parents this early on could blow up in both of our faces.

We were happy. Wasn't that what mattered most?

But I respected how much my boyfriend cared for my brother. And now that we'd taken things to the next level, he was insistent that it was time.

When I got to his house, he was sitting on one of the white Adirondack chairs on their front porch.

"Hey, what are you doing out here?" I asked as I walked up the three little steps to greet him.

"Waiting for you." He leaned forward and rested his cheek against my stomach and wrapped his hands around my waist, stopping to squeeze my butt which made me laugh.

Ricky opened the front door. He was Gray's favorite pledge, and I could tell that he worshipped my boyfriend. "Hey, guys. I'll see you after break. Have a good Christmas."

"You out of here?" Gray moved to his feet and pulled him in for one of those strange half boy hugs where they don't fully embrace, but sort of tease the idea.

"Yeah. I'm going to drive home now. You guys heading out tomorrow?"

"Yep," we both said at the same time.

"All right, be safe." He waved and made his way down the porch, and Gray reached for my hand leading me inside.

"Thanks for your help," Gray called out and Ricky turned back and gave him a thumbs-up.

"What are you up to?" I asked, as he scooped me up and threw me over his shoulder like I weighed nothing. He ran toward his room and I couldn't stop laughing as I smacked his ass.

He pushed his bedroom door open and set me on my feet. I gasped at the sight. His lights were off, and he had white twinkle lights running around the perimeter of the room. He put a little tabletop tree on his nightstand, and that was lit up as well. It was a dreary day, so there was very little sunlight coming through the windows, but the room was lit up like a Christmas wonderland.

"What is this?" I whispered, and my hands came over my mouth as I continued to scan the room. This hadn't been here when I left this morning. He'd set this whole thing up today.

He closed his bedroom door and took my hand, leading me to the bed. "I feel bad that I can't give you your gifts on Christmas morning because you've convinced me to wait to tell Cade until after Christmas. So, we'll have to act like we aren't together until then. But I wanted to do something special for you."

"I know you want to tell him right away, but it's only two days. I don't want to ruin Christmas if he does freak out." I continued scanning the room. "And this is so amazing. I love it."

"Well, if I didn't have the history that I have, telling your brother wouldn't be this big of a deal. This is on me."

"Hey, Cade has a track record too. That doesn't mean he isn't good enough for Camilla. Everyone has a past," I said as he pushed to his feet and walked to his closet. It pissed me off that telling Cade we were happy had to be such a negative thing. Who was he to judge? I loved my brother and he deserved to know the truth, but he also needed to stay in his lane.

Gray handed me a little box. I tore the paper off and opened the top to see the most beautiful rose gold necklace with a little heart dangling in the center. My heart raced and emotion welled. "Oh my gosh. This is stunning."

My hands trembled as I pulled it out of the box and studied it. Gray took it from my fingers and I lifted my hair for him to clasp it around my neck.

"You have my heart, G. I want you to know that. It's yours always." His words nearly brought me to my knees.

"You have my heart too." A tear streamed down my cheek and he caught it with his thumb.

"I think I've loved you for so long, I can't even remember a time when I didn't. And I want to give you everything. I know it's going to be tough when we talk to Cade, but we'll get through it. And hopefully your parents will be okay with it as well. That's what I want. I want this to be something we don't have to hide when we're home moving forward."

I smiled and reached for my backpack and pulled out three gifts. Mine weren't as fancy as his, but I did try to find things I thought he would like. I handed him the first one. He tore through the gift wrap and studied the leather-bound book. He flipped to the first page and his lips turned up in the corners. I'd printed out all the pictures we'd taken this semester and placed them in the book. Some photos were taken at the pottery studio when he'd gone with me, a few were taken in Willow Springs when we'd snuck away, and most were taken at his fraternity house. Lying in bed, cuddled up watching a movie—Gray and I were always together. He laughed when he saw the one that I took of him with a towel wrapped around his waist, water dripping down his body as he looked in the mirror.

"You little horn dog. Were you watching me?" he teased as he continued to flip through each page.

I leaned forward and smiled as I looked at the selfie we took. Gray's face was buried in my neck as he kissed me, and my mouth was wide open in laughter. As we continued to look at each photo, it reminded me that we'd come so far over the past few months. There was a comfort and a closeness that was impossible to miss.

"Maybe we should just let Cade see this book, and let the photos speak for themselves," I said when he flipped the last page over.

"I love this so much, G. And I promise I'm going to make this right with Cade."

"It's not your responsibility to make my brother understand. Yes, he deserves the truth, but that's it. He doesn't get to decide what's best for us. This is not up to him. It's ridiculous." I leaned forward and kissed him before passing him the next package.

"It's not ridiculous. Cade knows you're special, just like I do. And I wouldn't be okay with you dating me if I weren't so fucking crazy in love with you."

I rolled my eyes. "Now you're talking crazy. Here. One more."

He looked inside the gift bag and pulled out a book titled, *Idiot's Guide To Taking the LSAT.*

"Oh man, I needed this." He laughed as I handed him one more gift and he shook his head in disapproval as if I'd given him too much. Gray had a hard time receiving gifts, I'd noticed this over the past few months. He enjoyed giving and being there for the people he loved, but he expected very little in return, and that broke my heart. Because he deserved everything. He deserved my brother's approval, because he was a great friend to Cade and always had been. I wished Gray saw himself through my eyes.

He opened the last package and held up the T-shirt as he barked out a laugh. "My girlfriend is more badass than yours."

"True that, buddy." I laughed.

"You are a badass. Thank you. I've never gotten such thoughtful presents before." He tucked my hair behind my ear.

My chest squeezed. Gray hadn't been loved by his family the way he should have been, and I wanted to give him all that I had. "I love you. And don't be mad, but I have to leave for a few hours. I'll be back to have dinner with you though."

"What? Where are you going?"

"Tiffany is making me and Addy come clean the house before break. She's definitely not happy with me." I pulled at the edge of the comforter on his bed.

"Fuck that. Are you serious? Since when is that a thing? The day before we go home for break? Hell, half the student body has already left. Is it only you two that have to be there?"

"Yep. She said it's a *new thing* that she is implementing."

Gray picked up his phone and typed out a message. When his phone dinged, he laughed at the screen. "All right, let's go."

"Where are we going?"

"I just messaged Jett. Fuck Tiffany. We're going to help you bust this out. She can kiss my muscular, toned ass."

I laughed. "I see you're the president of the Gray Baldwin's butt fan club."

He nipped at my ear and I yelped. "Damn straight, baby. Let's go."

We'd just finished Christmas Eve dinner, and I was actually happy that Gray had convinced me to talk to my brother sooner rather than later because I was already tired of putting on an act. We'd come home yesterday, and it was unbelievably uncomfortable to pretend that we weren't together. I'd made every effort to convince Gray to sneak into my room last night, but he'd refused to do it because he didn't want to risk it. We'd laughed over the role reversal as he was the one trying to do this the right way, and I was willing to break all the rules. I couldn't stand being away from him.

Gray was going to talk to Cade the day after tomorrow. He wanted to do it on his own so if my brother lost his shit, which he most likely would, I wouldn't have to be around for it. He'd take him out to the lake and have a man to man, or a come to Jesus, or whatever one wants to call it. My stomach wrenched at the thought, but I was equally annoyed that it had to be such a big deal. Cade was stubborn and set in his ways, and I wasn't looking forward to him throwing a temper tantrum. I knew my brother well and he didn't like surprises. But I hoped he'd get over it quickly.

My hand rested on the table beside Gray's when my mom brought dessert out and set it down. His finger grazed mine, as if it were impossible not to touch when we were near one another. My foot found his beneath the table and I intertwined my leg with his. If Gray Baldwin was in my vicinity, I was going to be tangled up with him.

"These look so good," I said, trying to focus on anything other than the boy beside me.

"I thought I'd make a few choices this year." There was a tray of peppermint bark, frosted sugar cookies, and a gingerbread Bundt cake.

We tried samples of each as holiday music played through the surround sound, and the house smelled like pine and peppermint. Gray was going over to his house after dinner to have another dessert with his family. He wanted me to go with him, but we knew that would look suspicious to Cade. I just couldn't wait to have this out in the open. I knew my parents would be happy about it as long as we were both happy.

"I'm going to head over to Addy's to do our gift exchange with all the girls." I'd been meeting my best friends on Christmas Eve since we were young.

"Oh, that'll be fun. I hope you'll have them all over here while you're home as well." My mother reached for a cookie.

"Yes, I will for sure."

"And you're going to your mom's for a little bit?" Cade asked Gray as he bit the head off of a snowman cookie and sprinkles fell all around him.

"Yep. I'll be over there for a few hours."

"Okay, I'm going to head down to the lake and meet a few friends for a beer," Cade said.

"Never a dull moment in Willow Springs with you kids." My father scooped a healthy portion of whipped cream on top of his cake.

"Don't drink too much. I'm planning to be up early for presents," I said, rubbing my hands together and everyone laughed.

"Don't you worry. I'm in a fraternity, I can handle my booze." Cade pushed to his feet.

We cleaned up and everyone said their goodbyes as we all

went our separate ways. When I got to Addy's house, there was a text from Gray.

Gray ~ I can't wait to have this behind us. I hate lying to him. He deserves better.

Me ~ I agree. But it shouldn't be this big of a deal to tell him either. This is partly his fault that we've had to keep it a secret.

Gray ~ Love you, G.

Me ~ Love you xo

The girls and I had our gift exchange and oohed and aahed over all the cute gifts. I piled up my presents of makeup and fuzzy socks and jammies beside the table. We each had a matching stack of goodies, and we settled down for a quick chat over hot cocoa and cookies.

"So how is it at the house? I'm dying to know how you're surviving staying away from that sexy boy of yours," Coco said around a mouthful of pastry.

"It's very weird. We both feel uncomfortable. Gray hasn't been around as much as usual and I think it's because he feels all this guilt about Cade. He went to his mom's tonight but said he'd be back later."

"And you're telling him the day after Christmas, right?" Addy asked as she reached for a cookie. "I think it's ridiculous that you have to walk on eggshells around Cade. He should just be happy for you guys."

"I agree," Ivy said. "Cade isn't your father, and the fact that everyone has to worry about how he'll take it versus just being happy for you bothers me. I love your brother, but it's always been his way or the highway."

"Right? And no offense, G, but your brother was no saint in high school either. Before he met Camilla, he was a player too. So, he's a bit of a hypocrite if he doesn't take it well," Maura added.

"Yeah. A part of me wishes we had just told him from the start. Now it feels like this big lie, and he's going to blow up that he was left in the dark. But we didn't know it would turn into this... we wanted to give it a chance to see where it went."

"And oh boy, did it go somewhere. You two could heat a small country with those sparks you put out. I kind of want to smack your brother upside the head and ask how he missed it. Anyone with the slightest bit of awareness can see there's something there. Even his girlfriend is suspicious, and she barely knows you two." Coco sat back and shook her head.

We all laughed and made our plans for New Year's Eve before heading home. I texted Cade and Gray to see where they were. Cade was still out at the lake and said he wouldn't be back for a while, and Gray was on his way to my house. I met him outside, as his truck pulled in the driveway just as I jumped out of my car.

"Hey," I said, making my way over to him.

He glanced around and pulled me close before his mouth came over mine. "I hate this."

"Me too."

"We just need to get through tomorrow."

I pushed up and kissed him, tangling my fingers in his hair.

"What the actual fuck is this?" My brother's voice startled me from behind Gray's car. We were standing off to the side of the driveway near the bushes. I pulled back and turned to see Cade storming toward us.

"What are you doing here?" I said, and my words wobbled when I saw how mad he was. The driveway was dark, but the streetlight provided just enough light to make out his features.

I'd never seen my brother look so angry.

"What am I doing here? Last I checked, I lived here. Yeah, you thought I'd be at the lake, huh? Funny thing is someone mentioned that they saw you two home a few weeks ago, and you appeared to be very much *together.* Not the way a guy looks out for his best friend's little sister. They seemed surprised I didn't know." Cade's words slurred and I knew he was drunk, which was not going to help the situation.

"Dude, let me explain. We were going to talk to you after Christmas." Gray moved to stand in front of me and his hand came behind him to rest on my forearm.

Always the protector.

"How long?" Cade shouted, moving just inches from Gray's face.

"It's complicated. Let's go for a walk and talk this out."

"It's complicated? What the fuck does that mean? Why the fuck do we need to go for a walk?" Cade poked his finger hard into Gray's chest and I was not staying put any longer.

"You're being so ridiculous. Why don't you ask yourself why we felt the need to hide this from you? I'm a grown-ass woman, Cade. Stop treating me like a baby. And this is your best friend. Why can't you just be happy for us?"

"G, stop," Gray said, moving to stand in front of me again.

"You're not a grown-ass woman, if this is who you're choosing to date." Cade's voice was getting increasingly louder, and he was more agitated now that I'd spoken up.

"Fuck you. How dare you say that!" I screamed at him.

"Jesus Christ. You're fucking her, aren't you. *You fucked my sister,* you son of a bitch." Cade lunged forward and Gray gripped him by the shoulders.

"Gigi, get in the house," Gray said, his voice remained calm. "Don't talk about your fucking sister that way, dude."

"Don't you speak of my fucking sister in any way," Cade shouted, and his words were so loud I swore they ricocheted off the house. He turned and punched my car, which was parked in the driveway beside him. "Did you fuck my sister, you piece of shit? Tell me right now!"

"Get in the fucking house, G." Gray turned to look at me, and Cade dove on top of him with no warning. I stumbled out of the way. Cade punched him as he sat on top of him, and Gray did not fight back. He just lay there taking it. Cade threw at least three punches with absolutely no resistance from Gray.

"Stop it," I screamed.

The door flew open and my father rushed outside. "What in the hell is going on?" He yanked my brother off of Gray and looked between them.

"You want to hit me again and again, go for it," Gray said, his voice clipped and cool as he moved to his feet and wiped the blood from his nose. I moved to stand beside him and reached for his hand. "I'm in love with your sister, dude. This is not how I wanted to tell you. But you sure as shit didn't make me feel like there was any good way."

"You're fucking dead to me! We're done." Cade's voice could wake the dead as he shouted at both of us. My mother rushed outside to see what was going on. "Get in the fucking house, Gigi."

"Don't tell me what to do. You don't get to call the shots. I love him, whether you support it or not does not change that."

Cade lunged forward again, breaking free of my father, and took another shot at Gray who stumbled back, and I fell down right alongside him. I hit the pavement hard and heard my head crack against the cement.

"Jesus Christ, Cade. Get in the goddamn house. You're drunk and out of control." I'd never heard my father sound so angry. Cade stormed in the house and my parents were at my side, as Gray pulled me against his chest as he sat on the pavement.

"Are you all right?" he asked, feeling the back of my head and looking down to see blood on his hand. "Fuck, G. You're bleeding."

"Oh my god," my mom cried out. "What do we do, Bradley?"

"Go get a towel and some ice. Gray, I don't know what's

going on. Cade is clearly intoxicated, but I think you need to go home. I can't focus on Gigi with you two fighting."

"Don't blame him, Dad." My words broke on a sob, and my head pounded as Gray lifted me to my feet. "This is not his fault. He didn't do anything."

"I don't care whose fault it is. I need to make sure you're okay. We can work all of this out later."

"Your dad's right. Let him take you inside and check you out." Gray stroked my hair as he studied me before turning to my dad. "Will you call me and let me know how she is?"

"Of course, Son. I'm sorry about this."

My father hurried me into the house, and Gray disappeared into the darkness.

And he took a piece of my broken heart with him.

twenty-two

. . .

Gray

I WALKED into my mom's house after trying to clean up my face in the car, but I didn't have much luck. I tried to sneak in through the kitchen, but Simon was there, and Mariana was handing him a cocktail. My mother stood behind him and gasped when she saw me.

"Oh my gosh, Gray. What happened?" Mom hurried over to me, and Mariana rushed out of the room and I imagined she was grabbing a towel.

"I'm fine. It's not a big deal." My face stung, as Cade had gotten in several good shots. I didn't hit him back. He needed to get this out and I deserved what he served up.

The truth was, there was never going to be a good time to tell Cade about Gigi and me. If I'd told him in the beginning before anything even happened, he would have reacted the same fucking way. My best friend was a stubborn ass and he always had been. The bottom line was that Cade didn't think I was good enough for his sister. And he was probably right. But it wasn't going to stop me from trying, even at the cost of losing my friendship with him. That's why I finally realized I had to tell him, because regardless of the outcome, I wasn't walking away from Gigi.

And it sucked. Because he was family, and I loved the dude more than life itself.

But I loved his sister more.

And if he forced me to choose—I would choose her. I hoped it wouldn't come to that, but after the way he reacted tonight, I doubted we would ever be able to repair things. I kept checking my phone to see if Gigi or her father had texted me, but I hadn't heard anything yet. I couldn't believe she'd ended up hurt in this mess. I should have forced her inside before things escalated. I was pissed at myself for letting that shit go down in front of her.

Mariana brought a wet towel over and set an icepack beside me as she started cleaning up my face. "My goodness, you're going to be hurting tomorrow."

"Simon, can you grab some Tylenol from the medicine cabinet?" my mother asked as she gripped my hand.

"You want me to get it?" I could hear the disdain in his tone. "I think maybe it's best that he suffer a little. Maybe that will teach him a lesson to stay out of trouble."

"Simon," my mother hissed. "I did not ask for your opinion. I asked you to do something for me and I'm still waiting."

"Mom, let it go," I said, as Mariana dabbed at the gash on my cheek and I flinched.

My stepfather slammed something on the table, and I assumed it was the bottle of Tylenol. The douchebag didn't like being tasked, especially not for me.

"You coddle him too much," Simon barked.

Jesus. If I were any less coddled someone would report my mother to CPS. It was a strange phenomenon growing up with so much money, yet zero emotional support. And I knew I was fortunate that at least I had that. But in all honesty, I'd trade the money for a little love all day long. Less shit and more care would have gone a long way. And I wasn't a whiny bitch, I could deal with the hand that I was dealt, but I wasn't going to sit by and let him call me coddled. I took offense to that.

I looked up at Simon and shook my head. "You don't have a fucking clue who I am."

"Well, let me guess. You got drunk tonight and probably got in a fight with someone who will come knocking at my door tomorrow and it will be my mess to clean up. I'll have to bail your ass out. You're just like your father, Gray," Simon said, and for the first time, I realized his words were slurring.

Judgmental prick.

"For your information, I am completely sober. But you, on the other hand, might want to start taking it easy on the sauce. Glass houses, and all that shit, Simon." My phone vibrated and I looked down at the screen.

Bradley ~ We just got to the hospital. Gigi needs a couple stitches in the back of her head, but she should be okay. She's filled us in on the gist of what went on tonight, and I need you to know that we do not think any of this is your fault. I'm not happy with my son at the moment, but once he sobers up, I will speak to him. His behavior was unacceptable. Merry Christmas, Gray.

I pushed to my feet and kissed my mother and Mariana on the cheek. "Thanks for your help. I've got to go."

"What? It's Christmas Eve. Where are you going?" my mother asked as she studied me.

"I'm tired of being somewhere I'm not wanted." I turned to face Simon. "I'm sorry that you married a woman with a kid. And I'm sorry that you hate my father. He's made a lot of mistakes, but just because I want him to get better does not mean that I think what he's done is okay. I am a lot of things, Simon. But I am not my dad. And I don't need to prove that to you anymore. As long as I know who I am, I'll be all right. So, keep being good to my mom, Bea, and Penn, and we won't have a problem."

My stepfather stared at me but didn't speak, which was a

first. I was tired of battling the man. Tired of feeling like I didn't belong. And now that I'd fucked things up with Cade, I didn't belong at the Jacobs' house either.

But I belonged with Gigi, regardless of who thought so. And yes, this wouldn't make for a good Christmas, but I didn't fucking care. I was glad it was out in the open. I was tired of hiding who I was. Who I wanted to be. The one person I cared about most, Gigi, knew me. That's all that mattered to me.

"Are you going to the Jacobs'?" my mother asked, and Mariana stood behind her with tears streaming down her face. There were many times that she'd stepped up as more of a mother than my own mom had. But we all made choices and we all had our own struggles, so I wasn't judging my mother. I just knew that I didn't want to be here.

"Don't worry about it, Mom. I'm fine. I'm pretty good at surviving on my own. I've been doing it for a long ass time." I kissed the top of her head and walked out.

I drove straight to the hospital and made my way into the emergency room and found Katie Jacobs standing in front of a machine full of snacks. She had a pile on the chair beside her and she looked up when I walked in.

She set down the cookies in her hand with the rest of the snacks and hurried toward me. She hugged me so tight it was hard to breathe. It was the first time I'd relaxed in hours.

We stood like that for much longer than usual before she pulled back and swiped at the tears streaming down her face. She leaned up and ran her fingers over the cut on my cheek.

"You look terrible," she said over a chuckle.

I laughed. "Thanks. How's Gigi?"

"She'll be all right. She's in back with Bradley getting stitched up now. I think her heart hurts a lot more than her head."

I nodded. "Yeah. I get that. I'm sorry we didn't tell you."

"You don't need to be sorry, Gray. I know you love my

daughter. I think I knew it before either of you two did." She reached for the snacks and handed me a few to carry as we walked through the waiting room.

"We wanted to make sure it was something that would last before we told you guys—well, especially Cade."

She turned to look at me when we pushed through a set of doors to find Gigi. "I think you and Gigi are just the two people he's closest to in the world, and he doesn't know how to handle it. And trust me, I'm not making excuses for him. He acted like a jackass. He'll come around. You know how he is."

I wasn't so sure she was right about that, but I nodded. It was Christmas fucking Eve and we were in the fucking emergency room because Cade and I had gone to blows. I didn't need to add any more drama to this mess.

We stepped into the room and found Gigi and Bradley getting her things together to leave. She rushed into my arms when she saw me. "You're here."

"Of course, I'm here. *You're here.* Where else would I be?" I laughed as I wrapped my arms around her.

"Thanks for coming, Gray." Bradley clapped me on the back. "We'll give you two a minute."

"How do you feel?" I asked, pulling back to look at her. I turned her around and lifted her hair to see a small patch at the bottom of her skull shaved and eight or nine stitches were there. "Jesus. That's a big gash."

"Thankfully I have a lot of hair, so Dr. Darby said no one will be able to see it."

"I'm sorry you got hurt. I guess that went about as bad as it could have gone, huh?" I said as I studied her.

"He was drunk. He'll regret it in the morning. I'm so pissed at him I can't even see straight. The things he said to you, oh my gosh. Who does he think he is?"

"Listen, G. Your brother loves you so damn much, and I get that. Don't be too hard on him. He would never intentionally hurt you, we both know that. He's going to beat himself up something fierce for you getting hurt. Cut him some slack, okay?"

Her sapphire blues searched mine, and a little line formed between her brows as panic set in. "What? Where are you going?"

"I'm going to head back to school. Your brother needs time, and I can't be at Simon's anymore. I'd rather be alone than at that house," I said, resting my forehead against hers.

"I'll come with you. We can leave tonight."

"No, G. Do this for me. Stay here and mend things with Cade. Will you do that for me?" I asked.

She pulled back and tears streamed down her face. "Of course. I'd do anything for you. But I don't want you to be alone on Christmas."

"I've never cared much for the holidays, you know that." I laughed, trying to lighten the situation and the sadness I saw in her eyes. "Do this for me, please. I'll see you in two weeks, okay?"

The tears continued to fall. Her little hands settled on each of my cheeks. "You're not leaving me, are you?"

"Never, baby. I just can't stand the thought of coming between you and your brother. You need this time together, and I'll be waiting for you. I promise."

"Okay," she croaked.

"There's nothing to cry about. It's finally out there. The worst is over." I wanted to make her feel better, but I wasn't sure if that was true. Because if Cade never forgave me, it would be the worst thing to ever happen to me. But I'd still do it all over again for her.

I reached for her hand and we intertwined our fingers and I led her out of the room. Katie and Bradley stood there eating M&M's and they smiled when they saw us. We walked out to the parking lot and I turned and hugged them each goodbye.

"You know you can come back to the house," Katie said, as she reached up to touch my cheek.

"Not now, but I'll be back. Merry Christmas."

"I love you, Gray. You know that, right?" Katie asked.

"I do. I love you, too."

Bradley cocked his head to the side. "Are you going to your mom's house?"

"Nah. I'm going to head back to school early. I'll see you soon."

Bradley and Katie exchanged a look but nodded and got in the car.

"I don't want you to go." Gigi lunged at me one more time.

"You worry too much, baby. I'll call you in the morning, okay?" I needed to get her in the car and get out of there before she convinced me to let her come with me.

"Okay. I love you." She climbed into the car and I walked to my truck.

I started the engine and got on the road.

It's not the way I planned on spending Christmas.

But I was completely at peace with it.

I made it back late to the house and spent most of the drive on the phone with Gigi. She hadn't talked to Cade yet as he'd passed out drunk while they were at the hospital, and I knew he'd be waking up with a bitch of a hangover and a lot of guilt over his sister getting hurt. I was glad she was there, though she tried to convince me that she should drive here tomorrow, and I made her promise me again that she would stay and fix things with her brother.

I could handle Cade not forgiving me because I deserved it. But I couldn't handle coming between him and his sister.

They loved one another so much, and they needed to work through this.

I took a quick shower and crashed. My sheets still smelled like Gigi, and that made being here tolerable.

I slept late and woke up to a bunch of messages from my girl. There was also one from my dad, Mariana, Katie Jacobs, and Wren wishing me a Merry Christmas. My phone rang and Gigi's name flashed across the screen. It was a FaceTime call and I waited for her face to come in focus while I propped my pillows on my bed to sit up.

"Hey," I said. "Merry Christmas, beautiful."

"You're finally up. It's late. Merry Christmas. I miss you," she said, frowning at the screen.

"What's wrong? How's your head?"

"My head is fine, Gray. I just hate that you're there and I'm here."

"How was Christmas morning? Have you talked to your brother?" I asked.

"He tried. He only apologized for my head injury. I kind of still hate him, so not much more has been said." She fiddled with the heart charm that hung from her necklace and I smiled. I loved that she'd never taken it off since the moment I'd given it to her.

"Baby. Talk to him. Do not come back until you two are okay. You got it?"

"Why are you being so nice to him after what he did to you? He's such an asshole," she said.

"Because I've been an asshole enough times to know when someone deserves a pass. Give him a pass, G."

She rolled her eyes. "We had a visitor this morning."

"Oh yeah? Who?"

"Your mom." She raised her eyebrows and cocked her head to the side.

"My mom? On Christmas morning? What did she want?"

"She wanted to see you."

I shook my head. "Jesus. That's… surprising. I'm shocked Simon allowed that."

"She looked like she hadn't slept and said she was worried about you. She asked Cade if he knew what had happened to you last night."

"Shit. What did he say?" I asked.

"Keep in mind he's extremely hungover and no one in this house is speaking much to him. He just stared at her and shook his head before I asked him to leave us alone. I told her that you and my brother had a disagreement and that Cade was an idiot." She finally smiled and shook her head. "She thought you were here. I told her you went back to school."

I scrubbed a hand up the back of my neck.

"All right. I'll give her a call later. I'm going to call my grandparents and let them know I'm not coming by today."

"Okay. Will you call me later?" She looked tired and sad.

"Of course. Go talk to your brother."

She nodded. "I love you, Gray."

"Love you more."

I pushed up to walk to the bathroom to take a piss and brush my teeth. I glanced in the mirror to see a nasty cut and a bruise beneath my left eye. I'd been in fights before, and this wasn't terrible. Bruises healed. And hopefully time would heal the wounds between my best friend and me. I dialed my grandparents and they were disappointed they wouldn't see me today, but I promised to come home and visit soon. I called my dad next, and he told me he'd be moving to a halfway house tomorrow as he had completed the program. Well, he'd basically run out of money. Was he ready for the real world? Probably not. But at some point, he would have to find out if he would sink or swim.

My LSAT prep books had arrived in the mail and I pulled them out and got to work. May as well take advantage of the time and the quiet.

A few hours later, I realized it was well past lunchtime

and grabbed my keys to go pick up some food. I didn't know if anything would be open on Christmas Day, but I couldn't be the only asshole who was hungry. I pulled the door open and startled when I saw my mother walking up the steps to the fraternity house.

"Mom?"

"Hey. Merry Christmas," she said, and she held up a bag. "I have barbecue. Are you hungry?"

"What? Yeah. Come in. What are you doing here? Where are the girls?"

My mother had never been to campus. It just wasn't her thing. She was busy with Simon and the girls, and I always just went home. It had never bothered me—*it is what it is*. But I'd be lying if I said I wasn't happy to see her standing on my front porch.

She stepped inside and I led her to the kitchen. "I wasn't going to let you be alone on Christmas. No matter how many mistakes I've made in the past, I wasn't going to make another one."

I nodded and grabbed some utensils and two bottles of water and set them on the table. I wasn't sure how to respond. "You didn't need to leave the girls."

"You're my child too, Gray." She shook her head when she dropped in the seat beside me. "Simon can handle them just fine on his own. What you said to him last night, well, I want you to know he heard you. He has been drinking too much. We'd gotten into it a few months ago when he made that effort to go to dinner with you, but he's been falling back into those old habits over the holidays and it's not acceptable. And he can be a judgmental ass."

I barked out a laugh. My mom never cussed, and she never said anything negative about her husband.

"That's putting it mildly." I chuckled as I pulled the two containers out of the bag. The smell of barbecue sauce had my stomach rumbling. "But I'm glad he heard me. I can't do it anymore, Mom. I can't be there letting him take out his anger toward Dad on me. I get it. Dad fucked up. But I don't need Simon telling me that every fucking time I'm home."

She nodded and a tear ran down her face. "I agree, dear, and you're right. I should have spoken up a long time ago, and I'm sorry for that. But I will be more vocal with him from now on."

"Oh yeah? You're going to start putting Simon in his place?" I teased.

"I'm here, aren't I?" she asked as she swiped at her tears.

"You are. And I appreciate it."

"Merry Christmas, Gray. I love you."

"Love you too, Mom," I said, and we both dug into our food.

"Now tell me what's going on with you and Cade."

We spent the next two hours talking. I told her about Gigi and about my fight with Cade. She listened and she offered advice. She said she'd always thought there was something there with Cade's little sister and me, and we laughed about it. We talked about my father and his road to recovery. His past mistakes and my hopes for his future. It was the most we'd spoken in a long time, and it felt damn good.

Because even after all this time, it turns out I still needed my mom.

And she'd finally shown up when I needed her most.

twenty-three

• • •

Gigi

"CAN I TALK TO YOU?" Cade asked as he stood in my doorway and leaned against the frame. It had been three days since Christmas, and we had still barely spoken.

"I don't know. Are you going to throw a temper tantrum and punch someone, or can you have an adult conversation?"

"Come on, Gigi. He's my best friend. You're my little sister." He dropped down to sit beside me on my bed.

"So what, Cade? I get it. We should have told you. But do you see why we didn't? Look how you reacted. And Gray knew you'd never be okay with it. Trust me, he tried everything not to give in to the feelings we have for one another, and that's because of you. Because he loves you so goddamn much. And you treated him like shit. You act like he's unworthy."

"You don't know how many girls he's been with," he hissed, pushing to his feet and pacing my room.

"Once again, you're wrong. I know who Gray is. He's told me everything. I don't care about his past. I care about now. And how about you? You've been with a lot of girls, does that mean that Camilla shouldn't give you a chance? You're such a hypocrite."

He gasped and turned to face me. "He shouldn't have kept it from me. He should have talked to me about it."

I nodded. "Okay. So, had he come to you and said that he wanted to date me, what would you have said? Be honest with yourself, Cade."

"Fuck. I would have said no. But it's not because I don't think Gray is a great guy. Jesus. He's my best fucking friend. This is what I tried to explain to Camilla. I obviously think he's fucking awesome. He's like a brother to me."

"Yet you attacked him before you let him explain. People change."

"He was supposed to look out for you. He's a player. It's not going to last." He ran a hand through his hair.

"You're wrong. We love each other. Our only issue is my brother is being a jackass," I said.

"If he hurts you, I'll never forgive him."

"Do you hear yourself? You aren't even giving him a chance. This is not new, Cade. It's just new for you. And you can either get on board or lose both of us," I said, pushing to my feet because I was done with this conversation.

"Wow. You're taking this the whole way. You're that serious about him?"

"You know what surprises me? That you don't get it. He's your best friend, and you aren't willing to give him any credit. He's always been there for you. When you thought Camilla was pregnant," I whispered because obviously that was a secret that my parents didn't know about, "he jumped in his car and was there for you immediately. It didn't matter that he was in the middle of finals, or that he was dealing with so much stuff with his dad. He dropped everything for you. And you didn't even give him a chance when he tried to talk to you. Maybe you need to learn how to be a good friend and quit judging everyone else," I said, my gaze locking with his before I stormed out the door.

You could lead a horse to water… but maybe it would be better to just hit him over the head with a bucket.

My brother needed the latter.

I met the girls at The Rusty Pelican for lunch where Jett's mom, Mae worked. We loved her and had been eating here every week since we started high school. She wanted to hear all that was going on with us after our first semester at school, obviously she talked to Addy all the time because she and Jett were always together. But she had a million questions for the rest of us. We hugged her goodbye and made our way outside.

"Who wants to go with me to Lenny's for some hot chocolate?" Addy asked as she rubbed her hands together.

Lenny Balsalcki owned The Chocolate Fountain right down the street from the diner in town.

"I'll go," we all said in unison and laughed.

"Well, if it isn't my favorite Willows," Lenny said, surprising all of us because he was rarely full of holiday cheer. He was probably the most pessimistic person I'd ever known. The glass was not only half-empty… it was drier than dirt.

"You're in an awfully good mood," Addy said as she went around the counter and hugged him. They'd always had a special friendship.

"Am I? Well, it has nothing to do with the fact that the donut king next door just got written up by the health department for not being sanitary. The Chocolate Fountain has always received exemplary marks for cleanliness. That two-bit hustler thinks he can make his shop *'dog friendly',*" he said, using two fingers on each hand to show us quotation marks. "Well, karma is a biotch with a capital B. Don't you forget that, girls."

We laughed. He was one of my favorite people in town. We placed our order and found a table in the back.

"So how is it going with your brother? Any better?" Maura asked. We hadn't covered my drama just yet, as we'd been discussing the fact that Maura had gotten in a little fender bender this morning, with none other than Crew Carlisle. The Carlisles were enemies with the Bensons, Maura's family, and they had a long, bitter family history that no one really understood. She'd told us that he'd been a complete ass to her and recommended that the cops arrest her. *For a fender bender.* Thankfully Officer Powell was Maura's neighbor, and he found the whole thing hilarious and he'd sent her on her way in a huff.

"It's fine. We're talking a little more. But I'm still mad at him for how he's treating Gray."

"Your brother is lucky he's so fine. It almost makes me forget how freaking judgmental he is. Gray is like a brother to him and he's willing to throw their friendship away because you two are in love? He's ridiculous." Coco rolled her eyes dramatically and clapped when Lenny set down our hot chocolates before hustling back to greet some customers that walked in.

"How is Gray doing with everything?"

"He's been studying for the LSAT and insistent that I stay here and work things out with my brother. He made me promise. But I don't know that I'll ever get through to Cade. He's a stubborn ox. And I just want to go back to school and be with Gray."

"I think it's sweet that he wants to make sure you and Cade are okay. Who would have ever thought Gray Baldwin would be such a sweet boyfriend," Ivy said, shaking her head and smiling before scooping a huge pile of whipped cream on her spoon and devouring it.

"I know. He's so stinking cute with you. I love it," Maura said.

"So, fix things with Cade and then you can go back to school early and enjoy your hot, sexy boyfriend. Damn, I need to get me one of those." Coco closed her eyes and smiled, and we all laughed.

"Your parents are totally fine with everything, right?" Addy asked.

"Yes. I would have liked to talk to them myself, but thanks to Cade, I'm fairly certain they know we're sleeping together. I mean, why else would my mom suddenly feel the need to take me to the doctor and get me on the pill?" My mother had *the talk* with me a few days ago and insisted on taking me to see her gynecologist. I was fairly certain she'd overheard Cade's outburst about Gray and me and assumed we were sleeping together. *Thanks, brother.* "But yes, they are really happy that Gray and I are together. They love him. They can't believe the way Cade is behaving."

"He'll come around," Maura said. "And I think it's sweet your mom took you to the doctor. My mom would never talk to me about sex or boyfriends. All of that makes her so uncomfortable. She's so old school."

"Please. Have you met Cricket? She would never utter such nonsense," Coco said in her haughtiest voice and rolled her eyes. "She thinks sex is dirty. I'm actually shocked she has two kids. I'm guessing those are the only two times she's done it."

We burst out laughing.

"Maybe Cricket's a closet sexy girl," Ivy whispered as if she had just said the most sinister thing in the world.

"A closet sexy girl? Did you just call my mom a whore?" Coco said as tears streamed down her face and we continued to laugh some more.

Time with my girls always made me feel better. And they were right. I needed to fix things with Cade so I could get back to Gray. I missed him so much, and I was tired of letting Cade control the situation.

We finished our drinks and Lenny walked over. "All done, ladies?"

"Yes. We wish there was a Chocolate Fountain at school. I crave these when I'm not home," Addy said, smiling up at the older man.

"I'm sure. That cafeteria food is terrible. Filled with chemicals. Hell, it's a racket. They charge kids a fortune for crappy food. The world has gone to hell in a handbasket, I swear it has."

"Hey. What happened to cheerful Lenny?" Addy teased.

"Cheerful Lenny does not exist, my dear. Yes, I'm happy that weasel got served some papers, sure. But that doesn't make up for the Howards coming in here this morning and stiffing me on my tip. They said that I should try being a joy spreader. Can you imagine that?" He shook his head as we all pushed to our feet and tried to hide our smiles.

"Joy spreaders get old. We like you how you are, Len." Coco patted him on the back.

"You know what they say about the Howards, don't you?" He leaned in and whispered, a town gossip down to his toes.

"Do tell," Ivy said, her eyes wide as saucers.

"They're hoarders. You know… like you see on TV. They have piles of crap everywhere. It's a serious addiction."

Addy couldn't contain her laughter. "I've babysat for the Howards and I promise you they are not hoarders, Lenny. Their house is immaculate."

"Why do you always have to ruin the fun with all that sunshine, Addy?" he barked and even he couldn't hide his smile.

"Love you, Len," she said, leaning over to hug the crotchety old man. We all followed suit and hugged him goodbye.

"Stay warm, girls. There's a nasty bug going around. My cousin's daughter had to have her leg amputated last week because of it. You wouldn't want to be hobbling around on one foot, would you?"

We waved goodbye and practically fell out the door laughing.

"It's the people like Lenny that make me miss Willow Springs," Coco said, wrapping an arm around me. "All that gossip and negativity reminds me of home."

"Yeah. I love being home with you guys again." Ivy interlocked her arm with Maura and Addy, and we made our way down the street.

Nothing could beat time with my girls in Willow Springs.

Aside from time with my boyfriend.

I had a relationship to repair so I could get back to him.

And that's exactly what I planned to do. Starting today.

When I got home, it was quiet. My dad was at work and my mom was at a fundraiser meeting for the Willow Springs annual luncheon. I saw Cade's car in the driveway, and I peeked in his room, but he wasn't there. When I got to my room, he was sitting on my bed staring at a photo album of us when we were kids.

"Hey," I said, walking in and dropping to sit beside him.

"Hi. I hope you don't mind. I found it on your shelves."

"Of course not." I glanced down and laughed at the picture where Cade and I had cake all over our faces after my third birthday party. On the next page was one with Gray and Cade and me all covered in cake and icing.

He was there.

He'd always been there.

Cade closed the book and dropped back to lie on the bed. His legs hung off as his feet were still on the ground. He covered his face with his hands and groaned. "I fucked up, didn't I. Why do I always overreact?"

"Because it's who you are." I raised a brow and smiled when he looked up at me.

"It'll suck if it doesn't work out, because he's my best

friend and you're my sister. But you're right, G, he's been a really good friend to me. I just know all the dumb shit we've both done over the years."

"But I know about it too. Gray and I don't have secrets. And why can't you trust that I can make decisions for myself?"

"I don't know. Camilla says I'm mad because apparently I'm a control freak, and I didn't see this coming," he said, pushing up to sit.

"She's a wise woman."

"I guess you're right. She saw something there with you and Gray the first time she met you. And Mom told me she always saw it too. I guess I'm the idiot."

"No, you're not. I didn't see it. I was irritated with him more than I wasn't. But he said he always knew." I cocked my head to the side and smiled.

"You really love him, don't you?" he asked.

"I really do."

"And he didn't pressure you into anything?" he asked, and he looked away.

I waited until he looked up and my gaze locked with his. "Never once. He tried everything to push me away. Even after we were together, he wouldn't do, um, things…" I hesitated and he covered his ears.

"Gigi. I do not need the details."

"But you do, Cade. You need to know that he hasn't pushed me to do anything. Not ever. He's been so careful and loving. He's the one who was worried about you—much more than I was."

He barked out a laugh. "Oh really. And why is that?"

"Because it's not your business. Yes, we should have told you when it first started. But honestly, we've both never had a serious relationship, so announcing it to your brother when you don't even know if it's going anywhere seemed ridiculous. We wanted to give it a chance before we added that pressure, you know?"

"Damn. I get it. Camilla and I didn't tell anyone when we first started dating. Hell, I wouldn't even admit it to myself. I never thought I could be in a relationship like this."

"And can you imagine when you were first figuring things out if you had to get approval from your sister or your best friend?" I rolled my eyes.

"But Gray wrestled with it, didn't he? He's a loyal fucking bastard to the core. Fuck. I messed up." He fell back again and covered his face.

"You did. And he needs a friend right now, Cade. His dad is back out and living in a halfway house. Simon was a royal asshole to him after your fight because he assumed Gray got into trouble. So, he went back to school by himself. On Christmas Eve."

"Jesus Christ. I fucking hate myself. Why haven't you gone back yet?"

"Because he made me promise I would repair things with you before I went back. He's so worried about coming between our relationship."

"I suck."

"You really do," I said, over my laughter. "And he's the only one who isn't mad at you. He keeps sticking up for you, which pisses me off."

Cade sat up and pushed to his feet. "All right. Are we good?"

That was abrupt. "Um, sure?"

"That's not what I mean. I know what I need to do." He paced in front of my bed.

"Okay. Well, I think we've made some headway. I'm going to head back to school tomorrow."

"Can you hold off a day or two?"

"What? Why?"

"Because I'm going tonight? I need to make things right

with Gray, and it will be better if I can apologize without you there. I need to fix this. Can you let me do that?"

I smiled and lunged at him, hugging him tight. "Of course, I can. That will mean a lot to him."

"It'll mean a lot to me." He smirked before walking toward the door. "And don't call him and tell him I'm coming. Let me do this my way."

"Fine. But if you touch him again, you'll be dead to me."

"Oh, it's like that, is it?" He knocked on my doorframe and raised a brow.

"It's totally like that," I said.

Because it was.

But I'd be lying if I said I wasn't thrilled that my brother was finally being rational. I wanted things to go back to normal for him and Gray.

And it seemed like that was finally going to happen.

twenty-four

. . .

Gray

GIGI AND CADE had repaired things and I was relieved. It was the first time that I'd talked to her that she wasn't angry at him. I didn't know if he and I would get there any time soon, but I hoped we would. But for now, this was better than the alternative. I needed to make sure she and her brother weren't fighting over me. I couldn't live with that shit.

I shot Wren another text asking if he'd seen my dad. Wren had called me last night and said he'd been out with Mae Stone but had received a call that my father had been at the fight club and was hanging with those two dudes that had come looking for him once before. How many times could we do this?

My phone rang and I picked up when I saw it was Wren calling.

"Hey, any word?"

"It's not good, Gray. There was a big upset last night at the fight club. The guy that was a sure thing did not win, and a lot of people lost a shit ton of money. Your dad apparently bet on the losing guy and is in trouble. He's fucking around with the wrong people. He's playing with money he doesn't have, and I don't know how long I can protect him from this shit."

"Jesus. What is he even betting with? Credit cards? I mean, he sold his Rolex. Did you give him that cash yet?"

"No. He's been avoiding me since he moved into the halfway house. Obviously, he went back to placing bets with these guys and he didn't want me to know. But Gray, the stakes are a lot higher this time, from what I'm being told."

"What does that mean?" I asked, dropping to sit on my bed and scrubbing a hand down my face.

Here we go. It just seemed to get worse each time.

More booze.

More drugs.

More money.

"He's got thirty-five hundred bucks left from the sale of the watch. He has no assets, no car. He's sucked your grand-parents dry, and I've loaned him a chunk of money myself. But from what I'm hearing, he bet twenty-five grand last night and lost. I don't know what the fuck he's thinking. And these are bad dudes. I'm going to close up shop for a while because these guys are hanging out here all the time now—and they're bad news."

"Holy shit. Twenty-five grand? What the fuck? So, they're after him? Where the fuck could he be?" I asked, and I fought back the lump in my throat. I could go to Simon. I could beg for the money. But when would it end?

"I don't know, but I know they won't stop until they find him."

"All right. I'll come home. I'll help you look for him," I said.

"Hold tight, Gray. I don't want you getting mixed up with these guys. I've got a few of my employees out looking for your dad. I can have him hide out at my place until we figure something out. It's a lot of cash. Let me see what I can come up with."

"Okay. Maybe he could hide out here?"

"I think keeping your father away from you might be a better idea. I don't want you messed up with these guys."

"Fuck. I don't know what to do, Wren. Thanks for looking for him. I'm sorry about this."

"Don't apologize for the sins of your father, Gray. That is not on you. I speak from experience on this. Just keep your phone on you, and I'll keep you posted." Wren was a man many people in Willow Springs whispered about. He had his hands in a lot of pots, but he'd always been a stand-up guy to me and my dad. But the rumor mill was always flowing back home, and everyone had something to say about Wren.

"All right." I disconnected the call and buried my face in my hands.

I called Gigi and filled her in. Hell, I hated telling her how fucked up my dad was, but I needed her to tell me what to do. I trusted her. She told me to listen to Wren and hang tight. She was heading back to school tomorrow or the next day, and I couldn't wait for her to be here.

There was a knock at my bedroom door and Ricky peeked his head in. He and two other dudes were the only ones who had come back early. Most people were home with their families enjoying the holiday break. We weren't all that lucky. Although having my mom show up and spend two days here at a hotel had been an unexpected surprise. We'd talked about a lot of things and though we still had a way to go on repairing our relationship, we were both willing to try, and that was progress.

"Sorry to bother you, Gray. There's someone here to see you. He said to tell you he was your *dickhead best friend.* His words, not mine." Ricky shrugged.

"What?" I pushed up and saw Cade standing beside him.

"Can I come in?" he asked, and I'd never seen my best friend look nervous, but he did.

"Yeah. Of course." I nodded to Ricky to let him know it was good, and Cade stepped inside and shut the door.

He dropped to sit on my desk chair and faced me. "I was an idiot."

I chuckled. "No, you weren't. She's your sister. I get it. I should have told you."

"There would have been no way to tell me, and we both know it. As my sister so politely said, I'm an arrogant asshole. I fucked up, brother. And I need you to know that it wasn't because I don't think you're a good guy. Hell, you've been my best friend my entire life. It was never about that."

"Dude. Stop. I get it. Hell, I don't think I'm good enough for her either. But I'm damn well going to try." I dropped to sit on my bed to face him. This visit was a surprise, and I was happy about it. But my mind was reeling about my dad.

"Gray, that's not it. It was never about that. I just didn't think you would want to be in a committed relationship, and I didn't want you to fuck over my sister. It's Gigi, you know?" He looked so guilt-ridden, I wasn't used to that from him. Cade was a lot of things, but apologetic and humble were not the norm for him.

"Brother, listen to me. I get it. I understand why you thought that. I was worried about it at first too. But… the more I was around her, the more I knew I couldn't stay away."

"That's the thing. It wasn't my place to judge. Hell, I was a player myself. And I turned my shit around for Camilla. I shouldn't have said the things I said to you. I was wrong, Gray. You're one of the best people I know, and I should have trusted you."

Hell, I had not expected this.

"I appreciate it. And I understand it. Had I known what I know now—I would have come to you from the beginning," I admitted.

"And what do you know now?" he asked, quirking a brow in challenge.

"I know that I love your sister so much it's painful. There

isn't anything I wouldn't do for her. She's all I want, all I see." I shrugged.

"Okay, that's enough. I believe you. I do not need any more details about your obsession with my sister." He laughed and pushed to his feet. "I'm sorry, brother."

I stood and he pulled me in for a hug, clapping me hard on the back like the asshole he was.

"We're good," I said when we pulled apart. "Stop beating yourself up."

"All right. But if you hurt her, I will tackle your ass again."

Now we both laughed. "You do realize I didn't fight back. I let you take your shots because I had them coming. Next time you won't be so lucky."

"Yeah. I still see the bruising from my badassery. Nothing like fighting with your best friend and then causing your little sister to go to the hospital and get stitches. You can only imagine how Katie and Bradley are feeling about me right now." He shook his head and dropped back down to sit in the chair. His parents were two of the coolest people I knew, so having them disappointed in you would not be easy.

"That bad, huh? Gigi said you guys made up?"

"Yeah. She called me out on my shit, and I finally listened. She was right. She usually is. And Camilla wants a fucking medal because she called it the first time she met you guys. And my parents think I should cut back on the booze for a bit, which I'm doing. Taking a page from the Gray Baldwin pussy-whipped motherfucker book."

I barked out a laugh. "You're such an asshole. Come on, let's go eat. I'm starving. I'll fill you in on the shit show that is my father over lunch."

And just like that, things were looking up.

After filling Cade in on my father, he decided to spend the night. There were tons of open rooms at the frat house, and he didn't want to leave when we still hadn't heard anything about my dad. I appreciated it. I was happy we'd repaired things, and there was no one I wanted in my corner more than Cade. The dude had always had my back, and I counted on that.

I got up and called Wren. He said they hadn't had any luck finding him, and I didn't miss the concern in his voice. Cade was using my shower because he said the communal bathroom should be shut down for how unsanitary it was. I'd laughed because there was no doubt he was right about that.

I talked to Gigi and she was happy that Cade and I were back on track. As much as I liked having him here, I was ready for him to leave so my girl could come back. I missed the fuck out of her and seeing her face on a phone screen was not cutting it.

"Dude, you live like a king with this fucking shower. This is a sweet setup." Cade was dressed but was still towel drying his wet hair.

"I am a fucking king. Get used to it." I tossed my LSAT book on my bed because I was having a hard time focusing with my dad missing.

"No word yet?"

"No. Where the fuck could he be? I called my grandparents and I didn't want to panic them, but I thought maybe he was hiding out there."

"What did they say?" he asked, sitting down to pull on his socks and boots.

"They haven't seen him." My phone vibrated and I reached for it.

"If that's my sister again, I am putting you in the pussy-whipped Hall of Fame. Dude, you two talk a hundred times a day. It's ridiculous." He rolled his eyes.

I glanced down at my phone and my heart raced.

What the actual fuck?

I held up my phone as Cade read the message.

Unknown Caller ~ We have your father. He owes us 25 Gs, and he claims he doesn't have it. You've got till the end of the day to get that money together, or we'll cut off one finger at a time and send it to you. Or we could just personally deliver them to your pretty little girlfriend. Wouldn't mind a couple rounds with her. We know where you are, Gray. Get in your truck and get your ass to Willow Springs or you won't be seeing your dad any time soon. I'm sure your stepdaddy could front you the cash. Get to work. We'll send you a meeting location when you get closer. If you go to the police, you won't see your dad again, I can promise you that. We're watching you.

"Holy fucking shit," Cade whispered.

I dialed Wren. "Hey. I got a text. They've got him. They want the money. They told me to get in the truck and drive my ass there or they're going to start cutting off his fingers. They brought up Gigi. What the fuck, Wren. What do I do?"

"These motherfuckers. I am going to fuck them up, I swear to God. This is not okay," he shouted, and I heard something shatter in the background. "Call Gigi. Tell her not to leave the house. I'll get some guys over to the Jacobs' house just to keep an eye on things. I think this guy is trying to intimidate you. They aren't a big-time operation. It's two dumb fucking dudes that think they're fucking gangsters. They obviously have him because I've scoured this fucking town and I can't find him. You need to get in your truck and head here. Do what they say for now, and we'll figure this out. I have some guys on the inside at the police department. Let me work on things on my end."

"They said they would kill him if I called the police. They told me to get the money from Simon. They brought up Gigi. How the fuck do they know so much about me?" I was frantically pulling on my shoes and a baseball cap and searching for my keys as my best friend stood there listening to the call. I had Wren on speakerphone.

"These are bad dudes, but it's just the two of them as far as I know. I've heard from my guy on the inside that the cops have been after them, but I don't know how deep into this they are. Just get here. Call Gigi and give her a heads-up, and I'll have some guys drive by your mom's house as well. Just get here, Gray."

"Okay. See you soon."

Cade and I were out the door and on the road within minutes. I called Gigi and she was scared shitless. I told her not to leave the house, and of course, her girlfriends were on their way over to sit with her because they were loyal as shit. I was happy she had them.

"I'm guessing you're probably questioning the idea of me being with your sister right about now?" I asked my best friend when I merged onto the freeway.

"Fuck no. I know you have Gigi's back, Gray. This shit with your dad is not your fault."

"No, but it's still my reality. And anyone in my life has to deal with that."

"Gigi and I are in your life whether you two are dating or not. Stop trying to find reasons why you aren't deserving of good things. How many dudes would be doing this for their father? You're a good man, Gray. The best I know. I couldn't ask for better for my sister, if I'm being honest. But if you ever tell anyone I said that I will cut your balls off in your sleep."

If I had any ability to find humor in any situation at the moment, I would have laughed. But I couldn't right now. My girl was scared to death, my dad was being held hostage by these lunatics, and I didn't know how we were going to get him out of it this time. I didn't see a light at the end of the tunnel and that scared the shit out of me.

"I don't know why you aren't in your car driving home. You shouldn't be with me," I said, because I was still pissed that he'd jumped in the truck with me. The last thing I wanted to do was involve more people in my dad's fucked up mess.

"Dude. You're my day one. We're in this together. You were there for me during my shit with Camilla. I was freaking out, and you strolled in and handled everything."

"I think a pregnancy scare and some drug-dealing assholes holding my father hostage are on two completely different playing fields." I shook my head. "I'm dropping you at your house when we get to town."

"The hell you are. That's the worst thing you could do. Then you'll have me and my sister following your ass."

I couldn't think straight. I didn't know what to do. I hoped that Wren would come up with a plan before I made it to Willow Springs. My phone vibrated and Cade grabbed it from the cup holder.

"Good Christ," he whispered under his breath.

"What is it?"

"A photo of your dad tied up in some dingy place. Maybe a basement?"

"How does he look?"

Cade was quiet for a minute and I hissed at him to speak.

"He looks all right. Scared."

"But he doesn't look injured?" I asked as I slammed my fist against the steering wheel. How the fuck was I going to get him out of this?

"No. There's no blood or signs that he's been hurt."

The phone vibrated again, and Cade read the text message.

"You have three hours to get the cash together. We'll set up a meeting spot. You better be there."

"How the fuck am I supposed to come up with twenty-five thousand bucks in three hours?" I ran a hand through my hair.

"We could give them the title to my jeep. It's got to be worth that much?"

"I can't ask you to do that, brother. But I appreciate the offer."

"You didn't ask me to do it. I offered. And it's a viable option," he said.

We drove in silence as we both tried to process how the hell this would go down. It was getting dark and my mind was spinning with what to do. I needed a motherfucking miracle.

We exited the freeway, and I was shocked how quickly we'd gotten here. My stomach sank because I hadn't heard from Wren, and I was running out of options.

My phone rang and Cade put it on speakerphone and told me it was Wren.

"Hey, we just pulled into town. Any news?"

"My guy at the police station said they knew about your father being held."

"What the fuck does that mean? They know he's being held, and they aren't doing anything to get him out?"

"I don't fucking know. But we have the money for you. I'm at your mother's house now," he said, and he kept his voice low.

"You're at my mom's house? What the fuck is going on?"

"Jett called me. He and Gigi told me to meet them here," he said. "Gigi met with your mother and asked her for the money."

I pulled over on the side of the road and ran a hand down my face. There were so many moving parts, and I had no control over anything anymore.

"I told her not to leave her fucking house," I said, taking the phone from Cade.

"Yeah, I know. But she called Jett and had him come over and bring her here. He called me right away, so she was never in danger. And she's got a mind of her own. There's no talking her out of shit, I'm sure you know that."

"Welcome to my life," Cade whisper-hissed because he wasn't happy about her going rogue either.

"All right. Is Simon there?"

"Yeah. He's here. He's actually being helpful for whatever reason," he said, and I could tell he had a hand over his mouth to keep his voice low so no one would hear him.

"I'm on my way."

"Gigi is so fucking stubborn," Cade said as he punched the dashboard. "She shouldn't have left the house."

I nodded, but pride filled my chest. My girl was a lot more like me than I'd ever realized. She'd do anything for the people she loved. "She was smart. She called Jett. I trust the dude with my life. And he called Wren, so they were covered. Trust me, Wren has everyone in town on this."

Cade shrugged. "So, what's the plan?"

"I don't have a fucking clue."

And that was the truth. But I knew I'd do whatever I needed to do to help my dad.

Because he was my dad.

And no matter how fucked up he was, I wasn't going to turn my back on him.

It just wasn't an option.

twenty-five

. . .

Gigi

I WENT UPSTAIRS to check on Gray's sisters, who were busy coloring in their room with Mariana. My parents had just arrived after they'd been blowing up my phone, and I was forced to fill them in on what was happening. They wanted to be here for Gray. They loved him almost as much as I did.

I heard voices downstairs and hurried back down to see Gray and Cade walk through the door. My feet were moving before I could stop myself from lunging at Gray. I'd missed him so much, and I just needed to know he was okay.

His arms came around me and I knew everything would be okay. As long as I was with Gray, we would figure it out.

"Hey," he said, pulling back and tucking my hair behind my ear. "Didn't I tell you to stay put?"

I rolled my eyes. "Yeah, that didn't work for me. I wanted to help."

"Shocker," Cade seethed before his lips turned up in the corners just enough to show me that he was being his typical sarcastic self.

"Hey, sweetheart." Gray's mom hurried over, and he

pulled her in for a hug. "You didn't have to deal with this on your own."

"Apparently not," he said, and his gaze locked with mine and he quirked a brow. I didn't care if he was mad that I'd involved his mother. Gray couldn't do this on his own, and he shouldn't have to. Simon was a very wealthy man, and he had the financial resources to help out, and I just planted the seed with Gray's mother.

I knew she wasn't doing it for her ex-husband, she was doing it for her son. And Gray needed to know his mother would step up for him.

Wren and Gray were deep in conversation with the undercover cop who had arrived a few minutes earlier. Apparently, the guy that Wren worked with had brought them together, and for the first time today, I felt like there might be hope. I didn't want Gray walking into this alone. My stomach was in knots. I knew my boyfriend would not abandon his father. It wouldn't be an option. But knowing that there would be police officers watching this whole thing go down made me feel a lot better than Gray going in solo.

Simon stepped out of his office and dropped a duffel bag at Gray's feet. "This is twenty-five thousand dollars. It's yours."

Gray nodded and studied him before he spoke. "I appreciate it, Simon." The emotion and appreciation in my boyfriend's eyes said it all.

"I understand your need to help your father. I've been assured that the police will be monitoring your every move." I didn't miss the way his voice cracked, nor had I missed the worry lines that had formed between his eyebrows over the past two hours.

"That's what I've been told," Gray said as his phone buzzed in his back pocket.

He read the text aloud. "Drive to the parking lot at the warehouse where the fights take place, and a motorcycle will be waiting there. Do not get out of the car. You can follow him to the location. You better have that money with you or don't bother coming. There is no negotiation. You come alone, and if anyone follows you, your father dies. Leave now. The clock is ticking."

I sucked in a breath as tears streamed down my cheeks. This was actually happening. I dropped to sit on the bottom step and covered my face with my hands as I tried to muffle my sobs. What if Gray got hurt? They could kill him and his father. We didn't know what he was walking into.

Oh my god.

All the air left my lungs, and I couldn't breathe.

Cade came to sit beside me, and he whispered in my ear. "Don't make this harder for him, Gigi."

"Baby, it's going to be fine. In and out. They want the money, not me." Gray pulled me up to my feet and into his arms. I gripped his T-shirt in my hands, wanting to keep him close.

I couldn't find any words, so I nodded.

"All right. You sure you want to do this?" Wren asked, and Gray pulled back. "If you wait, they're going to assume you're up to something. You want me to get in your car and they can just deal with me whether they like it or not?"

"That could work," Simon said, and we all turned with surprise.

"No. They said no negotiating. We've come this far. We have the money. Let's not give them any reason to hurt him. I've got this."

"I agree with Gray, I've got my guys on the line. They've already got eyes on your father. He's okay. They are sitting in a car at the park, which is where we assume they are going to lead you." Officer Romero studied his phone as he spoke.

"So why even do this? Grab those son of a bitches now," Simon hissed and Gray's eyes bulged out of his head as he studied his stepfather.

"We need to catch them in the act. If we go in now," he looked at Gray and cleared his throat, "Dylan isn't the most reliable witness. We need Gray to hand them the money. It will be enough to put them away for a long time. We've been following these two for quite some time, and this is exactly what we've been waiting for."

"He's not your scapegoat," Simon shouted, and I reached for Gray's hand and he intertwined our fingers.

"We're going to keep him safe," Officer Romero said.

"All right. Let's do this." Gray kissed the top of my head and grabbed the bag off the floor. He turned back and glanced at everyone one more time before walking out the door with Wren and Officer Romero on his heels. Officer Romero got on the phone just as Gray jumped in his truck.

Sobs racked my body. I didn't know if I'd ever see him again. This wasn't fair. Gray shouldn't have to be put in a position to save his father.

"What are we going to do now?" I asked, and my words were barely recognizable as it was difficult to speak. The lump in my throat was suffocating.

"We're going to wait," Wren said, but the bleakness in his tone had chill bumps covering my body.

"He's going to be fine. He's the toughest dude I know." My brother paced in front of me and my parents moved on each side of me.

"These are bad guys, Cade. This is not a fraternity fight. These guys will kill his father, so what stops them from killing Gray?" I shouted as fear radiated from every part of my body.

"The police are following him, Gigi. They won't let anything happen to him," my father said.

"I agree. I spoke to my contact as well, and he said the whole force is in on this." Wren's gaze locked with mine.

"He's going to get through this. It's Gray we're talking about." Jett rubbed my shoulder and forced a smile.

I heard Simon yelling into the phone to someone and only made out part of the conversation. He was telling them to call in every favor they had. Simon was a powerful man, and I hoped he was doing something to help Gray.

Gray's mom sat on the couch in the living room, staring off into space. I hugged my parents before moving to sit beside her. I wanted to tell her that he'd be okay, but I didn't know if that was true. And I couldn't mask the absolute fear that was currently consuming me. I reached for her hand and she turned to face me. Tears streamed down her face and her bottom lip quivered.

"You love him, don't you?" she asked.

"Yes." I couldn't muster any other words in my current state.

"Good. He has something to fight for. I've failed him, you know that, right? Of course, you do."

"He loves you," I said as I swiped at the tears that were blurring my vision.

"Your family has been more of a family to him than we have." Her words were riddled with guilt, and I wanted to make her feel better, but I couldn't. Because it was the truth. Gray's family had failed him on more than one occasion, and here he was stepping up to save his father.

He deserved better.

He deserved the kind of love that he gave.

And that was the one thing that I could give him. Because I loved him more than I'd ever loved anyone or anything. More than I ever knew possible.

And I needed him to be okay.

Because I wouldn't be okay without him.

I buried my face in my hands and the doorbell rang.

I heard their voices before I saw them.

Addy, Maura, Ivy, and Coco rushed over to me.

They'd been with me when I'd called Jett for help. I'd

insisted they go home as I didn't want them involved. But here they were.

Addy was at my side, and Coco was crouched in front of me. Ivy and Maura moved behind me and wrapped their arms around my neck and hugged me.

"It's going to be okay," Addy said, her voice calm and stoic.

"What are you guys doing here?" I croaked.

"Jett told us you needed us. So here we are. How are you holding up?" Coco asked.

"I've been better. We're just waiting now."

Ivy and Maura moved to sit beside Gray's mom, and they did what they could to comfort her. Mariana set a bunch of water bottles out for everyone and went upstairs to check on the girls. I didn't miss the sadness in her gaze when she'd patted me on the shoulder.

Wren and my father paced around the room, Simon was shouting into the phone, Officer Romero stared down at his screen, my brother had his face buried in his hands, Jett dropped to sit on the chair, and my girls surrounded me.

I wished Gray could see just how loved he was.

But right now… it was a waiting game.

And I was out of patience.

twenty-six

. . .

Gray

WHEN I ARRIVED at the desolate parking lot, there was a man waiting there on a motorcycle, just as expected. I followed him out to Willow Springs park, and I prayed like hell that my father was okay. I knew there was a chance that we'd both die tonight. I had made peace with it, because regardless of the outcome, I would do it again for my dad. For a chance to get him back.

But fuck if my mind didn't stop going to Gigi. The sadness in her eyes when I left. The awareness that I had something amazing to stick around for. For the first time in my life, my future was brighter than I'd ever imagined. I'd been studying for my LSAT and I was determined to go to law school. I had a kick-ass internship set up for the summer, but most importantly, I had a girl that I loved more than anything. A girl that made me want to be better. She made me want to fight for all the things I'd never thought I deserved.

Because she believed I deserved them.

But here I was in the middle of a shit storm that was so far out of my control, I had no idea what I was walking into.

The dude on the motorcycle stepped off his bike and I got

out of the truck, duffel bag in hand. He didn't speak. He motioned for me to follow him down the dark tree-lined path. He didn't take his helmet off, but I was able to see that he was a bit shorter than me, but probably had fifty pounds on me. I tried to assess the situation one step at a time. We walked in silence, and the sound of gravel moving beneath my feet was the only audible sound. My heart raced, and I wiped my sweaty palms on my jeans.

Stay calm.

I glanced over my shoulder, but I didn't see any officers in sight. I hoped like hell they were somewhere nearby, but at this point, I was on my own for all I knew. The man in front of me came to a stop beside a tall evergreen tree, and the streetlight a few feet away shone just enough to allow me to make out a man wearing a ski mask. My father was down on his knees and he croaked when his gaze locked with mine.

"Shut the fuck up, Dylan," the man said to my dad then turned to me. "You followed the directions well, Gray. You're already a lot wiser than your dumbass father."

I tried to keep my composure. Showing these guys fear would just give them an edge they didn't need. They held all the power right now. My reaction was the only thing they couldn't control.

"What the fuck happens now?" I snarled.

"Oh, we're feeling brave, are we?"

"I'm not the one with my face covered, am I?" Where the fuck did that come from? I sure as shit didn't need to piss them off.

"You don't want my mask off, Gray. Not when money is involved. That would mean I'd have to kill you, and I'm trying not to go there unless you give me reason otherwise."

"I've done everything you've asked." I dropped the bag of money on the ground and the guy wearing the motorcycle helmet reached for it.

He unzipped the bag. I'd never even checked it. I'd trusted that Simon put the money in. Nerves engulfed me with each passing minute, but I forced myself to push that away.

Don't show fucking fear.

I repeated the words over and over in my head as the dude that was hovering over the bag pushed to stand. "It's all there."

I let out a breath I hadn't even realized I'd been holding for the past few minutes.

I didn't know if this was my father's rock bottom, but I knew without a shadow of a doubt that it was mine. If I made it out of here alive, I would not be looking back.

I was done being his savior.

He would have to save himself.

"What have we learned here, Dylan?" The man yanked my father to his feet.

"I will cover what I owe you moving forward." My father's words wobbled, as he had no fight left in him.

Moving forward? This isn't his rock bottom? How much lower could we go?

"That's right," the man said, shoving my dad toward me. "You are fucking with the wrong man. Do you hear me?"

My father had chased his demons into hell.

And I'd followed him here.

I heard a ruckus behind me, and everything happened in a blur. Bright lights filled the space as a couple dozen men rushed the area. Someone yanked me back and my fists came up in response, before I realized it was a police officer. He hurried me into the tree line as shouts rang out around me.

"Drop your weapon," someone yelled.

The sound of three gunshots had me turning and I tried to run toward my father, but two men held me back. I was shoved to the ground and shielded by the officers.

A helicopter appeared overhead, and a bright light shone down on all of us. The sound of the propeller mixed with muffled voices.

"We've got them both. We're clear," another voice called out.

I pushed up to look for my dad and saw a few policemen down on the ground with him.

The place was chaos in a matter of seconds. Fire engines and police sirens arrived on the scene. A group of paramedics were rushing toward my father, and I shook the officers away and ran toward him.

"For God's sake, Gray. Let us get this under control," a man shouted as he gripped my shoulders hard.

"Was he shot?" I asked, dropping down to squat beside my father.

"He's all right. Looks like the bullet just grazed his leg." Three guys lifted my father onto a gurney.

"Dad, can you hear me?" I asked, and I swiped at my face when I realized tears were blurring my vision.

I couldn't believe I was walking out of here.

I just hoped my father would be okay.

"I hear you." His words were slurred.

"His blood pressure is dropping. We need to get him out of here," the paramedic said, as they placed a mask over his mouth.

I followed them toward the ambulance and glanced over to see a slew of officers with the two assholes that had held my father captive. They were cuffed and being shoved into two different squad cars. This was surreal. It felt like I was having an out-of-body experience, but I knew that it was happening.

"Do you want to ride with your father?" one of the officers asked, and I nodded. "We'll talk to you at the hospital."

"Gray," my father called out as they loaded him in the ambulance.

"I'm here." I reached for his hand and stood beside him.

The siren sounded and lights had my father's face going from red to blue as we sped down the road toward the hospital. When the doors opened, three people in scrubs stood there ready to take him. One turned to me with empathy. "We need to take him inside. We'll find you when we know more."

I jumped down from the ambulance and a blur in my peripheral had me turning to see blonde hair flying around as she sprinted toward me. Gigi lunged into my arms as sobs racked her body.

"Oh my god, you're okay?" She pulled back, running her hands down my arms and chest.

"I'm fine, G." I wrapped her up and breathed in all that goodness.

All the reasons to walk away from this darkness.

"I was so worried. We heard shots were fired. You weren't hurt?" she asked, hugging me tighter.

"No. I'm okay. My dad was shot in the leg. Looks like it just grazed him and isn't too bad. The two guys were arrested. How did you even know what happened?"

"Officer Romero kept us updated. Simon and Wren also had people giving them updates. They had everyone on it. I snuck out the back door. Coco drove me here." Her breaths were labored, and I pulled back to look at her.

"So much for staying put, huh?" I chuckled as I used my thumbs to swipe away the tears from her cheeks.

"Jesus, girl. Do you ever do what you're fucking told?" Cade came running up the sidewalk and rushed toward me. He wrapped his arms around me. "Glad you're safe, brother."

"I was not going to wait there when we could be at the hospital," she snipped, moving back to settle against me.

"You know, you two might just be perfect for one another. Neither of you ever fucking listens or follows a goddamn rule." Cade waved a hand over his head to let his parents know where we were.

"Damn straight," I said, pulling my girl even closer.

Wren, my mom, the Jacobs, Jett, and Gigi's best friends were all there as we made our way into the hospital to wait to hear about my father. Even Simon walked in and dropped down to sit beside my mother. He looked up at me and smiled. I couldn't remember the last time he'd smiled at me. Or even if he ever had.

"Glad you're okay, Gray. You gave us a scare, but that was really brave what you did. Really brave. Son." He nodded before turning his attention back to my mother.

This night just kept getting crazier.

Three days later, I'd gone to the hospital to check on my dad. He was getting discharged, and I didn't have a fucking clue what he would do. How would we make sure this didn't happen again? And how involved would I allow myself to be, after all that had happened?

I dropped to sit down in the chair beside his bed.

"I don't know what to say, Gray. You saved my life."

I nodded. We could have both died, and that reality did not sit well with me. I'd stayed up the entire night after holding Gigi while she cried. I'd made her a promise that I'd never put her through that again, but I knew what that meant.

It was time for my dad to sink or swim.

He was out of options.

"Can't go there with you anymore, Dad." I looked up to see tears streaming down his face as the words left my mouth. "I have too much to lose. So, you're going to have to make a decision about your own life. Those two assholes might be in jail, but there are always going to be more. This is your second chance, take it or leave it. But if you leave it, you will be standing alone in that darkness."

"I don't have a lot of options, Son."

"I'm here to give you a new one," a voice said from behind me, and I turned to see Simon walk in the room. He reached for the other chair and slid it beside mine before dropping to sit.

"What are you doing here?" I asked, stunned by his presence.

"I'm here to offer your father an out." He turned to face my dad. "I have a private plane chartered to take you to Florida to a rehab facility for ninety days. I will fund your program for as long as you remain vigilant. If you leave once, that offer is off the table. If you complete the program, your housing and therapy will be covered for as long as you remain clean. But it will not be in the state of Texas or anywhere near your son."

I stiffened at his words but allowed them to sink in. He was doing this for me, not for my father.

But why?

"So, I just never see my kid again? Is that what you want?" Dad hissed as he struggled to sit forward.

"If you remain sober and clean, I will fly Gray to see you as often as he wants. But no, you will not live here on my dime. You almost killed your son, Dylan. I won't allow you to put him in that danger again. But because he loves you so damn much, I'll do this. I'll give you one more chance. It's your choice." Simon clapped his hands together and shrugged. "It's a good one. You'd be wise to take it. Plane leaves in an hour."

Fuck me.

What was happening?

Dad looked at me and nodded. "I'll take it. Thank you."

Simon pushed back and left the room.

"I'll be right back." I moved out the door to find him.

"Simon," I shouted, and he turned around and walked toward me. "Why are you doing this?"

"Because you deserve it. You know, Gray, I realized something when you walked into that situation to save your father."

"What's that?"

"You're a lot braver than me. I think I resented you for a long time because you never gave up hope on your dad the way that I did on mine. I thought you were being weak, but in reality, you were being strong. You're a good kid. I've been too tough on you. And you know I rarely admit when I'm wrong," he said, clapping me on the shoulder before turning to leave.

I looked up, half expecting pigs to be flying overhead.

"Thank you," I said, and he held a hand up and waved at me as he continued toward the elevator.

I made my way back to the hospital room and my father laughed. "Well, that was unexpected. I guess the asshole likes you more than we thought."

I rolled my eyes. Was he serious? "Fuck, Dad. He just offered you an out. Do you not get that? He's doing a really good thing here, which is more than I can say for you. You almost got us both killed."

Something in my chest squeezed because for the first time since I met Simon, he actually showed me a different side of himself. A human side.

And if I could forgive my father for his sins, why shouldn't I do the same for Simon?

"You're right, Gray. Yeah, I'm sorry, but I'm going to turn things around."

I questioned my dad's sincerity and wouldn't be holding my breath. I'd lost the ability to hope when it came to my father.

The ball was in his court now.

Gigi and I drove back to school together because Cade had taken her car back for her so that he could get his jeep and head back to school. It felt like so much time had passed since my fight with Cade; yet in reality, it had only been a few days.

But everything had changed.

Cade and I were fine, and he was completely okay with Gigi and me being together. It was amazing what a traumatic experience could do to help you see things more clearly.

And I was seeing things clearer than I ever had.

My dad had boarded a plane that Simon chartered for both of them. Simon flew with my father to Florida and personally checked him into a program there. Dad was getting a second chance on my stepfather's dime, and the distance helped me breathe easier. I didn't have to worry about getting calls from Wren anymore about my dad being in trouble.

Wren and I had grown closer than ever, and in some ways, he had been more of a father to me than my own dad or Simon had ever been. But all of this taught me that everyone had their own shit, and everyone deserved a chance at redemption. Hell, I was all about second chances these days.

"You know what I'm looking forward to?"

"What?" I asked, my fingers intertwined with hers as I merged onto the freeway.

"Dating out in the open. Not worrying about Cade or your dad or Tiffany or anyone. Just you and me."

I nodded. "That sounds fucking fabulous to me. You sure you don't mind being tangled up in my mess?"

She laughed. "Gray Baldwin, I'll get tangled up with you any day of the week."

"You're so cheesy, baby. And I fucking love it."

Her head fell back in laughter, as she scooted closer. "I love you."

"Love you, G. Always have, always will."

And I was a man of my fucking word.
This girl was my past.
My present.
And my future.

twenty-seven

. . .

Gigi

EIGHTEEN MONTHS LATER

"GRAY DYLAN BALDWIN," the dean called out, and Gray made his way across the stage. He was graduating with honors and had already been accepted into The Texas University School of Law. We were both thrilled because I had two more years of classes, and now we'd be able to stay at the same school.

The past eighteen months had been amazing, because we had no more secrets and no more dark clouds hovering above us. And when it was just Gray and me… it was magic.

I'd found my forever in the boy I'd despised most of my life. Don't get me wrong, Gray still liked to push my buttons, he was jealous and bossy—and I wouldn't change a damn thing. I loved everything about this boy. Cade still gave us a hard time about any PDA, because we couldn't seem to keep our hands away from one another when we were together, and I made no apologies for it.

We cheered and screamed as he crossed the stage. My parents had come to see him receive his diploma, and Cade and Camilla were there as well, as they were both graduating the following weekend and we'd be there for that special moment too. Gray's mom and Simon sat on the other side of me with Bea and Penn.

Simon had stepped up, which had surprised the heck out of my boyfriend. Once Dylan made it through the ninety-day program, Simon found him a job and a place to live. He flew Gray and me out there several times, but Dylan had experienced a relapse two months ago and was back in rehab. Simon had stepped up once again and covered the cost, even though he'd said it was a one-time offer, and I knew he'd done it because he loved Gray. Simon and Gray had formed an unexpected friendship. Gray acted like it wasn't a big deal, but he'd broken down to me a few times about how much it meant to him.

Because behind all that tough exterior was a teddy bear.

Gray was all bark and no bite—unless you wanted him to.

I digress.

I had a hard time keeping my mind out of the gutter when it came to Gray. He was romantic and sweet and would move the sun and the earth if I asked him to. But if someone looked at me wrong, he was the first one to take their head off.

My gentle giant.

When Gray walked over, he moved past everyone and lifted me off my feet. "Love you, G. Couldn't have done it without you."

I laughed. He was ridiculously charming. "You did this all on your own, fool."

"Well, I wouldn't have wanted to do it without you. Is that better?"

"Get a room, for God's sake. No one needs to see you two gushing all over one another," Cade hissed before he pulled my boyfriend in for a hug. "Proud of you, brother."

Gray made his way through the group thanking everyone for coming.

Gray and Simon shared a hug that lasted much longer

than usual. Their relationship had changed since the night Gray had gone to save his father.

Turned out that sometimes tragedies brought people together.

I was just thankful that we'd made it through and come out on the other side stronger than ever.

I couldn't wait to see what the future held.

Because as long as I was with Gray—I was happy.

He'd been with me my whole life, and I hadn't even known that I loved him back then.

He'd been my nemesis.

My friend.

My lover.

But most importantly—my happily ever after.

epilogue

. . .

Gigi

EIGHTEEN MONTHS LATER

WE WERE home for winter break, and all of us were heading to Addy's house for a Magic Willows meeting. I'd just left Gray at my house with Cade, and he was pouting because he didn't want me to leave.

He knew spending time with my best friends was important to me, but it didn't stop him from pulling out all the stops to make me late.

He'd tackled me on the bed and tried to make me stay. Kissing my neck and teasing me, knowing exactly what I liked.

What I needed.

But girl time was also important to me, and he'd laughed when he'd finally let me up to leave and made his way to the living room to hang out with Cade.

I jogged when I saw Coco just up ahead, and we both complained about how ridiculously cold it was outside. I pulled my coat tighter around my neck before we walked into Addy's basement together. Maura and Ivy were already there.

We all dropped down in our usual spots, just like we always did.

Maura and I were on the shaggy rug across from Coco, Addy, and Ivy who sat on the couch. Addy had a tray of Christmas cookies sitting on the coffee table and hot cocoas set out for each of us.

"Okay, let's get down to business." Ivy flipped the leather-bound book open.

"Well, I have news," Maura said, giving us that look as if we needed to prepare ourselves.

"What? You're finally breaking up with that dud of a boyfriend, Will?" Coco said, holding her hands together as if she were praying and closing her eyes.

We all burst out in laughter and then righted ourselves when we realized that Maura wasn't laughing.

"Stop hating on Will. He's fine," she huffed.

"People do not write romance novels about *fine*," Coco said with a knowing look. "The dude is boring AF. You are settling. I'm just the only one who has the balls to admit it."

"I have balls too," Ivy said with irritation and we all laughed.

"Of course, you do. But can we please not talk about your balls or my boring boyfriend." Maura shook her head. "This isn't about Will."

"Oh my gosh. You hooked up with that hot Italian guy and finally had good sex for the first time in your life." Coco clapped her hands together before leaning forward to study Maura as if this was the most exciting news in the world.

"Are you drunk? The hot Italian guy is my thirty-year-old professor. I did not hook up with him."

"You do seem to be a bit sauced." Addy smirked at Coco and made no attempt to hide her laughter. "Did you pour some Baileys in that chocolate?"

"Girls, I am drunk on life, as we all should be. We're hot. We're graduating from college in six months. I already have a fabulous job offer in Houston and I'll never need to move back to this godforsaken town. No offense. I know you guys plan on coming home at some point. *I'll visit.*" Coco winked.

"Focus, Co. What's going on, Maura?" Ivy asked, pen in hand, ready to play scribe and write down whatever she said.

"Remember I told you that my counselor said they were going to place a few students for certain internships this last semester?"

"Don't be humble. They were placing the top one percent of your class. You are freaking brilliant, and I knew you'd get picked," I said, smiling at her because she never gave herself enough credit.

She waved her hand in front of her face. "Well, it turns out the most coveted internship in the program is shadowing the assistant to the president at the largest advertising agency in Dallas. And I was selected. It's an amazing opportunity and turning it down would be completely disrespectful. My counselor was so excited. She just called to let me know that I was nominated by all of my professors. It's the highest honor." She shook her head in disbelief.

"So why aren't we celebrating with a little something-something in this hot chocolate? Scratch that. Grab the tequila, let's do some shots." Coco raised a brow. "What's the problem?"

"My father. He's going to lose his shit," Maura explained.

"Why?" Ivy asked.

"I would think he would be so proud that you were selected. He's always pushing you so hard to study and be prepared. This is what he's wanted for you." Addy did not hide the confusion in her gaze.

"The internship is with the Carlisle Ad Agency. I will be the assistant to that freaking cocky asshole, Crew Carlisle. *He's* the president of the company. Apparently his grandfather retired two years ago, and he's running the show now."

"Oh my. I'm sweating. That guy is so hot. He's got that

arrogant, I-know-my-shit-don't-stink, let me give you all the orgasms thing going on. Oh, what that man could do with those hands. I saw him chopping down a Christmas tree for his family last week out at Evergreen Farms and I couldn't stop staring at his hands. They're almost as big as his feet." Coco winked before falling back in laughter. "You know what they say about big hands and big feet. Can you just imagine what else that man is packing?"

"The last thing I'm doing is thinking about what he's packing. He is such a jerk. Remember when he called the cops on me for that fender bender? I can't stand him. And my father absolutely despises the Carlisles. I'm just terrified that once Crew realizes that I'm the candidate from the school, he's going to tell them he doesn't want me, and then I won't have anything lined up. But I can't even imagine working for him. What am I going to do?"

"You are going to do nothing. You probably won't have to see him much. You'll be shadowing his assistant. You can stay under the radar," I said.

"Maybe. I don't even know. My dad keeps asking if I have anything lined up yet. I told him my counselor was working on something for me. But what am I going to tell him?"

"You just tell him you landed a gig at a local advertising company. Your dad doesn't know anything about that business and he just wants to know that you got a position. He doesn't have to know the details. It's six months. You'll be coming home after graduation and he'll be none the wiser." Addy reached for a cookie.

"That's true. And you can continue hating Crew when you work for him." I raised my mug. "I think we should toast to that. It's amazing that your professors chose you, even if you hate the guy you work for."

"Or you can have hot, angry office sex on his desk. I'll drink to that," Coco said, and we all laughed some more.

What can I say, the girl had a way with words.

"Okay, it's all in the book. You don't tell your father unless you absolutely have to. He's not that great of a listener anyway. He just wants to know you got a gig so he can brag to all his friends at the club," Ivy said as she scribbled on the lined white paper.

"Thanks." Maura chuckled, even though we all knew it was true. Maura was the baby of the family with two older brothers, and those were tough shoes to fill. Her father was a bit of an intimidating guy, and he barked more than he listened.

"I can't wait to see what we all do after graduation," I said. Gray and I would be staying one more year in Austin until he graduated from law school. We both wanted to come back to Willow Springs, where I hoped to open an art studio and Gray wanted to practice law. We'd been together for three years now, and it didn't really matter as long as we were together.

"Me either. Jett's gotten a couple offers at accounting firms in Austin, but he knows I want to come back and write for the Willow Springs paper. Hell, they already offered me the on-air news anchor gig, so we're still talking about what we want to do."

"That's because that reporter, Judy Jones, is older than dirt. I was watching the news last night and I swear she forgot to put her dentures back in. Ratings would pick up quite a bit if they put your fine self on air, and they all know it." Coco ate the head off of a reindeer cookie and chewed dramatically.

"I agree. And I have news." Ivy set her pen down.

"What is it?" I asked.

"Loraine Applebee phoned me this morning. She wants me to take over her event planning business. My dad said he would front me the money to buy her out." Ivy shrugged as if this wasn't her absolute dream to be living back in Willow Springs after graduation and planning weddings and parties for everyone in town. She was born to be an event planner, and I was so happy for her that she was chasing her dreams.

We all cheered and raised our mugs once again.

"Looks like we all have a plan. Cheers to us," Addy said.

"Magic Willows for life." Maura held her glass up high and we all clinked them together.

"Magic Willows for life."

THE END

Do you want to see Maura go to work for Crew Carlisle, in the small town, enemies-to-lovers romance…

Read Charmed HERE https://geni.us/Charmed

acknowledgments

Greg, Chase & Hannah, thank you for being my biggest supporters and always believing in me and encouraging me to chase my dreams! YOU are the reason that I work hard every day!! I love you ALWAYS & FOREVER!!

Annette, Pathi, Natalie, Abi, Caroline, and Doo, thank you for being the BEST beta readers EVER! Your feedback means the world to me. I am so thankful for you and all of your feedback! I would be lost without you!

Thank you, Sarah Hansen (Okay Creations) for working your magic once again! I absolutely LOVE this cover!!

Sue Grimshaw (Edits by Sue), Thank you for your encouragement, your guidance and your support. Your feedback is always spot-on and I am so incredibly thankful for you! Thank you for believing in me and in this story and for helping me get that ending right!! I appreciate you more than you know!!

Ellie (My Brothers Editor), I am so thankful for you!! I appreciate all that you do for me!! Thank you for always fitting me in and for all of your positive feedback, and most importantly, your friendship! Love you!

Tamara Cribley (The Deliberate Page), so thankful to get to work with you again. I love all of the little details that you add to the formatting and appreciate your patience and support so much!! Thank you, my friend!

Willow, I would absolutely be lost without you!! Thank you for always making time to read my words and make them shine!! So thankful to be on this journey with you!! Love you!!!

Sarah Ferguson (Social Butterfly PR), Thank you for all of your help and guidance!! It means the world to me!! xoxo

Ashlee (Ashes & Vellichor), Thank you for bringing Gigi and Gray to life!! I appreciate you more than you know!!

Danah Logan, Thank you for the beautiful graphics and for bringing this story to life with the teasers!!

Dad, you really are the reason that I keep chasing my dreams!! Thank you for teaching me to never give up. Love you!

Mom, thank you for your love and support. Love you!

Sandy, thank you for reading and supporting me throughout this journey. Love you!

Lisa, Julie, Eric, Jen and Jim, I am very thankful to have such supportive and encouraging siblings in my life. Love you!

Eric, there is no one that listens and supports me more than you!! I appreciate the encouragement more than you know!! Love you, E$!

Pathi, I am so thankful for you! You are the reason I even started this journey. Thank you for believing in me!! Love you!

Natalie (Head in the Clouds, Nose in a Book), Thank you for supporting me through it all! I appreciate all that you do for me from beta reading to the newsletter to buddy reading so we can talk about all of the trauma!! Hahahaha Love you!

Willow and Catherine, our daily chats keep me laughing and keep me moving forward!! Thank you for your friendship! I love you both so much! #lovechain

Kalie & Korrie, your support and love means the world to me!! I am so thankful for you both!!

Sammi, Marni, Adriana & Alison, Thank you for being so supportive and encouraging along this journey!! It truly means the world to me!!

To all the bloggers and bookstagrammers who have posted, shared and supported me—I can't begin to tell you how much it means to me. I love seeing the graphics that you make, and the gorgeous posts that you share. I am forever grateful for your support!

To all the readers who take the time to pick up my books and take a chance on my words…THANK YOU for helping to make my dreams come true!!

keep up on new releases

Linktree Laurapavlovauthor

Newsletter laurapavlov.com

other books by laura pavlov

Magnolia Falls Series

Magnolia Falls Series
Loving Romeo
Wild River
Forbidden King
Beating Heart
Finding Hayse

Cottonwood Cove Series
Into the Tide
Under the Stars
On the Shore
Before the Sunset
After the Storm

Honey Mountain Series
Always Mine
Ever Mine
Make You Mine
Simply Mine
Only Mine

The Willow Springs Series

Frayed

Tangled

Charmed

Sealed

Claimed

Montgomery Brothers Series

Legacy

Peacekeeper

Rebel

A Love You More Rock Star Romance

More Jade

More of You

More of Us

The Shine Design Series

Beautifully Damaged

Beautifully Flawed

The G.D. Taylors Series with Willow Aster

Wanted Wed or Alive

The Bold and the Bullheaded

Another Motherfaker

Don't Cry Spilled MILF

Friends with Benefactors

follow me...

Website laurapavlov.com
Goodreads @laura_pavlov
Instagram @laurapavlovauthor
Facebook @laurapavlovauthor
Pav-Love's Readers @pav-love's readers
Amazon @laurapavlov
BookBub @laurapavlov
TikTok @laurapavlovauthor

Made in the USA
Columbia, SC
16 April 2024